Regency Belles of Bath

From shopkeepers...to Cinderella brides!

On a quiet street in Bath, you'll find a small, unassuming biscuit shop. And, if you walk in, you'll have the chance to taste a small slice of perfection. Belle biscuits are like nothing you could imagine! Though the shop would be nothing without the women who run it...

But it's not just confectionery delights that customers fall in love with—it's the shopkeepers, too! From a captain about to become an earl, to an officer who has just stepped back onto shore, there's an unexpected love story around every corner...

Escape to the Regency streets of Bath with...

An Unconventional Countess

and

Unexpectedly Wed to the Officer

Both available now!

Look for Beatrix and Quinton's story

Coming soon!

Author Note

Unexpectedly Wed to the Officer is the second book in my four-part Regency Belles of Bath miniseries, a collection inspired by my grandparents, the city of Bath, and my own profound and enduring love of biscuits. It also references the huge amount of maritime literature I read at university by featuring a naval hero, although I've made Sebastian's experiences quite tame by comparison to real-life events.

When the first book in the series, *An Unconventional Countess*, came out, a number of readers requested more of the indomitable Lady Jarrow. Having just finished the third book, I promise you she'll be back!

JENNI FLETCHER

Unexpectedly Wed to the Officer

Recycling programs for this product may not exist in your area.

ISBN-13: 978-1-335-50595-8

Unexpectedly Wed to the Officer

This edition published by arrangement with Harlequin Books S.A.

For questions and comments about the quality of this book, please contact us at CustomerService@Harlequin.com.

Harlequin Enterprises ULC
22 Adelaide St. West, 40th Floor
Toronto, Ontario M5H 4E3, Canada
www.Harlequin.com

Printed in U.S.A.

Jenni Fletcher was born in the north of Scotland and now lives in Yorkshire with her husband and two children. She wanted to be a writer as a child but became distracted by reading instead, finally getting past her first paragraph thirty years later. She's had more jobs than she can remember but has finally found one she loves. She can be contacted on Twitter, @jenniauthor, or via her Facebook author page.

Books by Jenni Fletcher

Harlequin Historical

The Warrior's Bride Prize
Reclaimed by Her Rebel Knight
Tudor Christmas Tidings
"Secrets of the Queen's Lady"

Regency Belles of Bath

An Unconventional Countess
Unexpectedly Wed to the Officer

Sons of Sigurd

Redeeming Her Viking Warrior

Secrets of a Victorian Household

Miss Amelia's Mistletoe Marquess

Whitby Weddings

The Convenient Felstone Marriage
Captain Amberton's Inherited Bride
The Viscount's Veiled Lady

Visit the Author Profile page
at Harlequin.com for more titles.

To my own little chatterbox.

Chapter One

Belles Biscuit Shop, Bath—November 1806

The door hit Sebastian Fortini squarely on the nose.

It was, he considered, a case of monumentally bad timing. If he hadn't been looking sideways, wondering why the dresser that had spent two decades in one particular corner of the kitchen had suddenly moved to the wall opposite, then he wouldn't have turned so sharply at the creak of a floorboard in the hallway, which meant that the door, when it opened, would have had only its own and not his additional impetus to wield against him. But unfortunately he had, and he was, so it did.

If only the chain of catastrophes had ended there…

Alas, his nose proved to be just the first victim as the full and somewhat considerable weight of a heavy oak door being violently rammed rather than gently pushed open knocked the rest of him off his feet and into an inelegant heap on the floor.

Between the impact of the wood on his face and the stone flagstones on his posterior, it was actually difficult to tell which was the most painful, a fact that did nothing to curb the flow of expletives that immediately burst from his lips, which appeared to be coated in some warm, sticky substance.

He reached a hand to his nose, felt blood and sucked in a breath, readying himself for a fresh burst of eloquence, when a female figure suddenly sprang out of the darkness of the hallway, armed with what appeared to be the contents of a coal bucket.

'Get out!'

Sebastian raised himself up on his elbows, squinting at his attacker through the murky flickers of light cast by the still-glowing hearth. Unexpected as it was to find himself being threatened in the dead of night by a shovel and pair of fire tongs, he was frankly more perplexed than alarmed. His sister's voice, he was further surprised to notice, had developed something of a west country burr in the two years since he'd last been home on shore leave. More bizarrely, she'd grown in height, too. In fact, her whole appearance had undergone some kind of radical transformation…

'What the blazes?' He drew his brows together, belatedly acknowledging that she was not, in fact, his sister after all. Not unless the blow to his head had affected his sight, which seemed unlikely since there was nothing blurry about the vision of golden loveliness before him. She was about as different in appearance to Anna as it was possible to be—willowy, golden and, at that moment, clad in a white nightgown short enough to reveal a pair of slender, shapely calves and positively minuscule ankles. In other circumstances he might have been quite delighted to find himself lying beside them. Unfortunately, she'd just knocked the sense out of him and the words racing through his mind were a great deal less than charitable. Ankles be damned, his nose felt as though it was about to explode.

'Oh!' She started forward at the sight of blood and then checked herself, jerking her chin upwards and scowling defiantly instead.

'You might give a man some warning when you're about to open the door.' He scowled back, clenching his jaw against the impulse to swear some more. He'd barely scratched the surface of his extensive sailor's vocabulary. 'I think you just broke my nose.'

'Good!' Her grip on the shovel only tightened. 'That'll teach you to break into people's property in the middle of the night! Now get out or I'll scream for the night-watchman.'

'Wait!' He reached into his jacket pocket and pulled out a handkerchief, waving it in the air like a flag of surrender before using it to wipe the blood off his face. After two days of travelling in a series of cramped stagecoaches from Plymouth, the last of which had arrived three hours late thanks to a loose wheel, being hit in the face by a door wasn't the welcome home he'd been hoping for, but, injured party or not, the last thing he wanted was to be hauled off to gaol in the middle of the night. 'I didn't break in. I have a key and I was trying *not* to make any noise, if you must know, only things seem to have moved around since I was last here.'

He threw another speculative look around the kitchen. The pale yellow walls, oval-shaped oak table and threadbare armchair by the hearth were familiar, but actually quite a *lot* had changed since he was last there. To begin with, there was the broom he'd knocked over when he'd opened the back door, then there was the sack of flour he'd stubbed his toe against, then a set of shelves he *definitely* hadn't seen before, not to mention the dresser… Presumably his sister had decided to move a few things around, but where was she anyhow?

'Where's Anna?' He cocked his head to one side enquiringly.

'You know Anna?' The woman blinked, apparently surprised enough to lower the shovel a few inches.

'All my life.' He glanced from her face to her makeshift weapons and then back again. It didn't seem as though she had any real intention of using them, but considering the various sharp edges and their potential uses, it was probably best to be sure. 'By the way, would you mind putting those tongs down? I'm afraid to ask what you intended to do with them, but they're making me want to cross my legs.'

'Oh.'

His lips twitched as a furious blush spread across her cheeks. Now that the pain in his nose was receding, it occurred to him that if he really *had* to be hit in the face by a woman, then she might well be the one he would have chosen to do it. Even scowling and wielding a pair of tongs, she was quite stunningly pretty. Beautiful in fact, with delicate, elfin features set in a peaches and cream complexion, albeit one that was currently claret-coloured.

'No!' She was adamant despite her embarrassment. 'Not until you tell me how you know Anna.'

'Well…' He braced his hands on the floor, pushing himself to his feet so abruptly that she leapt part way into the air, the tongs wobbling precariously in her grasp. 'I believe that we first met in the cradle. She used to sing me lullabies, as I recall. Allow me to introduce myself. Sebastian Fortini, at your service.'

'Anna's little brother?'

'The one and only.' He winked and made an elaborate bow, enjoying her gasp of surprise as he flourished the now bloodstained handkerchief out in front of him. 'As for you, I can only assume that you're a figment of my imagination caused by the blow to my head.'

'Oh, dear.' A horrified expression crossed her face. 'Sorry about that. I really thought you were a burglar.'

'Quite understandable.' He lifted his shoulders, conceding that it was, in fact, *entirely* understandable since he hadn't sent any advance notice of his arrival. There hadn't seemed much point when he could travel in person just as fast as a letter, but then he hadn't reckoned on his coach's late arrival. That *had* struck him as somewhat unfortunate, coinciding as it did with the middle of the night, but he'd assumed that he could simply let himself in, sleep in the armchair by the hearth and wait to surprise his sister in the morning. What he *hadn't* expected was to trip over half the kitchen furniture and wake anyone else up.

'My name's Henrietta Gardiner.' The woman placed the tongs and shovel down by the hearth and clasped her hands together primly in front of her.

'Delighted to meet you, even under the circumstances.' He suppressed a smile at the primness. There was something charmingly incongruous about it when she was standing in front of him wearing nothing more than a white nightgown, particularly one that, whilst not exactly sheer, did only a partial job of concealing the luscious curves beneath. He allowed himself a few seconds of appreciation before pulling his gaze reluctantly back to her face. 'So, Miss Gardiner, has my sister employed you to guard the shop against night-time marauders?'

'Not exactly. I'm the new manager.'

'Manager?' He forgot instantly about the nightgown, seized with a rush of panic. 'Why is Anna employing a manager?'

'Because she's—' She stopped mid-sentence, regarding him askance. 'Wait, didn't you get any of her letters?'

'No. My ship's been stuck out in the Pacific for the past year. I haven't heard anything from home in the whole time. What's happened?' He took a step forward impatiently. 'Is she all right? Has something happened to our mother?'

'Oh, no, everything's all right. They're both perfectly well, only—' She stopped for a second time, sucking her bottom lip between her teeth in a way that made him acutely conscious of her nightgown again. 'I think I'd better put the kettle on. Are you hungry? There are some leftover biscuits somewhere.'

'You mean Belles?' He pulled a chair out and settled himself down at the table, feeling relieved by her assurances. The thought of one of his family's famous biscuits was comforting, too, telling him he was finally home at last. 'I can't remember the last time I had one of those. I hope Anna hasn't been messing around with the recipe.'

There was a conspicuous pause before Miss Gardiner answered, a glint of amusement in her eye as she deposited a plate of biscuits on the table in front of him. 'You might be surprised by what Anna has done. Welcome home, Mr Fortini, we have a lot to talk about.'

* * *

'Let me get this straight. My sister—*my sister Anna*—who despises the aristocracy and everything they stand for, married an earl and now she's a countess?'

Sebastian wasn't sure how many times he'd repeated the question—or repeated the same combination of words in a variety of different ways. He'd started off with the vague idea that if he kept *on* repeating them, then they might start to make sense, but the tactic seemed to be having the opposite effect. Everything that he'd heard over the past half an hour was so bewildering and unbelievable that he was seriously wondering whether he ought to consult a doctor about the blow to his head, after all.

'I know it's a lot to take in and it sounds far-fetched, but I assure you it's all true, Mr Fortini.'

Miss Gardiner was regarding him across the table with an expression of tolerant sympathy, her delectable figure now modestly hidden beneath a green woollen dressing gown, more was the pity. *She* struck him as somewhat unbelievable, too, and not just because he'd been living among men for so long. If he'd tried, he could hardly have dreamt up a more exquisite-looking specimen of femininity, although, considering the circumstances, she surely *had* to be real. If she were a figment of his imagination, then they'd be doing a lot more than drinking tea and eating biscuits at midnight. They'd be on the same side of the table for a start, if not on top of it, and she wouldn't be wearing that dressing gown either. Not to mention that he'd be far more intimately acquainted with those ankles...

'But a *countess*?' He dragged his mind back to the subject in hand.

'Of Staunton, yes.' In addition to her more obvious attractions, Miss Gardiner appeared to have limitless amounts of patience. 'They held the wedding here in Bath six months ago. I was a witness.'

'You were?' He leaned forward. 'Tell me, how did Anna seem?'

'Very happy.'

'Are you certain? Forgive me, but I know how Anna feels about the aristocracy. She detests the whole lot of them. Are you sure she wasn't coerced into anything?'

'Coerced?' Miss Gardiner looked baffled. 'I believe that she had mixed feelings at first, but I've never heard of a shopkeeper being *coerced* to marry an earl.'

'No, but perhaps there was some compelling reason...?'

She stared at him blankly for a few seconds before emitting a high-pitched squeak of indignation. 'Absolutely not!'

'What about financial reasons, then?' Sebastian wasn't prepared to let the subject drop so easily. 'Perhaps she felt she needed the security?'

'Anna would *never* have married for money!' Miss Gardiner pushed her chair back, apparently on the verge of storming away. 'Or for any reason except affection and respect! It's insulting that you would even suggest such a thing!'

'I would never insult my sister.' Sebastian held his hands up in a placatory gesture. 'I just need to be sure that she got married of her own free will and that she was happy about it. I'd hate to think of her being forced into anything because I wasn't here to help her in a difficult situation.'

'Mmm.' She sat down again, her expression softening slightly as she tucked her chair back under the table. 'Well, in that case, you can put your mind at ease. Anna's marriage was a love match. She married the Earl despite his rank, not because of it.'

'That's a relief. Still, a countess...' He shook his head. 'You have to admit, it sounds pretty unbelievable and not just about Anna, but my mother, too. How is it possible that after twenty-five years of being disowned by her family, she's gone to live with her mother, my so-called grandmother? A dowager duchess, of all people?'

'I don't know, but she has, at your uncle's house, Feversham Hall in Yorkshire. Anna says they're all very happy together. As is she.'

'Well, damn it all.' He winced. 'Pardon me, Miss Gardiner.'

'That's all right.' She gave him an arch look. 'It's really nothing compared to the things you said earlier.'

'Ah...you mean when the door hit me? Sorry about that, although, to be honest, I've forgotten what it was exactly. Nothing too shocking, I hope?'

'That would probably depend on how easily a person is shocked, but I've chosen to regard it as educational. I never realised that my vocabulary was so lacking before.' One corner of her mouth curved upwards, revealing a dimple in her left cheek. 'But you're forgiven. All of this must have come as quite a shock.'

'That's an understatement.' He tipped his chair on to its back legs. 'You know, as pleasant as tea is, I believe that the situation might call for something stronger.'

'You mean to drink?' The dimple disappeared as

two spots of colour blazed across her cheekbones. 'I'm afraid we don't have anything like that.'

'Not even some port? There always used to be a bottle tucked away on the top shelf in the pantry.'

'Ye-es.' Her gaze flickered to one side. 'There *was* a bottle, only I took it down a few months ago. I believe I might have poured it away.'

'You poured it away?' He dropped his chair back to the floor in surprise. She was looking curiously guilty, too, although, considering her healthy complexion, he found it difficult to believe that she was a hardened port-drinker or anything-drinker. Probably the opposite was true and she disapproved of alcohol entirely, which given his current desire for a drink was more than a little unfortunate. Still, since it couldn't be helped… 'Never mind. I can see that you've made quite a few changes.'

'Yes. Anna said that I could do whatever I liked and I thought that the dresser—'

'It wasn't a criticism, Miss Gardiner,' he interrupted as her spine stiffened defensively. 'Just an observation. Now that I look at it, I wonder why my mother never thought to put the dresser over there herself. It makes the whole kitchen look bigger.'

'That's what I thought.' She looked pleased, the vivid red of her cheeks fading to a dusky and extremely fetching shade of pink. 'And with the table here, we can see through to the shop when we're baking.'

'*We?* You have an assistant, I presume.'

'Nancy, yes. She was a kitchen maid, but the Earl's grandmother sent her to help with the baking for a while and she liked the work so much that she stayed. Now she lives here, too.'

'She's a deep sleeper, I take it?'

'Very.' The dimple made a fresh appearance. 'And she hates to be disturbed. That's why I didn't wake her tonight. I thought perhaps I was just imagining noises down here.'

'I'm relieved that you *didn't* wake her.' He lifted a finger to his nose and pushed it tentatively from side to side. 'You're quite ferocious enough on your own.'

'Oh, dear. Do you really think that it's broken?'

'Probably.' He felt a twinge of guilt at her contrite expression. 'But not to worry. It's not the first time and I doubt it will be the last. I actually forget how my face looked originally. For all we know, this might be an improvement.'

She gave a low, throaty laugh and then leaned across the table suddenly, her eyes alight with curiosity. 'Did you break it before in the navy? Anna said that you were a lieutenant.'

'Only *acting* lieutenant, I'm afraid. I was promoted by my captain, not the Admiralty, and I never got an opportunity to sit any exams. Now, thanks to Trafalgar, the navy has a surplus of officers so I've been discharged from duty. Not that I'm complaining about our victory, but it might have been easier to swallow if I'd actually been there instead of...' He bit his tongue. 'In any case, I'm back.'

'So you're not going back to sea?'

He lifted his shoulders in a shrug. It was a good question. He'd finally come home to help Anna run Belles, but apparently that ship had sailed, too. He wasn't needed here any more than he was in the navy. Which was ironic considering how guilty he'd felt about being away over the past few years. Now it appeared he was a completely free man. Free from family obligations, naval orders *and* commitments. It was a strange, somewhat exuberant feeling. He could do anything he wanted, go anywhere he wanted. He was still only in his early twenties, young enough to find another career. He could…

'Mr Fortini?'

He started. 'Forgive me, I was just thinking. To be honest, I've no idea what I'll do yet. Maybe I'll just enjoy my freedom for a while.'

'Anna and your mother will be thrilled to see you again. They've been so worried. The Earl even went to the Admiralty to ask about your ship.'

'Really?' Sebastian had to make a conscious effort not to clench his jaw at the words. If that were the case, then it was possible his new brother-in-law already knew what had happened to the *Menelaus*. The question was whether or not he would have told Anna. He hoped not, and fortunately Miss Gardiner seemed to have no idea…

'I'm afraid there was no way for me to send word any earlier.' He shifted forward in his chair, splaying both of his hands out on the table in what he hoped was a masterful way of steering the conversation. 'But I'm here now. Only it appears that I've come to the wrong place.'

'Not *wrong*. It's still your family's shop. They're just…'

'Not here?'

'No.' She smiled apologetically. 'I'm afraid not.'

Their gazes locked across the table and he found himself instinctively smiling back. Her eyes were a luminous and vibrant blue, he noticed, as clear and enticing as the tropical seas he'd seen on the other side of the world, like warm pools he might willingly dive into. Something about them made him completely forget what they were talking about. If he hadn't known better, he would actually have thought they had some kind of hypnotising effect… He couldn't take his own off them.

'More tea?' She broke the spell, reaching for the teapot. 'I think there's a little left.'

'No, thank you.' He stood up, suddenly aware of the impropriety of their situation and wondering if her eyes weren't perhaps a little too enticing for their own good. 'I ought to be on my way.'

'You're leaving?' She looked startled. 'But it's the middle of the night!'

'True, but under the circumstances I can hardly stay here. It wouldn't be proper, or so my mother would tell me anyway.'

'No, I suppose not.' A series of expressions passed over her face before settling into one of resolve. 'But I can't possibly throw you out into the cold. Belles belongs to your family, which makes it your home even more than it is mine.'

'Miss Gardiner…'

'I admit that the circumstances aren't ideal…' she spoke over him '…but it's not as if Nancy and I are ladies. Nobody cares what we do. There's really only the shop's reputation to think about, but as long as we smuggle you out discreetly in the morning, then who's to know you were ever here?'

'I still don't think…'

'But I *insist*.' Her chin jutted upwards mutinously. 'Most decent establishments will be closed at this time of night and, even if they aren't, it's likely to be freezing outside. Improper or not, I'd never be able to look Anna in the face again if anything happened to you. No, Mr Fortini, I simply cannot allow you to leave, not when there's a perfectly serviceable sofa in the parlour.'

'The green one? I remember.'

'Good. Because I'm putting my foot down.'

'So I see.' He rubbed a hand over his chin, recalling his earlier glimpse of ankle and feeling rather impressed by her speech. It seemed a shame to gainsay her after all that—besides, who was he to argue when a beautiful woman insisted that he stay for the night? Even if it wasn't *quite* in the way he might have preferred. An image of lithe female limbs wrapped around his own floated into his mind… He didn't want to think about how long it had been since *that* had last happened…or since he'd done anything with a woman for that matter. No wonder he was fantasising about ankles!

'Well then…' He cleared his throat huskily. 'I appreciate your hospitality, Miss Gardiner.'

'You do?' She looked vaguely surprised by her own success. 'I mean, good. I'll go and fetch some blankets and meet you in the parlour in a few minutes.'

'I'll see you there.'

Sebastian watched her go, dropping back into his chair to take stock of the events of the night. His nose was possibly broken, there were going to be bruises on sensitive areas of his body, he was no closer to being reunited with his family and he was about to sleep on a sofa that, if memory served, was a good foot too short to be comfortable. He *ought* to be wishing he'd stayed in Plymouth. Instead, he felt quite unexpectedly happy.

It must be the shop, he reasoned in bewilderment. Only that could explain this powerful, strangely profound sense of being home.

Chapter Two

The scream cut through the silence of the early morning like a knife. Not a blunt butter knife either, more of a bloodthirsty dagger, piercing Henrietta's eardrums and bringing her back to consciousness with a start.

Heart thumping, she flung her quilt aside and leapt out of bed, remembering to grab her dressing gown this time as she sprinted out of her small attic room and down the stairs. After making up a bed on the sofa for Mr Fortini, she'd returned to her own, confident in her ability to wake up early enough to tell Nancy what had happened during the night, not to mention who to expect in the parlour, but her nocturnal adventure had obviously caused her to oversleep. Now the muffled exclamations and thuds coming from below made it sound as though a wildcat had been let loose in the parlour, which she had to admit was a pretty accurate description of her flaming-haired, flaming-tempered assistant.

'Stop!' She burst into the parlour just in time to snatch a vase out of Nancy's hands and prevent her from hurling it like a missile across the room. 'He's a guest!'

'What?' Nancy spun around indignantly, still looking ready to do battle with her fists.

'A guest! This is Mr Fortini, *Anna's* brother. He arrived in the middle of the night and I said he could sleep here.' Henrietta looked around the parlour with dismay. The sofa was lying on its side, there were books and ornaments strewn everywhere and a porcelain figurine of a cat was balancing precariously on the edge of a coffee table. 'He didn't know that Anna and his mother have moved out.'

'How could he *not* know that?'

'Because he's been at sea and he never received any of their letters!'

'Oh.' The fiery light in Nancy's eyes dimmed slightly. 'Well, how was I supposed to know that?'

'You weren't.' Henrietta sighed. 'I was going to tell you when I woke up, but I slept longer than I expected and… Mr Fortini?'

She looked across the room to where the object of Nancy's wrath was bending over, hands pressed against his knees, apparently struggling and failing to contain a burgeoning sense of mirth. He was also, she noticed with a quickly stifled gasp, in a state of considerable undress. Thankfully, he was still wearing breeches, but his jacket, waistcoat and cravat were all neatly folded to one side, while his plain white shirt was unbuttoned and gaping open to reveal an expanse of broad and muscular chest, liberally sprinkled with hair the same midnight shade as the dishevelled and curly locks on his head.

'Are you *laughing*?' She gaped at him in disbelief.

'Just a little.' He let out what could only be described as a guffaw.

'But why?'

'Why?' It was several moments before he could answer with anything resembling calmness. 'Because I've spent the past five years in His Majesty's Navy and I've been attacked more in the past six hours than I have in almost the whole of that time. You two are more dangerous than the French.'

'I should think so.' Nancy folded her arms belligerently. '*I* could deal with Napoleon.'

'I'm sure you'd be a worthy opponent. The Emperor wouldn't stand a chance.' Mr Fortini pushed himself upright and wiped his eyes. 'I don't think I've ever been tipped out of a bed before. Not even a hammock.'

'Oh, dear.' Henrietta winced. 'I hope it didn't hurt.'

'Not too badly. Fortunately, I was distracted from the pain by the avalanche of books on my head.'

'They were the first things that came to hand, but if you really are Anna's brother then I'm sorry.' Nancy slid the porcelain cat back to safety. 'By the way, I think I might have damaged your nose.'

'No, that was me.' Henrietta shook her head miserably. 'I hit him with a door in the night.'

'Really?' Nancy looked impressed.

'Really,' Mr Fortini confirmed. 'She threatened to impale me with some tongs, too, though fortunately she relented. Altogether, it's been a somewhat strange homecoming, but I'm delighted to meet you, Miss…?'

'MacQueen. Nancy MacQueen.'

'Sebastian Fortini, at your service.'

'Hmmm.' Nancy gave him a long, interrogatory stare. 'No hard feelings, then?'

'I wouldn't dare.'

'Good. In that case, I'd better go and get breakfast

started. We won't get the baking done on an empty stomach.'

Henrietta shuffled her feet self-consciously as Nancy disappeared down the lower flight of stairs to the kitchen and shop floor. It felt strange to be alone with Mr Fortini again. To be alone with any man for that matter. She'd made a point of avoiding situations like this for the past eight months and yet she'd spent at least an hour in *his* company during the night without any anxiety at all. She'd felt instinctively comfortable with him, probably because he was Anna's brother—so much that she'd actually asked him to stay! It seemed so unlike her, these days anyway, that if it hadn't been for her rude awakening then she might have suspected him to have been part of some dream. The whole situation was bizarre, but he looked too large and robust to be anything *but* real. Not to mention that there was an overturned sofa at his feet.

'I really am sorry.' She peered across at him sheepishly. 'I'm usually the first one to wake up. It never occurred to me that I'd sleep longer.'

'Since I was responsible for you being tired, I can hardly blame you for that.' He lowered his voice conspiratorially. 'Just promise there aren't any more assailants lying in wait. I'm not sure my nerves could take it.'

'I promise.' She caught her breath as he leaned in towards her, one hand on his chest as if he were genuinely concerned about his nerves, which only drew her attention back to that part of his body, not to mention the row of powerful-looking stomach muscles underneath... Quickly, she lifted her gaze to his face, though that was hardly much better. He looked rugged and rumpled and, well, *bruised*, with a masculine appeal that went beyond merely handsome, not to mention a roguish glint in his eye that made her feel as if she'd just been running. Which to be fair, she had down the stairs, but that had been several minutes ago.

'Well then...' She bent down, grasping one end of the overturned sofa in an attempt to hide her face while she got her breath back. The whole parlour seemed somehow smaller and airless with him in it. 'Perhaps you'd like to sleep some more? We'll try not to make too much noise in the kitchen.'

'Allow me.' He flipped the sofa over as if it were just a piece of toy furniture. 'No, I'll get up now, too. I should probably be going before your neighbours arrive to see what all the commotion was about.'

'If anyone asks, I'll tell them a cat got into the house.' She gathered up the books and stacked them back on the shelves, struck with a combination of relief and regret at the thought of him leaving. It seemed impossible to decide which was dominant. There was something both appealing and unsettling about him, something about his bare chest and playful, slightly lopsided smile that caused a peculiar fluttering sensation in her stomach. She wasn't sure whether she liked that either, but surely good manners compelled her to offer him some refreshment?

'Would you care for some breakfast before you go?' The words were out of her mouth before she could stop them. 'It's the least we can do after attacking you twice in one night.'

'That's a good point.' He smiled in a way that made her heart perform a somersault in her chest and her head instantly regret the offer. 'I'd be delighted, Miss Gardiner.'

* * *

'I didn't think I had a choice, especially after I hit his nose,' Henrietta explained to her assistant ten minutes later. 'He needed somewhere to sleep and this *is* his family's shop.'

'Did he demand to stay?' Nancy looked suspicious again.

'No-o. He was going to leave actually, but I offered to make up the sofa.' She reached for a piece of toast and smeared butter across it. 'Do you think I shouldn't have?'

'Not necessarily, but did you ask him for any proof?'

'Proof of what?'

'That he's who he says he is.' Nancy lifted her eyes to the ceiling. 'He doesn't look much like Anna, except for dark curly hair and brown eyes, but a lot of people have those.'

'He has a similar way of speaking, too, and his lips are *exactly* the same shape as Anna's.'

'You've obviously been paying more attention than I have.' Nancy gave her a quizzical look. 'I can't say I've looked that closely at his lips.'

'Neither have I.' Henrietta felt a wash of colour spread over her cheeks. 'I just think they look similar, that's all…'

She applied another, unnecessary layer of butter to her toast. Now that the shock of the night and that morning had worn off, she was starting to think that perhaps she *had* been somewhat foolish in encouraging Mr Fortini to stay. Even if he was Anna's brother, which she was inclined to believe he was—either that or a very convincing impostor—who was to say that he was the kind of man she *ought* to have let stay under the same roof? Neither Anna nor her mother had ever told her anything untoward about him, but then he'd been away at sea for five years! If there was anything bad, they might not have known about it. And it had never even *occurred* to her to ask for proof of his identity! Instead, she'd been so taken aback by his arrival that she'd let her guard down and gone back to her old ways. She'd been too trusting. Too stupid. Too naive. More unworldly than ever. Good grief, even *he'd* thought that his staying was a bad idea! What must he think of her now, especially after the way she'd been staring at his chest that morning? What if she'd given him the wrong idea about her and her motives for inviting him to stay? What if he thought—?

'Sorry about the books, by the way.' Nancy interrupted the rising tide of panic. 'I shouldn't have thrown them.'

'Don't worry.' Henrietta was too relieved by the interruption to scold. 'Anna took all of her favourites when she left. It's not as if we can read them anyway.'

'*You* can. You're still having lessons with Miss Pybus, aren't you?'

'Not recently. I haven't had time.'

'Humph.' Nancy's lips set in a thin, disapproving line. 'Your brother doesn't deserve you.'

'Yes, he does.' Henrietta dropped her toast back on to her plate. 'He practically raised me on his own and you know he's been in a terrible state since Alice died. It's as though he's broken inside.'

'I know he's not helping to mend himself either.' Nancy's expression was part-sharp, part-sympathetic. 'My stepfather's a drunk. I recognise the signs.'

'David's not a drunk. He's just having a hard time taking care of himself and the boys at the moment.'

'Well, I don't think it's fair the way he expects you to go every day and take care of them. My mother works herself to the bone for her worthless husband, too, and all she ever gets in return is misery. You'll never catch me throwing my life away on a man, father, brother, husband or whatever you want to call them. If you ask me, the whole lot are a thousand times more trouble than they're worth...' Nancy speared a hard-boiled egg violently on the end of her fork. 'Speaking of which, our guest needs to be on his way. It'll be bad for business if people think we entertain sailors at night.'

'Anyone who thinks us capable of that obviously has no idea what time bakers get up in the morning.' Henrietta sighed. 'But he said he'll be leaving after breakfast anyway, travelling north to see Anna and his mother, I expect.'

'My mother first.' The man in question appeared in the kitchen doorway suddenly, smartly dressed and with his curly hair swept back into a low, slightly dishevelled queue. His square jaw, on which there had been a veritable swathe of black stubble that morning, appeared to have been quite ruthlessly shaved, making the now infamous shape of his lips even more noticeable.

Henrietta turned her attention back to her plate before she could notice anything else. Even with a bruised and off-centre nose, he looked quite disconcertingly handsome. Words like *strapping* and *virile* sprang to mind.

'There's no rush, however,' Mr Fortini continued. 'I came straight here from Plymouth and I've no desire to be shut up in a stagecoach again too soon. I thought I might actually stay in Bath for a few days, although somewhere else, naturally. Is the Wig and Mitre still open?'

'Yes, but it's not very fancy.' Nancy lifted her eyebrows. 'Wouldn't a hotel suit you better?'

'Not really. I may be an officer, but I'm not exactly what you'd call a gentleman.' He winked. 'Now, if that coffee's sufficiently brewed, allow me to pour, ladies.'

'Thank you.' Henrietta took a deep breath as he placed a cup in front of her, trying to quell a fresh burst of fluttering in her chest now as well as her stomach. She'd felt quite comfortable with him during the night, except for one oddly intense moment when their gazes had locked over the teapot, but now it was downright unnerving, not to mention irritating, the way her body seemed to react whenever he winked or smiled or even so much as looked in her direction for that matter. She hadn't felt so unnerved since…well, since Mr Hoxley, and look how that had turned out! She'd learned her lesson about men eight months ago and learned it thoroughly, too, or so she'd thought. Only something about Mr Sebastian Fortini seemed to place her in danger of forgetting it.

She picked up her coffee cup and blew steam across the surface. Frankly, the sooner he left for Yorkshire the better for her peace of mind—and body—it would be.

'Well, this is pleasant.' He sat down in the chair next to hers, a discreet distance away, yet close enough to make the whole right side of her body tingle with awareness. 'You know, Anna told me about you, Miss Gardiner.'

'She did?' She looked around at the words. 'But I thought you said you hadn't heard from her for a year?'

'I haven't. It was before that, in the last letter I received. She'd said that she'd taken on a new assistant to replace the formidable Mrs Padgett and that you were a breath of fresh air. Now I can see why.' He tipped his head closer. 'I only hope she wasn't too much of a tyrant to work for.'

'Not at all.' She stiffened despite his teasing tone. 'I always loved working with Anna.'

'I'm delighted to hear it. What about you, Miss MacQueen? Do you know my sister?'

'A little.' Nancy gave him an appraising look before continuing. 'I got to know your mother quite well, too, when I first came to work here. She used to tell stories about you, like the time you and a friend climbed on to the roof and threw Belles at the houses opposite. She said that you were aiming for the chimneys, but the people in the street below thought it was raining biscuits.'

'Ah...yes.' Mr Fortini rubbed a hand around the back of his neck. 'I suppose I wasn't always the most responsible youth, but I promise to be perfectly well behaved today. In fact, I thought I might go and visit a few of my old haunts if the two of you would care to join me?'

'Us?' Henrietta almost poured coffee into her lap.

'Why not?'

'The shop...'

'Can be closed for one day. Anna and my mother might not be here, but I must have some kind of authority. I'll take the blame anyway.'

'I still don't think...'

'Why don't just the two of you go?' Nancy chimed in unexpectedly.

She felt her jaw drop in surprise. Considering her assistant's earlier comments, Henrietta thought it was the very last thing she would have expected her to say. 'But I couldn't possibly leave you to do everything. It wouldn't be fair.'

'It is when I'm offering and it would be silly for us both to miss a trip out. I can manage on my own as long as we get the baking done first.'

'And I can help with that,' Mr Fortini offered.

'You can bake?' Henrietta looked from him to Nancy and then back again. If she hadn't known better, she might have suspected them of conspiring together.

'I grew up here, didn't I?' He was already rolling his sleeves up. 'Admittedly, it's been a few years since I last wielded a rolling pin, but I haven't forgotten how. Between the three of us, we'll get it all done in no time.'

Chapter Three

Henrietta stared unhappily into her bedroom mirror. She'd changed out of the plain brown muslin she used for baking and into her best cotton day dress, but her reflection looked all wrong. The turquoise-blue shade of the fabric matched her eyes perfectly, complementing her skin tone and even somehow accentuating the strawberry threads in her hair, but those very things in themselves made her uneasy. She didn't *want* to match or complement or accentuate anything. And she didn't want to go for a walk either!

She stuck her tongue out at her reflection. It wasn't that Mr Fortini wasn't good company. On the contrary, he'd proven himself extremely *good* company that morning, chatting, joking and even singing a few verses of opera while he'd demonstrated his formidable skill in the kitchen. It wasn't that the weather was poor either. The world outside her window looked cold but sunny, surprisingly so for November. Annoyingly perfect for a promenade. It was just...*why* had he asked her to accompany him? *Why* did he want to go for a walk with her? What if she really *had* given him the wrong impression during the night and he thought she was the kind of woman who might welcome male attention? What if he wanted to flirt with her, or worse?

On the other hand, she reassured herself, he'd included Nancy in the invitation, too. *That* would have been acceptable, enjoyable even, if it hadn't been for her assistant's out-of-character suggestion that just the two of them should go. They'd have to discuss that later, Henrietta thought darkly, but right now she had more immediate problems. Such as the fact that she was going for a walk with a man, a gentleman even, which he *was* no matter how he described himself.

Anna had told her the story a few months before, about how their mother, Lady Elizabeth Holden, the only daughter of a duke, had run away with an Italian footman twenty-five years before and been disowned by her family right up until that past summer. *That* made Mr Fortini a gentleman, of sorts anyway, although whether he was or wasn't was beside the point since she no longer went for walks with *any* kind of man, no matter how ruggedly handsome she might find them.

No, she decided, unbuttoning her dress despite the fact that she'd already wasted five minutes simply staring and worrying, she *couldn't* wear anything so flattering. Or *anything* that might enhance her appearance at all! As much as she wanted and strove to be modest, it was impossible to deny the effect her looks seemed to have upon men. If she could have given some of her beauty away, she would have done so—and gladly. Maybe *then* she would have stood a chance of knowing who was interested in her real self and not just her appearance. Up until a few months ago, she hadn't understood the difference, but now she knew that all most men saw or cared about was her face and figure. They all wanted the same thing, too, something she wasn't prepared to give, and it didn't take much for them to confuse friendliness for encouragement. She'd learned *that* from experience, too, and had no intention of making the same mistake again.

Quickly, she slid the blue dress over her hips and replaced it with the most shapeless item she owned, a scratchy grey woollen gown that irritated her skin, but was eminently sensible for a winter's excursion, then wrapped a dowdy old shawl around her shoulders and topped the effect with an even dowdier jockey cap bonnet. *There*, she thought with satisfaction, taking a second look in the mirror before starting down the staircase, that was much better. Or, if not better, then at least nothing that could be misinterpreted. If Mr Fortini was like most other men and judged by appearances, her outfit would tell him everything he needed to know about her. She looked like what she was determined to be: a serious and respectable shopkeeper, not someone to be flirted with and absolutely *not* the kind of woman who flashed her ankles while accosting men in her nightgown.

Of course, it was possible, she realised upon entering the shop, that she was somewhat overdoing the statement. Or definitely overdoing it if the roll of Nancy's eyes was anything to go by. If Mr Fortini hadn't already been leaning against the shop counter, waiting for her in a surprisingly thin-looking jacket and black top hat, she had a feeling she might have been marched back up the stairs and made to change. Again.

'Ready, Miss Gardiner?' Mr Fortini's own expression didn't waver as he opened the shop door.

'Quite ready, thank you.' She threw Nancy a pointed look and stepped outside, albeit wondering whether the eye roll was appropriate and she *was* overreacting a little. After all, Mr Fortini was Anna's brother and it wasn't as if he'd suggested anything scandalous. They were simply going for a walk around the city in broad daylight, a stroll down memory lane for him and a pleasant change to the daily routine for her. And Bath in the winter was more spectacularly beautiful than ever, the long rows of limestone buildings glowing a pale honey-gold shade wherever the sun kissed them. It would really be a shame not to enjoy such a gorgeous day while it lasted. There was nothing for her to be worried about and she really shouldn't—

'Shall we?'

The appearance of an outstretched arm made her shriek as if a wild animal with razor-sharp teeth and blood-stained claws had just hurled itself across her path.

'Miss Gardiner?' Mr Fortini looked justifiably confused.

'Oh, excuse me. I thought I saw a...snake.'

'A snake?' A pair of black eyebrows disappeared beneath his top hat.

'Yes.' She came down off her tiptoes and cleared her throat awkwardly. It was the first wild animal that had come to mind, but still, a snake in *Bath*? Even a slowworm was somewhat far-fetched.

'I see...' The eyebrows showed no sign of coming down again. 'Well, stranger things have happened, I suppose. Fortunately it appears to have slithered away.'

'Perhaps I imagined it.'

'Or a trick of the light, maybe?' He extended his arm a second time, bending his elbow with what appeared to be deliberate slowness.

'Ye-es.' She lifted her chin and curled her hand cautiously around his bicep, trying to ignore the flicker of heat that immediately sparked in her abdomen and darted outwards, along her arms to her fingers and down her legs all the way to her toes. If she wasn't mistaken, even the top of her head was in danger of overheating. Her whole body felt strange, the way it had that morning when she'd caught a glimpse of his bare chest, a memory she'd intended to repress as quickly as possible, but which seemed determined to keep intruding upon her consciousness like one of those tunes that got stuck in your head. Or like a particularly quote-worthy line from a poem, not that his chest was inherently poetic, just unfortunately unforgettable... Oh, dear. Her thick woollen shawl was starting to feel somewhat redundant.

'Shall we head towards Pulteney Bridge?' He strode onwards, appearing not to notice any change in temperature, possibly because he hadn't even bothered to fasten his jacket. 'I want to see what's changed over the past few years.'

'Not too much, I think.' She hurried to keep up, relieved to put the subject of snakes behind them. 'But then I suppose you don't always notice changes when you live in a place from day to day. I suppose even Belles must seem very different to you.'

'Yes, although that doesn't necessarily mean the changes are bad ones.' He gave her a sideways smile.

'Some of them are actually quite pleasant. Once the initial pain has worn off, obviously.'

'Oh…yes. How *is* your nose?'

'*Not* broken.' His expression was faintly triumphant. 'You'll have to try harder next time.'

She blinked, uncertain about how to respond to the joke, especially when she was still trying to regain her equilibrium and accept his arm for what it was, *just* an arm, no matter how sturdy or sinewy or astonishingly muscular it felt beneath her fingertips. None the less, she had the alarming impression that he was trying to compliment her, which meant that she needed to change the subject and quickly.

'Oh, look!' She was seized with a sudden burst of inspiration, pointing across Great Pulteney Street to the shopfront opposite. 'That's Redbourne's new general store. They moved premises last year. Now it's one of the largest shops in the city.'

'Is that so?' Mr Fortini sounded interested. 'Tell me, does old Mr Redbourne still manage the place?'

'No, his son took over a while ago.'

'Even better…' He acknowledged the words with a wicked-looking grin. 'Remember that story about me and a friend throwing biscuits across the street? Jem was my partner in crime.'

'Mr *James* Redbourne? But he always seems so…'

'Good and responsible? I know. His father always thought I was the bad influence, if you can believe that, but Jem was more than capable of getting into trouble on his own. He was just better at hiding it.' His grin widened. 'I'll have to pay him a visit and see if I can lure him back into old ways.'

'Maybe I ought to warn him.' She couldn't help but

smile, unable to resist his good humour. 'I could send a message, only not with Nancy. They don't get along.'

'Really? Has she been throwing books at his head, too?'

'She probably would if she could, but I don't know what she has against him. It's a mystery.'

'Now that sounds like a challenge...but enough about them. Tell me more about yourself, Miss Gardiner. I'm curious. Have you always lived in Bath?'

'No-o.' She stopped smiling and drew her brows together, wondering what to make of the question. She'd had similar enquiries from men before—not so much out of interest, she'd realised eventually, more to work out if she had some kind of protector—but Mr Fortini looked as if he were simply making conversation. And there was no harm in telling him a few details, surely? 'I grew up six miles away in Ashley.'

'I know the village. In fact, I believe I travelled through it yesterday, although it was hard to tell in the dark.'

'It's a pleasant place, but Bath is my home now.'

'Mine, too.' He looked around as if he were trying to take in every detail of the street. 'You know, it's funny. I spent most of my youth longing to escape and see the world, but I missed this place the moment I left. As much as I wanted to go, part of me has been homesick ever since.'

'That must have been hard.'

'Fortunately, I had plenty of distractions. The navy doesn't like to let grass grow under your feet. Or lichen anyway. So what made you leave Ashley and move to the city?'

'I had to. After our parents died, my brother and I needed to find work. That was ten years ago.'

'I'm sorry.' His voice softened. 'It's always hard to lose a parent, but you must have been very young, too. Eight? Nine?'

'Nine, but it was worse for David, my brother. He's eleven years older than me and had to take care of both of us. Fortunately, I found a job on a market stall, selling cloth. Then when I was seventeen I got a position in a dressmaker's...' She frowned at the pavement, wondering why she'd just told him that when she usually avoiding thinking about it herself. It wasn't a pleasant memory, one she had to shake her head to get rid of. 'Then I came to Belles.'

'I see. Why di—?'

'What made you join the navy?' She spoke before he could finish the question.

'Mmm?' He looked mildly surprised at the interruption. 'Oh, the spirit of adventure, I suppose. I always loved the idea.'

'Did the reality match up?'

'It wasn't quite what I'd expected.' A strange, inscrutable expression passed over his face. 'Some parts were better than others, but I got to travel, to find out what I was made of, too. Unfortunately, it came to feel somewhat tainted.'

'Tainted?'

'Yes. My father died not long after I joined, but when I got the news I was already at sea and couldn't come back.' He paused, his voice sounding rougher when he spoke again. 'By the time I had shore leave he'd been buried a year.'

'Oh.' She tightened her hand on his arm. 'I'm sorry.'

'So am I. Sometimes I think it was selfish of me to have left Bath in the first place.'

'What do you mean?'

'My father always worked too hard. I knew that. Maybe I should have stayed and forced him to retire.'

'But did he enjoy working in the shop?'

'He loved it. Belles was his pride and joy.'

'Then maybe you couldn't have forced him to stop.' She looked at him steadily. 'What about the navy? Did he object to your joining?'

'No, he was happy for me. He knew how much I wanted to get out on my own and travel like he had. My mother wasn't so enthusiastic, but at the time...well, Anna and my father were a good team in the shop and there didn't seem any need for me to stay. He seemed in perfect health, too. There was no way any of us could have known what would happen, but when it did...' He paused for a moment as they crossed Pulteney Bridge. 'Miss Gardiner, if I ask you a question, would you promise to give me an honest answer?'

'Of course.'

'Thank you. You see, after my father died, I felt that it was my responsibility to come back and help run the business. That was what he would have wanted, but it's not so easy to leave the navy, especially in wartime. There was nothing I could do to help except send money home, but I'd still like to know...how difficult have things been for Anna and my mother over the past few years?'

'Oh...' Henrietta sucked in a breath slowly. She didn't want to make him feel bad by admitting the truth, but that was what he'd asked for and what she'd promised to give. 'I believe that Anna *did* have a hard time running the shop on her own. The swelling in your mother's hands and feet got so bad that it became impossible for her to help with the baking and they couldn't afford to pay anyone else for the hours. Not for a while anyway.'

'So Anna had to do it all by herself?'

'Ye-es, but then she met the Earl and I moved in, so…' She tried to sound positive. 'It all worked out in the end.'

'No thanks to me, but I appreciate your honesty, Miss Gardiner.' A muscle clenched in his jaw. 'So, what happened at the dressmaker's?'

'What?' She almost tripped over her feet at the question. She'd thought they'd moved past that particularly unpleasant subject. 'What do you mean, what happened?'

'I just wondered why you left.' He reached his other hand out to steady her. 'Presumably you decided you preferred biscuits to dresses?'

'Not exactly. That is, I *do* prefer working at Belles, but I had other reasons for leaving. Anna understood them.'

'Ah.' He gave her a sidelong glance, seemingly on the verge of asking something else before changing his mind. 'Tell me about my new brother-in-law, then. Do you like him?'

'Lord Staunton? Yes, very much.'

'Good. Although he has another name, I presume?'

'Samuel, although I never dare to call him that no matter how many times he tells me to. I'll always think of him as Captain Delaney.'

'Captain?' He stopped walking abruptly.

'Yes. He was Captain of the *Colossus* at Trafalgar.'

Mr Fortini adjusted the brim of his top hat, let out a low whistle and leaned against a wall looking out over the River Avon. 'That was involved in some of the worst fighting. I like him better already, but how did a sea captain-cum-earl become acquainted with my sister in the first place?'

'He came to the shop. You could see that he liked her straight away, but she wasn't so sure.'

'Why not?'

'Well...' She hesitated, her stomach churning in the way it always did when she thought of that day. Life-changing as it had been for Anna, it had been well-nigh disastrous for her. 'She thought that he was a rake.'

'Was he?' His expression sharpened at once.

'No, but she thought so because of his companion, Mr Hoxley. As it turned out, she was right about him.'

'I see.' Mr Fortini held on to her gaze for a few seconds. 'You know, you provoke a lot of questions, Miss Gardiner.'

'Do I?' She laughed nervously. 'I don't think I'm that interesting.'

'On the contrary, I think you might be *very* interesting.'

'No.' She swallowed convulsively. There was a softness to his voice suddenly, an almost liquid quality that made her stomach twist and tighten even as it set alarm bells ringing in her head. 'You're mistaken. I'm really not.'

'Which is a polite way of telling me to mind my own business, I suppose.' He leaned slightly towards her. 'Forgive me. It's been a while since I've been in the company of a young lady.'

'A lady?' She shook her head at the description. 'I'm hardly one of those either.'

'And now you sound just like Anna. I've always thought that most people fundamentally misunderstand the word. Personally, I take it to mean honest, kind and thoughtful, all of which qualities you've already demonstrated. No, Miss Gardiner, I have to disagree. You seem quintessentially ladylike to me.'

Henrietta was aware of a strange duality of feeling, as if one side of her body were burning hot and the other icy cold. His words were unexpectedly touching, but she didn't want to be touched, either metaphorically or literally, and she didn't know whether to trust such a compliment either. He sounded sincere, but rakes always *sounded* sincere. Just because he was Anna's brother didn't mean that he wasn't just the same as Mr Hoxley underneath! Or Mr Willerby for that matter… Or any of the other men who came to the shop trying to flirt with her!

'Shall we go up to the Crescent?' He turned his head in that direction, smiling again. 'I'd like to be seen by as many people as possible. It's not every day I have such a beautiful young lady on my arm.'

Beautiful? Henrietta took a step backwards, bumping into a pedestrian walking behind her as she tore her hand away from his arm. That did it! If there was one thing she'd made sure of that morning, it was that she did *not* look beautiful!

'Mr Fortini.' She apologised to the pedestrian before wrapping her shawl tightly around her shoulders like a suit of armour. 'I agreed to come for a walk because I thought you simply wanted a companion.'

'I do.' He looked faintly bemused by her indignant tone.

'Then I'd like to get one thing clear. No matter what impression I might have given during the night, I am not *that* kind of woman.'

'What kind of—?'

'I do not have loose morals!'

'The thought never entered my mind.' His bemusement faded instantly. 'Miss Gardiner, if I've offended you then I'm truly sorry. It was unintentional, I assure you.'

'You haven't offended me.' She blinked a few times to hide the lie in her eyes. 'But just to be clear, I invited you to stay last night as a favour to Anna, nothing more. I may be an independent woman, but I do not care to be flirted with and I'd appreciate your putting any thoughts of that nature aside.'

'Consider it done.' He sounded sombre, though with a hint of confusion, almost enough to make her believe that he meant it.

'Good... And no more compliments.'

'Understood.'

'Thank you.'

'Well then, shall we continue?' He cleared his throat after a few moments of heavy silence, disturbed only by the fierce torrent of the river over the weir below. 'Perhaps you'd allow me to buy you a cup of tea to make amends? As I recall, there used to be quite a good tea shop on Milsom Street.'

Chapter Four

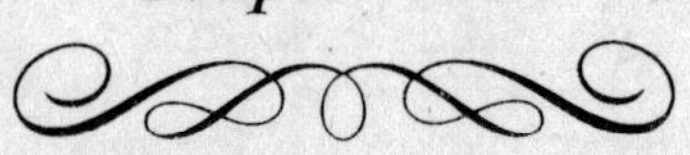

'Here we are, Miss Gardiner.'

Sebastian found them a small, octagon-shaped table in one corner of the tea room and tried to think of some innocuous subject to talk about. His companion was pursing her lips so tightly that she resembled a strait-laced and highly strung governess, a look exacerbated by her frankly appalling taste in clothes. She'd seemed tense from the moment they'd left Belles—since he'd come down to breakfast, now he thought about it—but he'd believed that she'd been starting to relax in his company. Obviously not. Whatever camaraderie they'd established during their walk was now completely gone. She seemed a whole different woman from the one who'd accosted him with fire tongs at midnight and he had no idea what the hell had gone wrong.

He folded one long leg over the other and bit back a sigh. In all honesty, he was having regrets about inviting her to walk at all, but ironically, he'd *wanted* to spend more time with her. Hard as it was to believe or remember why at that moment, he'd *wanted* to enjoy his newfound freedom with her and a walk in the sunshine.

Now he had the impression that she was regretting it, too. If he wasn't mistaken, she was actually counting the minutes until he took her back to the shop, which didn't say a great deal for his company, but then he supposed he was somewhat out of practice in talking to the opposite sex.

Months on end at sea with eight hundred other sailors tended to have a somewhat coarsening effect on a man's manners, which was probably why he'd ended up offending her, although calling her beautiful wasn't *such* a terrible thing to do, was it? Especially when he'd been entirely serious. She would have been stunning wearing a sack. And he didn't even know where to begin with her declaration about *loose morals.* She was acting as if he'd just tried to seduce her in the street in broad daylight!

Not that he would have been entirely averse to the idea…

'Thank you.' Miss Gardiner managed a half-smile as the waitress placed two cups of tea on the table in front of them. 'And you, too, Mr Fortini. This is very kind.'

'Don't mention it.' He nodded tersely. At least he'd got *one* thing right that morning. 'My mother always liked this tea shop. I'm glad it's still here.'

'Yes.' She took a sip and then placed her cup back in its saucer with a loud rattle. Or at least it seemed loud in the silence that followed since neither of them appeared to have any idea what else to say next.

'Tea in the navy is appalling.' He groaned inwardly as the words emerged from his own lips. Why not just talk about the weather?

'Really?'

'Yes, the leaves get weaker and weaker over the

course of a voyage. We had to give up on them eventually on my last ship. Quite a calamity for an Englishman.'

'I suppose so.' Her lips un-pursed slightly. 'Nancy and I were thinking about selling tea at the shop. Or coffee, perhaps, to go with the biscuits. I thought I might suggest it to Anna the next time she visits. Of course, we'll probably have to hire another assistant, but the shop's doing well enough that I think we can afford it...' Her voice trailed away as if she thought she'd just said too much. 'We'll see.'

'It sounds like an excellent idea to me.' He shifted forward in his seat. 'Miss Gardiner, about before—'

'It's quite all right,' she interrupted quickly. 'Perhaps I overreacted. In fact, I probably did. It's just that I prefer *not* to be complimented.'

Sebastian resisted the urge to raise his eyebrows at such a curious statement. Surely a woman who looked the way she did received dozens of compliments every day? And compliments were generally considered to be good things, weren't they? Why would she object? Then again, why would a beautiful woman deliberately dress herself in a garment that resembled nothing so much as an old coal sack? Not to mention a bonnet that seemed intended to drain all the colour from her complexion. Unless she was wearing them deliberately to discourage him from offering any form of flattery? Because she didn't want to look attractive? He thought back to her earlier protest. *I'm not* that *kind of woman...* What the hell kind of impression did she think she'd given him during the night?

He gave a jolt, realising that she was still waiting for an answer. 'Of course.'

'In fact, I'd prefer it if you'd speak to me as you would to Anna, as if I'm your sister.'

This time he had to wrench his eyebrows firmly back into place. Apparently, he really *had* lost his touch with the opposite sex if she was experiencing fraternal feelings towards him. Not that it ought to matter since he was leaving Bath soon anyway, but a man had his pride. Still, if fraternal was what she wanted, then fraternal was what he would give her. Which meant, first and foremost, that he needed to stop paying quite so much attention to her lips. Even pursed, they were still decidedly tempting: plump in the middle, with a peaked cupid's bow that he wanted to run his finger along. What would it be like to kiss her? he wondered. To slide his hands into her hair and bring her face to his, to press his own lips against her forehead and cheeks, maybe the tip of her nose, then finally her mouth…

'Very well.' He cleared his throat, feeling hot under the collar all of a sudden. 'But I should warn you this gives me licence to pull your hair and untie your apron strings.'

There was a faint spark in her eye. 'Then I'll just have to keep my bonnet on and be vigilant.'

'Excellent idea. You can't be too careful.' He leaned backwards, relieved that they'd cleared the air slightly at least. 'So where shall we wander to next? Up to the Circus?'

The spark faltered and then went out. 'I think perhaps I ought to return to Belles. I'm not happy about leaving Nancy to mind the shop all alone.'

'Ah…' He inclined his head. It seemed she really was counting the minutes, after all, although perhaps she was right and it *was* better to put their promenade out of its misery before they ended up talking about tea again. 'As you wish. In that case, I'll escort you back.'

'There's really no need.'

'There is to me.' He picked up his teacup with a terse smile. 'I said I wasn't much of a gentleman, Miss Gardiner, but I do make a bit of an effort. We'll leave whenever you're ready.'

'Sebastian Fortini?' A strapping, chestnut-haired man wearing a leather apron put down the barrel he was carrying and strode across the shop floor to greet him. 'What are you doing here?'

'I came to visit an old friend, but I can't see him anywhere.' Sebastian made a show of looking around. 'You look a *bit* like him, but you can't be. The James Redbourne I knew was a scrawny lad, all skin and bones.'

'I was a late developer.'

'*Late?* You must have grown at least a foot since I left.'

'A foot and a half, actually.'

'Well, it's good to see you again.' Sebastian found himself enveloped in a bear hug. 'Even if you *are* taller and broader than me these days.'

'Without any obvious bruises either.' His old friend peered at his face. 'What happened to your nose? Have you been fighting?'

'No. For once in my life, I've been entirely innocent of wrongdoing. Unfortunately, that doesn't seem to make any difference to the result.'

'Then I want to hear all about it. Come on.' James draped an arm around his shoulders, jerking his head at one of the women behind the counter as he steered him towards a small and pristinely tidy office.

'Take a seat.' James gestured towards a green leather-backed chair in front of a mahogany desk and then sat down behind it, extracting a bottle and two glasses from one of the drawers. 'Whisky?'

'I wouldn't say no.' Sebastian eased himself into the chair with a contented and approving sigh. 'The place looks good.'

'It's a new start.' James poured amber liquid into the two glasses and nudged one across the table. 'Our old premises were getting cramped so, once I took over the business, I decided we had to move.'

'I'm impressed. I thought your father would never retire.'

'So did I, but in the end my mother made the decision for him. Something to the effect of waiting fifty years for his attention and it was either her or the shop. Now they have a cottage in the country and are both happier than I've ever seen them. He's even taken up gardening. Delphiniums are his speciality.'

'Good for him. And even better for you. You're obviously a hands-on kind of manager.'

James glanced down at his leather apron and grinned. 'We had a delivery of brandy this morning.'

'I'll drink to that.' Sebastian raised his glass. 'Apparently I came home at just the right time.'

'Cheers!' James swallowed a mouthful and then gave him a searching look. 'But what are you doing in Bath? Shouldn't you be in Derbyshire, visiting Anna? Or the Countess of Staunton, I suppose I should call her now.'

'*That's* going to take some getting used to.' Sebastian rolled his eyes. 'The truth is I didn't know that she'd left, or that she'd got married either for that matter. I only found out when I got back to Belles last night and my mind is still boggling.'

'You only got home last night?'

'*During* the night, yes. That's how I ended up with this bruise.'

'Don't tell me, the charming Miss MacQueen?'

'Miss Gardiner actually.'

'Miss Gardiner?' James spluttered on his drink. '*She* hit you?'

'Not directly. She used a door. Then she threatened to castrate me with a pair of fire tongs.'

'You must have made quite an impression.'

'She thought I was a burglar, though in all fairness, she saved me from having a vase smashed over my head this morning. That *was* Miss MacQueen.' He put his glass down on the table for a refill. 'It was an eventful night.'

'It sounds like it.'

'Do you know her at all?'

'Miss MacQueen?'

'Miss Gardiner.'

'Oh.' If he wasn't mistaken, his old friend's cheeks flushed slightly. 'No, not very well. She was quite friendly when we first moved in, but she's been a lot more reserved since she took over Belles. One of my men tried flirting with her once and she almost bit his head off. Now they call her the ice queen, but no one really knows what to make of her any more.'

'I'm glad I'm not the only one.'

'Anna trusts her anyway.'

'What makes you say that?' Sebastian paused with his glass halfway to his lips.

'Nothing.'

'Nothing means something. I know you, James. What is it?'

His friend swallowed another mouthful of whisky and sighed. 'There were some rumours a while ago. Something to do with her previous place of employment. A milliner, I think.'

'A dressmaker. What kind of rumours?'

'I don't like gossip, Seb.'

'Neither do I, but if she's running my family business then I have a right to know.'

He winced inwardly, feeling a twinge of guilt at the words. They sounded pompous, not to mention faintly hypocritical given that he hadn't been involved in the business for so many years. In retrospect, Miss Gardiner *had* seemed somewhat defensive when he'd asked about her previous employment earlier, although she'd also told him that Anna knew her reasons for leaving. All of which meant that it was none of his business. In this case, however, curiosity appeared to outweigh conscience.

'All right, but it doesn't go outside this room.' James stood up and closed the door. 'They say there was some kind of scandal involving her and the owner's son.'

'*They* say?'

'One of my staff heard a story. Something about the mother accusing her of being a fortune hunter, of trying to seduce and trap him into marriage, but as to whether it's true...' He lifted his shoulders. 'In any case, she was sacked without references. That part's definitely true because I remember she came to the old shop looking for work. Unfortunately, my father wasn't sympathetic.'

Sebastian frowned into his glass, swirling the liquid around as he mentally negotiated his way through a confusing blend of emotions—indignation, surprise and something else he couldn't quite put his finger on... He didn't want to pay any heed to gossip and it was frankly hard to believe that the guarded and prickly woman he'd spent the morning with could ever have done something so scandalous, but it put her words about loose morals into some kind of perspective, especially if she'd been accused of them before...

If that were the case, however, then she'd either been unjustly accused or she was a reformed character, but surely *something* must have happened for her to be sacked without references...and damn it if the other emotion wasn't jealousy!

Jealousy? How could he be jealous over a woman he hadn't even met this time yesterday? The very idea was outlandish. Laughable, really. And yet something about it rang true.

'So, are you back on dry land for good?' James seemed eager to steer the conversation into a different channel. 'Or are you still restless?'

'Not as much as I used to be. To be honest, I'd reconciled myself to the idea of coming back to help Anna with Belles, but it appears I'm surplus to requirements. It's been taken over by two attractive, but extremely violent females.' He made a wry face. 'It could have been worse, I suppose. As for the navy, I'm pretty sure my chances of finding another post were scuppered alongside Napoleon's fleet.' He frowned. 'Although I'm not entirely sure I'd want to go back anyway.'

'So, what next?'

'Next I'll go north to visit Anna and my mother. After that...who knows? The world's my oyster apparently, although I thought I might loiter in Bath for today.'

'I was hoping you'd say that.' James grinned. 'In that case, you should stay with me tonight. I have rooms upstairs.'

'You're inviting me to stay in a building that's just received a fresh delivery of brandy?'

'Actually, when you put it like that...'

'Too late. I accept.' Sebastian laughed, resolving to put all thoughts of Miss Gardiner, fortune-hunting seductress or not, out of his mind. Aside from her obvious lack of interest in *him*, her past was none of his business and he had other things to think about. What to do with his future for a start. His sister was happily married, his mother ensconced with her family in the north and Belles appeared to be running smoothly. The world really *was* his oyster...and the last thing he needed was to be distracted by a woman, especially an ice queen.

He lifted his glass and tossed back the last of his whisky. He'd go and pick up his bag from Belles later, but after that...well, he doubted he'd be sharing anything more than pleasantries with Miss Gardiner again.

Chapter Five

'What went wrong?'

Henrietta's heart sank as Nancy confronted her, hands planted firmly on hips, at the bottom of the stairs. She'd been relieved to spy several customers in the shop when she'd come back in through the kitchen earlier, allowing her to sneak up to her bedroom and change into her yellow shop dress unnoticed, but now it seemed she wasn't going to escape an interrogation so lightly. Which was the very last thing she wanted, especially after she'd just made such a fool of herself in front of Mr Fortini.

'I don't know what you mean.' She smoothed her hair, making sure it was tucked neatly behind her ears while she maintained a calm and collected expression. 'Nothing went wrong.'

'*Something* must have happened for you to be back here so soon.' Nancy looked unconvinced. 'I said that you should take your time and enjoy yourself. Where *is* Mr Fortini anyway? Why didn't he escort you back?'

'He escorted me to the end of the crescent, if you must know, but I insisted on walking the rest of the way by myself. I'm sure he has better things to do than spend his time with me.'

'He seemed pretty keen on your company this morning.'

'I'm sure he was just being polite.'

'I doubt it.' Nancy gave a sceptical snort as they made their way through to the shop. 'Men are never that polite to me.'

'He invited both of us.'

'He was looking at you while he said it. I'm not blind. It was perfectly obvious it was you he wanted to walk with, just like every other man who comes in here, I might add. It's a good thing I *don't* want a husband or working with you could prove extremely frustrating.'

'You shouldn't put yourself down. You're very pretty.'

'No, I'm not, but you're a good friend to say so.' Nancy removed her hands from her hips finally. 'My hair is too red, my face is covered with freckles and I have an awful temper. Men don't like any of those things, or so my mother tells me.' She grimaced. 'Not that she's an authority on men, but my aunt said it, too. And my grandmother.'

'I'd rather that men *didn't* look at me.' Henrietta sighed. 'Or at least it would be nice if one of them could actually see *me*, the real me, I mean.'

'Is that what that awful outfit was about? You know you can be the real you without dressing like a scarecrow.'

'I dressed for the cold.'

'It's not *that* cold. I'm surprised birds didn't peck at you.'

'Well, they didn't.' Henrietta braced her hands

firmly on the counter. 'I might have looked a bit severe, but I didn't want any misunderstandings, that's all.'

'And why do you always assume misunderstandings are your fault? You're not responsible for what other people think. If men get the wrong impression, then that's their problem, not yours.'

'I know. Or I sort of know. I just don't want to make any more mistakes or feel stupid again.'

'I understand.' Nancy placed a supportive hand on her arm. 'But you're *not* stupid, you never have been and you don't need to hide away or pretend to be anyone other than who you are. You don't see me pretending to be calm and patient, do you?'

'Not often, no.' Henrietta found her lips twitching. 'Only you're not getting out of this argument so easily. I didn't *want* to go for a walk with Mr Fortini and you shouldn't have suggested it. You were the one who said that men were more trouble than they're worth!'

'Most of them are.'

'Exactly! You weren't even convinced that he was Anna's brother this morning.'

'Yes, but once I looked closer, I could see that you were right about the resemblance. And if he's her brother, then that means he won't be anything like...' Nancy paused and clucked her tongue '...like some men whose ears I'd like to box and will if I ever see them. Even *I* can accept there are a few exceptions to the rule. Besides, I thought you liked him.'

Henrietta gawked in surprise. 'What on earth made you think that?'

'Like I said, I'm not blind. You kept sneaking glances at him over breakfast.'

'I did not!'

'Yes, you did *and* you were fidgeting, but if it makes you feel any better, he was doing the same thing. It was putting me off my breakfast watching the pair of you.'

'You were imagining things.'

'I never imagine things. I'm not an imaginative person.' Nancy looked infuriatingly smug. 'And I'll admit that he's handsome in a rough kind of way. Is he coming to say goodbye?'

'I've no idea.' Henrietta started to tidy an already neat pile of boxes on the counter, chiding herself for the way her stomach clenched and then seemed to perform a jig at the thought. 'Although he left his belongings upstairs so I suppose he'll be back to—'

'What?' Nancy clamped her eyebrows together as she stopped mid-sentence.

'There she is again.' Henrietta pointed towards the window.

'Who?'

'The woman I told you about yesterday. She's been out on the pavement every day this week, just standing there or walking up and down. She's peered in at our window a few times, but she never comes in. I think she might be hungry.'

'She's dressed like a lady.' Nancy moved to one side of the window, peering out surreptitiously. 'Odd that she's wandering about without a maid, though. Maybe she's in some kind of trouble.'

'She keeps looking up at the boarding house as if she's waiting for someone to come out.'

'*Definitely* in trouble, then.'

'In that case, we should help her.' Henrietta nodded decisively, wrapping half a dozen Belles in a muslin cloth before heading for the door.

'Wait a minute.' Nancy put a restraining hand on her arm. 'For all we know, she might be a dangerous criminal.'

'I don't think so. She only looks about the same age as us.'

'*We* could be dangerous criminals if we wanted.'

'I'm still going to talk to her.' Henrietta lifted her chin, holding the door open for a group of septuagenarian ladies, then waited on the edge of the pavement for a few moments while a cart rolled past before crossing the road. The woman was facing in the other direction, a large, heavy-brimmed bonnet obscuring her face so effectively that Henrietta had to go and stand directly in front of her just to make eye contact.

'Excuse me.' She smiled, trying to look friendly as the woman let out a startled gasp. 'I don't mean to bother you, but I wondered if you'd like a biscuit?'

'I'm sorry?' The woman's face, which looked altogether too gaunt and pale against her sombre outfit, appeared panic-stricken.

'They're a new variety,' Henrietta lied, opening up the muslin. 'We're asking people what they think. Please...take them all.'

'I really shouldn't.' The woman lifted a hand hesitantly, as if she suspected some kind of trap.

'You can come into the shop, too, if you like?' Henrietta offered as the hand wavered in mid-air. 'It's cold out here.'

'No.' Her voice was the barest of whispers. 'No, thank you.'

'We might be able to help. Perhaps if there was someone in particular you were looking for?'

'How do you know—?' The woman's large, hazel-hued eyes widened like saucers before she grabbed two of the biscuits, spun on her heel and ran.

'Maybe he's forgotten about his bag.' Nancy sank down on a stool behind the counter and sighed wearily. It was the end of the day and there was still no sign of Mr Fortini. 'It seems an odd thing to forget about, though.'

'Mmm.' Henrietta turned the sign on the door over to *Closed*, wondering if perhaps she'd been too severe with him earlier and he didn't *want* to come back. Apparently she was scaring everyone off today.

'But I'm sure he'll remember it eventually,' Nancy continued. 'Then you can fix whatever happened between you.'

'I told you, *nothing* happened.'

'I know what you told me, but admit it, you *want* to see him again.'

'I admit nothing of the kind.' Henrietta straightened her shoulders. 'Anyway, I ought to visit David this evening.'

'Again?' Nancy scowled. 'You shouldn't be wandering about the city on your own. It's dark already.'

'I've done it plenty of times and…' she paused awkwardly '…well, I've been thinking that perhaps I ought to move back in with him.'

'What?'

'I know it's not ideal, but he's struggling and he needs me. His neighbour, Mrs Roper, has been helping to look after the boys in the afternoons, but I can't expect her to do it for ever.'

'And you've been paying her too, I expect?'

'Just a little.'

'Oh, Hen, I don't want to sound harsh, but *he's* their father and you already spend most of your free time there. Not to mention your money—and don't tell me it's *just* a little.' She threw her hands up in the air with a look of exasperation. 'Why is it always women who are supposed to drop everything whenever a man needs them? As if they think we don't have lives and ambitions of our own!'

'Because most of them *do* think that.' Henrietta sighed. 'But David's different. He needs me.'

'What about Belles?'

'I could still work here. I'll just have to be a bit more organised.'

'You couldn't *be* any more organised. You'll work yourself into the ground just like my mother. Besides, you can't be traipsing across the city before dawn to do the baking every morning. I won't allow it. No, we'll have to think of something else.'

'I've tried, believe me, but I *do* need to go now. I want to be sure the boys have a proper meal before bed.'

'All right, but don't be too long or I'll worry.'

'I promise.' Henrietta planted a kiss on the top of her head. 'What would I do without you?'

'Break men's noses with doors? You'll have to teach me that trick.'

Henrietta laughed, scooping up a bonnet and shawl before heading out of the back door and retracing the steps she'd walked earlier that day with Mr Fortini. Her brother had a small house in the Avon Street district, only a quarter of an hour away, less if she walked quickly, which she did, weaving her way through the other pedestrians so that she was tapping on the front door in less than ten minutes. To her dismay, however, there was no answer.

'David?' She lifted the latch and pushed the door open cautiously, but there was no sign of anyone inside, only a solitary rushlight flickering on a scratched and severely battered old table.

'He's asleep,' a small voice piped up through the gloom, though it was impossible to tell where it was coming from.

'Peter?' Henrietta looked around in consternation. 'Is that you?'

'It's Michael.' A head poked out from beneath the table. 'Peter's watching Papa. He said he ought to do it because he's two years older than me.'

'Why is he watching your father?' She crouched down, holding her arms out for a hug.

'He's been drinking again.' Michael's eight-year-old voice was matter of fact. 'All day, Mr Roper said. He brought him home and said that we should watch and be sure to roll him over if he's sick.'

'Oh, Michael.' She tightened her arms around her nephew, feeling nauseated herself at the words. 'I'm sorry.'

'It's all right. Mr Roper said he'll be right as rain in the morning, but we should talk quietly.'

'Ye-es.' Henrietta frowned as a new thought occurred to her. 'But how can your father have been drinking all day? Wasn't he at work in the mews?'

'Um...' A guilty expression crossed the little boy's face. 'I'm not s'posed to tell you.'

'Tell me what?'

'He lost his job.' Another voice emerged through a hole in the ceiling, closely followed by a pair of legs descending the ladder. 'Two days ago. They said he was a disgrace.'

'What?' Henrietta looked between the two boys in dismay. 'But I was here that evening. Peter, why didn't you tell me?'

'Papa said not to.'

'Oh.' She frowned. 'Well, that's not your fault. Where's Oliver?'

'Asleep in his cot.' Peter looked as if he were struggling to maintain a stoical expression.

'Aunt Henrietta?' Michael's tone turned wheedling. 'Did you bring any biscuits?'

'What kind of aunt would I be if I hadn't?' She reached into the folds of her cloak and drew out a small bundle. 'Cinnamon Belles for you, Comptessas for Peter and one of everything for Oliver.' She glanced towards the hatch in the ceiling, tempted to go up and deposit a bucket of cold water over her sleeping brother. 'Have you had a proper meal today?'

'Mrs Roper gave us some toast and cheese.' Michael shook his head as he dived into the parcel of biscuits.

'Right.' Henrietta straightened up, looking around the frigid and messy room with a burst of determination. She was going to have to break her promise to Nancy, but she'd deal with that later. 'First, we're going to stoke up the fire, second I'm going to make us all a nice meal and third... Well, third, I'm going to decide what to do with you.'

Chapter Six

'Good evening, Miss MacQueen.' Sebastian removed his hat and bowed as he entered Belles through the back door into the kitchen. 'I trust that you've had a pleasant and profitable day?'

'We've sold out of biscuits, if that's what you mean.' The pugnacious redhead glanced up from where she was polishing a brass plate beside the hearth.

'It wasn't, but I'm glad to hear it.' He threw a subtle look towards the hallway.

'If you're looking for Henrietta, she's not here.'

'And why would I be looking for Miss Gardiner specifically?' Maybe not so subtle, after all… 'It's a delight to see you again, too, Miss MacQueen.'

'If you say so.' She gave him an openly sceptical look. 'Your bag's over there. I brought it downstairs, but I was starting to think you'd left it for us as a souvenir.'

'Sorry about that. I spent the day with an old friend and lost track of time.' He reached down and swung the sack containing his few belongings over his shoulder. 'However, thank you again for your hospitality. If you need me, I'll be staying at—' He stopped, puzzled by the way she was chewing her bottom lip between her teeth as if she were worried. She didn't strike him as a particularly nervous person, but he had the distinct impression that she was preoccupied with something.

'Is everything all right, Miss MacQueen?'

She looked up again, holding his gaze for a few seconds before shaking her head. 'No.'

'No?'

'It's Henrietta. She promised she wouldn't be gone long, but that was two hours ago.'

'What do you mean *gone*?' The words caused his stomach to drop almost painfully. 'Do you know where she went?'

'To visit her brother over the bridge. She helps out with her nephews most evenings, though I keep telling her she shouldn't be walking around in the dark.'

'Do they live far away?'

'Around Avon Street.' The crease between her brows deepened. 'It's not the most salubrious area. I grew up there, so I ought to know.'

'I see.' Sebastian put his bag down again, gripped with a new sense of urgency. 'Then perhaps you and I should take a walk in that direction? Hopefully, we'll meet Miss Gardiner on her way home. Otherwise, you can direct us to her brother's house.'

'I knew it!' Miss MacQueen was already on her feet and reaching for her hat and bonnet.

'Knew what?'

'That you like her!'

'Of course I like her—as an acquaintance,' he added hurriedly. 'At this moment, however, I'm mainly concerned about her.'

'*Because* you like her and not just as an acquaintance.'

'Miss MacQueen, if I've given you the wrong impression…'

'Oh, don't start with all that.' She gave the ribbons on her bonnet a vigorous tug. 'Only a word to the wise. If you *do* like her, don't comment on her appearance or give any compliments if you can help it. I know it sounds odd, but she doesn't like them.'

'I noticed. This morning I told her she looked beautiful and—'

'*Never* say that!' Miss MacQueen practically hissed, shoving past him towards the door. 'That's the *worst* thing you could possibly say!'

'That she's beautiful?'

'Yes!'

'But why?'

'Because…' She opened her mouth and then clamped it shut again. 'That's *her* business. Just remember not to— Oh!'

He never discovered what not to do as the back door flew open suddenly and the woman in question herself bundled in, flanked by two young boys and carrying another, smaller one in her arms.

'What on earth…?' Miss MacQueen's mouth fell open. 'What happened?'

'David's lost his job.' Miss Gardiner sounded breathless. 'And when I got to his house he was—' She stopped, her eyes widening in surprise as they settled on Sebastian.

'Sozzled.' One of the boys finished her sentence for her. 'Bosky. Three sheets to the wind. Stewed. That's what Mr Roper said.'

'Mr Roper's one of the neighbours,' Miss Gardiner explained with a pained expression. 'I gave his son a shilling to stay and keep an eye on David tonight, but I didn't want to leave the boys. I was going to make them a meal, but…'

'It looked like a pigsty,' the same boy piped up again. 'That's what Mrs Roper said.'

'It *was*.' Miss Gardiner looked faintly mortified and then sighed. 'I thought about tidying up, but there was so much to do and it was getting late so I decided to bring them here for a bath and something to eat instead. They can sleep in my bed tonight.'

'And you can share with me.' Miss MacQueen had already removed her outdoor clothes and was rubbing her hands together briskly. 'Right, boys. Come with me and I'll show you where you can put your things.'

'Let me help, too.' Sebastian stepped forward, holding his arms out for the sleeping child in Miss Gardiner's arms and feeling somewhat shaken by the intensity of his emotions. He'd been so relieved at the sight of her that he'd actually found himself unable to speak for a few moments. 'This one looks heavy.'

'I'm not!' a sleepy voice protested from over her shoulder.

'Only because you're such a strapping young man.' He smiled as a youthful face turned to peer at him. 'You'll soon be carrying ladies about yourself, I'll wager. How old are you? Fifteen?'

'Five.'

'No! That's incredible.' He turned back to Miss Gardiner as the boy giggled. 'Please? You look as though you're about to collapse.'

'I admit I am a little tired.' She hesitated for another moment before handing the boy over with a sigh of relief.

'Your nephews, I presume?'

'Yes. This is Oliver and the other two are Michael and Peter.' She gave a tentative smile. 'Michael's the talkative one, but I'm sorry for bringing them here. I hope you don't mind.'

'Why would I mind?'

'Because Belles belongs to your family. You should know, I would never have brought them if it hadn't been necessary.'

'Miss Gardiner.' Sebastian bounced Oliver up on one arm. 'I abnegated responsibility for Belles when I joined the navy. You're the manager now and this is your home, which means that you may treat it as you see fit. If my sister trusts you, then so do I. That's all there is to it.'

'Thank you.' The expression in her eyes softened in a way that caused an abrupt lurch followed by a warm glow in his chest.

'Now let me find somewhere cosy to put this young man and I'll help to prepare that bath.'

'You don't have to do that.'

'Ever hear the phrase "all hands on deck"?' He arched an eyebrow. 'You're the captain here tonight, Miss Gardiner. Just give me your orders and I'll endeavour to see them fulfilled.' He flashed a quick grin. 'Anna will have my head if I don't.'

'I never thought of that.' Her lips curled and the dimple he'd noticed the previous night appeared for the first time that day. *Aha!* he thought with a definite sense of triumph, there she was. *There* was the woman he'd met during the night, the one he'd *wanted* to walk with that morning. She was back and she couldn't have looked any less like a fortune-hunting ice queen. And maybe, just maybe, Miss MacQueen was right.

Mr Fortini, Henrietta decided, was going to make an excellent father some day. His light-hearted, easy-going manner seemed infectious, so much so that her nephews took to him instantly. During bathtime, an event that had soaked a considerably greater area of the kitchen floor than she would have liked, he'd regaled them all with stories about fantastical sea monsters, each one of which he claimed to have confronted, outwitted and finally defeated in hand-to-fin or hand-to-tentacle combat. After that, he'd bundled them into clean sheets and then sat them down at the kitchen table for steaming hot platefuls of pie and gravy while she'd washed their clothes in the remaining bathwater. Despite her concern for David, it had proved a strangely enjoyable and entertaining hour's work. Even Nancy had laughed on more than one occasion.

All in all, she had to admit that it was possible she'd misjudged Mr Fortini's character. He seemed to genuinely want to help—surely a man who was only interested in flirtation wouldn't inconvenience himself to such an extent? It was hard to imagine either Mr Willerby or Mr Hoxley going to so much trouble. Maybe he was a man who could be trusted, after all…

'There we go,' she announced finally, pegging the last pair of trousers up on a rack above the hearth. The boys' stockings, she noticed, were almost threadbare in places, though she'd only darned them again a couple of weeks ago.

'Anyone for a glass of milk before bed?' Nancy stuck her head out of the pantry.

'Yes, please!'

'That doesn't mean you have to wolf down the rest of your pies,' Henrietta admonished them quickly. 'The milk isn't going anywhere, we promise.'

'Is there anything else I can do to help?' Mr Fortini stole a chunk of pie crust from Peter's plate and popped it into his mouth with a wink.

'You've already done more than enough.' Henrietta shook her head, feeling self-conscious again as he got up and came to stand before her. 'I'm very grateful. We all are.'

'It's been my honour to serve.' He reached for his jacket and drew it over his shoulders. 'Now, if you need me, I'll be staying at Redbourne's store tonight.'

'Redbourne's?' Nancy's head poked out of the pantry again.

'Yes. James Redbourne and I were best friends growing up. He's given me a bed for the night.' One of his eyebrows quirked upwards. 'I believe the two of you are also acquainted?'

'We've met.'

'Well...' He shrugged when no more comment appeared to be forthcoming. 'That's where I'll be.'

'Just for tonight?' Henrietta was dismayed by how awkwardly high-pitched her voice sounded.

'Yes. I'll be taking the stagecoach north tomorrow.'

'Oh.' Somehow the words made her feel deflated inside, as if she'd just lost something important. If she could have gone back to that morning, then she had a feeling she would have behaved very differently, but it was too late now. The opportunity was gone and the realisation felt like a cold lump in her stomach. 'Then I suppose this is goodbye.'

'I suppose it is.' He inclined his head though his eyes never left hers. 'It's been a pleasure to meet you, Miss Gardiner.'

'You, too, Mr Fortini.' She was horribly aware of colour rising up her throat and over her cheeks. Even with Nancy and the boys in the kitchen, the situation felt too intimate, as if some unspoken communication were passing between them. Only she wasn't sure what exactly they were trying to say either. It was less of a conversation and more of an awareness…one that was raising goose pimples on her skin and causing more fluttering than ever. 'Sorry again about your nose.'

'What happened to his nose?' Michael chirruped from the table.

'I hit it with a door.'

'For perfectly good reasons.' Sebastian averted his gaze finally. 'Your aunt thought I'd broken into the shop to steal all the biscuits.'

'Like a pirate?'

'*Exactly* like a pirate. But now I can leave safe in the knowledge that she has three young men to protect her.' He lowered his voice confidentially. 'Can I trust you all to act as my marines?'

'Yes, sir!' Peter and Michael both sat up straighter at once.

'Very good. Carry on then, men.' He raised a hand in a salute before bowing to Henrietta and Nancy. 'Miss Gardiner, Miss MacQueen. I'll leave through the shop if you don't mind?'

'Of course not.' Henrietta smiled, though for some reason she felt more like crying. 'Goodbye, Mr Fortini.'

'Goodbye,' Nancy added, waiting until he was out in the hallway before giving her a sharp nudge in the ribs. *'Well?'*

'Well what?' Henrietta lifted her chin.

'You know very well what *well* means!'

'What does it mean?' Michael looked between them both quizzically.

'Nothing. Finish your milk.'

'Go after him.' Nancy wasn't so easily put off. 'Say goodbye properly.'

'I just did.'

'With about as much warmth as an icicle!'

'*Don't* call me an ice queen!' Henrietta whirled on her. 'You know how I hate that.'

'All right, but he deserved better and I don't say that about any man very often. He was very worried about you earlier.'

'He was?'

'Yes! We were going to go and search for you when you arrived.'

'I still don't think...'

'Go!' Nancy pointed an imperative finger towards the hallway. 'Say it properly and *without* an audience. You'll regret it if you don't.'

'Mr Fortini?'

Sebastian had one foot out of the door and on to the pavement when Miss Gardiner came hurrying through the shop towards him. After all the commotion of the evening, she was looking somewhat dishevelled. Still beautiful, but with a few golden tendrils hanging loose around her face.

'Miss Gardiner?' He shifted his weight back over the threshold. 'Did I forget something?'

'No, but I...' She stopped a few feet away and clasped her hands together, seemingly reluctant to meet his eyes. 'I had a message for Anna.'

'Indeed?'

'Yes. If you don't mind, that is?'

'Not at all.' He waited a few seconds. 'Only you might have to tell me what it is first.'

'Oh...of course... Just tell her that everything's all right here. With Belles, I mean. And please give her my best wishes.'

'I'll be sure to pass that on.'

'Thank you.'

'Was there something else?' He lifted an eyebrow when she didn't move.

'I... Yes.' She pulled her shoulders back and looked at him finally. 'I wanted to say thank you for being so kind to my nephews. They've been through a great deal over the past few months.'

'Peter told me about their mother, that she passed away in the summer. I'm sorry.'

'But the way that you spoke to them tonight, telling them to take care of me like that... I think you've made them feel ten feet tall.'

'I hope so. There are a lot of boys in the navy around Peter's age. Powder keggers, cabin boys, servants... It's not uncommon for them to feel lost away from home, but giving them a sense of purpose always helps.'

'Well, you've helped them—and me.' She cleared her throat. 'Which is why I also want to apologise for the way I behaved this morning. There are certain subjects that I'm a little sensitive about. Oversensitive, perhaps.

I thought that you…' She stopped and gave her head a small shake. 'It doesn't matter what I thought. What matters is that I misjudged you and I'm sorry.'

'I see.' He regarded her steadily for a few seconds before closing the door softly behind him. 'Then shall we shake hands and be friends?'

Her shoulders seemed to sag with relief. 'Yes. I'd like that very much.'

'As would I.' He extended a hand and she took it, placing her fingers in his with a smile that seemed to spread and then falter abruptly. Which was strange, he thought, because he was aware of his own smile doing the same thing at the exact same moment. The very ambience in the room seemed to shift suddenly, as if some of the air had been sucked out of the door when he'd closed it.

Standing all alone, cocooned together in the dimly lit shop, he had the bizarre impression that they were the only two people in the world and that something significant and irrevocable was happening. The mere touch of skin against skin seemed to have set all of his nerves thrumming, so much so that he could actually hear blood rushing in his head. It was like the feeling before a thunderstorm, the atmosphere stretching and crackling with tension. If he'd been on board a ship, it would have been time to start battening down the hatches. On dry land, he didn't have the faintest idea what to do.

All he knew was that he couldn't look away from her or move his gaze even an iota to one side, as if she were hypnotising him the way she had on that first night. Not that she *had* actually hypnotised him, obviously, but whatever strange effect she'd had then seemed to be happening again… He had a powerful urge to wrap one of her golden tendrils around his fingers and draw her closer.

Fortunately, she blinked first. Several times, in fact, enabling him to look away.

'Do they have any family on their mother's side?' He cleared his throat, deafeningly loudly, or so it seemed in the silence.

'Not close by. Alice came from Taunton and I'd hate to send the boys so far away.' Miss Gardiner's throat appeared to need clearing as well. 'They can be quite a handful, but they're good boys really. My brother just isn't able to pay them much attention at the moment.' Her chin wobbled slightly. 'I'm afraid he grieves for his wife very much.'

'Ah. You mean that he drinks often?'

'Yes.' Her whole face seemed to crumple. 'More and more since Alice died. I've been telling myself that he'll stop eventually, but now he's lost his job and I can't see any way for things to get better.'

Sebastian started to reach a hand out and then stopped himself. The atmosphere still hadn't quite returned to normal and, after that morning, he didn't want to risk any more misunderstandings between them.

'What happened to your sister-in-law?' he asked softly instead.

'She thought it was another baby at first, only she got thinner instead of bigger. The doctor was never sure why.'

'Poor woman.'

'It was dreadful. She was so young and such a good mother. She'd be horrified if she knew how David was behaving now.' She wrapped her arms around her waist, hugging herself as if she were cold. 'I try to help as much as I can, but it's not enough. I know that I ought to do more, that I should go and live with him and take care of the boys and the house, but…'

'But you have your own life?'

'Yes!' Her eyes shot to his, a glimmer of pain swirling in the depths. 'I feel so torn. I don't see how I can do that and run Belles properly, but they're my nephews and I love them, too. And who will take care of them if I don't? It's wicked of me to want to do otherwise.'

'It's not wicked at all.' This time he couldn't stop himself from reaching for one of her hands, clasping it tight between both of his. 'I understand about feeling torn. I don't know your brother, but I expect he is, too. Sometimes people drink to forget their pain. I've seen it happen more times than I can count. Maybe your brother's not ready to face reality yet.'

'But he *needs* to be ready!' An angry expression crossed her face before she clapped her other hand over her mouth. 'Oh! I shouldn't have said that.'

'Why not? It's the truth. He has three sons to care for and a sister who's desperately worried about him. You've every right to be angry, but he's only human. Knowing how we ought to behave and actually doing it are often very different things. He'll face reality when he's ready.'

'What if he drinks himself to death in the meantime?' Her voice caught as her expression turned anguished again.

He squeezed her hand, unable to find an answer for that and unwilling to voice empty platitudes. He wanted to comfort her, if only he knew how…

'I'm sorry. I didn't mean to burden you with any

of this.' She drew her fingers away abruptly, her eyes welling with tears as she took a few steps backwards, retreating towards the kitchen before he could say or do anything to stop her. 'Goodbye, Mr Fortini. Have a good journey.'

Chapter Seven

'What now?' Nancy rolled a lump of cinnamon-flavoured biscuit dough out on the table. 'I don't mind the boys staying here, but we can't look after them *and* manage the shop.'

'I know.' Henrietta drew a flour-stained wrist across her forehead. 'They go to the charity school in the mornings and then Peter and Michael used to go and help David in the mews, but now he's lost his job...' She heaved her shoulders and cut out a row of perfectly square Comptessa biscuits. 'I'll go and speak to him after I take them to school, before he has a chance to start drinking again.'

'Good idea.'

'Hopefully it won't take long, but I'm sorry to leave you alone again.'

'Pshaw.' Nancy waved a hand dismissively. 'Don't worry about me, but what will you say?'

'I'm not sure yet.' She began to arrange the biscuits on a baking tray. 'Mr Fortini said that some people drink when they're not ready to face their pain, but David can't go on as he is and I can't take the boys home until I know that he's better. I need to make him understand that. In any case, I'll bring the boys back here this afternoon.'

'I'll find them some jobs to keep them out of trouble.' Nancy looked thoughtful. 'Maybe we could offer complimentary shoe-shining with every bag of biscuits?'

'I'm not sure how Mr Redbourne would feel about that, considering he has a shoe-shiner outside his store.'

'Does he? I hadn't noticed.' Nancy's tone was altogether too uninterested. 'Speaking of Mr Redbourne, I wonder if Mr Fortini has left yet. Did he say what time his stagecoach was leaving?'

'Does it matter?'

'Not to me, no.'

Henrietta kept her eyes on her dough. She'd been trying, unsuccessfully, not to think about Mr Fortini for most of the night and since she'd woken up that morning, still mortified by her near tears the previous evening. He'd been so sympathetic and understanding that she'd been strongly tempted to rest her head on his shoulder and start sobbing. Strangely enough, she had a feeling that he would have let her, too, despite the way she'd behaved on their walk. What would he have thought of her then? What would he have reported to Anna? That she was an emotional mess, most likely...which she was starting to think wasn't so far from the truth.

'If he hasn't left by now then I'm sure he'll be on his way soon.' She tipped her head to one side as if she expected to hear a stagecoach rolling past at any moment. 'I don't suppose we'll be seeing him again.'

* * *

'Breakfast is served.' James set two plates of sausages and egg on the table with a flourish.

'You know, I could get used to this.' Sebastian lifted his feet off a neighbouring chair and picked up his fork with a grin. 'Don't you have a maid to cook for you?'

'No. I can't see the point when I can manage perfectly well by myself.'

'Spoken like a true bachelor. It's funny, but I would have thought you of all men would be married by now.'

'Why me of *all men*?'

'You always seemed like the marrying type, that's all.'

'Maybe I just haven't met the right woman.'

'Really?' Sebastian paused in the act of spearing a sausage. There was something distinctly evasive about his friend's tone. 'Why don't I believe you?'

'Because you never could mind your own business.' James gave him a swift kick under the table. 'As it happens, I *thought* I had met the right one once, only it turned out the feeling wasn't reciprocated.'

'Well, plenty more fish in the sea.' Sebastian stopped and put his utensils down again. 'What a ridiculous phrase that is. I wonder who came up with it?'

'A sailor?'

'Probably, but it's not true, is it? I mean, there are fish and then there are *fish*.'

'Succinctly put.'

'What I mean is that it makes women sound interchangeable when they're clearly not.'

'True. I suppose some of them are mackerel and some are sharks.'

'You're not bitter, then?'

'Maybe a little, but I can't blame her for what happened. She never gave me any encouragement, I just hoped, that's all.' He laughed ruefully. 'So the stagecoach leaves at nine. It goes to Bristol first, I presume?'

'I think so, but the truth is, I was wondering whether you'd mind me staying for a few more days?'

'Not at all.' James gave him a searching look. 'I'd like to think it was for the pleasure of my company, but something tells me it has more to do with Miss Gardiner. Is the ice thawing a little?'

Sebastian didn't answer, vaguely surprised by his own request. He really ought to be heading north. He *wanted* to see his mother and Anna again and to start enjoying his newfound freedom, too, yet he couldn't quite bring himself to leave. Miss Gardiner needed his help and somehow that seemed more important. He wasn't quite sure what she'd meant when she'd said she'd misjudged him, but they seemed to be friends again and he couldn't just abandon a woman in trouble, especially one who worked in his family's shop. In the absence of Anna, it was *his* responsibility to help, surely?

Yes, that was it, he reassured himself. He felt compelled to stay because she was Anna's employee and Anna would want him to help. It had nothing to do with *her* specifically. He was attracted to her—it would have been frankly ridiculous to pretend otherwise—he liked her, even, but that had nothing to do with his decision, especially since she'd made it clear that flirtation was out of the question. He would have helped Miss MacQueen in a similar situation, too. Probably.

'It's not that difficult a question.' James gave him a

puzzled look. 'The food's going to get cold if you keep staring at your plate much longer.'

'Sorry.' Sebastian came back to himself with a jolt. 'It *is* to do with Miss Gardiner, as a matter of fact, only not in the way that you think. She needs help.'

'With the shop?' James looked surprised.

'No, some trouble with her brother and nephews.' He picked up his knife and fork again. 'It'll probably only be for a few more days, just until I know that she's all right. The end of the week at the most. It's what Anna would want me to do.'

'Naturally.' James smirked over the rim of his coffee cup. 'What other reason could there possibly be?'

'Do we *have* to go to school?' Michael complained as Henrietta marched him and his brothers out of the shop and along Swainswick Crescent. 'Can't we stay and help you sell biscuits?'

'No. Learning is more important.' She clutched Oliver's five-year-old hand firmly in hers. 'Besides, it's only for the morning. Then you can come back and do some jobs for me.'

'Will you teach us to bake?'

'If you like.'

'I'd rather learn about life in the navy,' Peter interjected. 'I'm going to be a sailor one day.'

'Really?' Henrietta glanced at him in surprise. 'I didn't know that you liked the water.'

'He wants to run away to sea like Sebastian when he grows up. He said so last night.' Michael smirked, elbowing his brother in the ribs and earning himself a fist in the arm back.

'No fighting, the pair of you!' Henrietta jabbed a hand between them. 'And it's *Mr* Fortini to you.'

'He said that we could call him Sebastian.'

'That's not the point.'

'But he said so!'

'It's true, I did!' a familiar deep voice called out from behind them. 'As may you, Miss Gardiner, if you wish?'

'Oh!' Henrietta whirled around in surprise, spinning Oliver along with her. 'Where did you...?'

'Come from?' He grinned lopsidedly. 'The same place as you, only I went into Belles through the back way and Miss MacQueen told me you'd just left through the front. I have to admit, it was quite a challenge to catch up with your fast pace.'

'We're late for school,' Michael informed him.

'But I thought you were leaving?' Henrietta gasped and then winced at the sound of her own words. 'Not that I wanted you to leave. Or to stay,' she added quickly. 'I just...' She shook her head, wondering what was the matter with her tongue. Not to mention her stomach, which seemed to have bounced all the way up to her chest, lifting her spirits along with it. Even her pulse seemed to be accelerating, pounding so fast it was actually hard to draw enough air into her lungs. Despite the embarrassment of the previous night, she felt quite ridiculously, ludicrously happy to see him again—and somehow unable to stop smiling. 'Forgive me, I'm just surprised, that's all. I thought you'd be on your way north by now.'

'So did I.' He shrugged in a faintly bemused manner. 'Only I decided I wasn't quite ready to leave yet. I have a few old friends I'd like to catch up with, as well as three young cadets to train.'

'Really, sir?' Peter's face lit up. 'Will you teach us to be sailors?'

'As long as you go to school first and *without* any complaining.' Sebastian winked at him. 'I actually wondered if you'd allow me to walk with you, Miss Gardiner? To signal the start of our new friendship?'

'You should call her Henrietta,' Michael interjected. 'If she's allowed to call you Sebastian. It's only fair.'

'I wouldn't presume...'

'But Michael's right. It *is* only fair.' She found herself smiling even wider in agreement. 'I'd be delighted if you'd escort us... Sebastian.'

'Then it would be my pleasure.' He tilted his head to one side, his dark eyes gleaming with what looked like satisfaction. 'I'd offer you my arm, but it appears this young gentleman has beaten me to it. What do you two say?' He held his hands out to Peter and Michael. 'Will you walk with me instead?'

'Yes, Sebastian!'

Henrietta led the way, laughing softly as he was immediately bombarded with questions about life in the navy. Just like the evening before, however, he seemed completely relaxed and at ease, impressing his young audience so much that she was half afraid they might both enlist before the end of the week.

She was so preoccupied with listening that she almost walked straight into another woman hurrying around the railings at the corner of the street.

'Pardon me.' She looked up, straight into the eyes of the woman from the pavement the day before.

'Oh! No, it was my fault.' The woman hesitated, her

lips parting as if she wanted to say something else, before she noticed Sebastian and scampered quickly onwards again.

'An acquaintance of yours?' he asked quizzically when she was out of earshot.

'Not exactly.' Henrietta looked back over her shoulder for a few seconds and then carried on walking. As much as she wanted to help anyone in distress, her nephews needed to get to school and she needed to speak to David. At that moment, she had more than enough problems of her own to deal with.

Chapter Eight

Henrietta found Sebastian exactly where she'd left him, leaning casually against a red brick wall opposite the schoolyard. In broad daylight, he looked even more ruggedly handsome than she'd remembered. His coat was hanging open as usual and his dark hair was swept away from his face, all except for one black curl that seemed determined to take up residence over his nose. That appendage was also looking noticeably less bruised today, allowing her to focus on his twinkling dark eyes as she approached.

There was something slightly wicked about them, she thought as she came closer, or, if not wicked, then definitely mischievous. Yes, that was a much better word. There was no malice in them, although now that she'd got past the initial pleasure of seeing him, she wondered if she was simply being naive again.

He'd said that he was staying longer in Bath to visit old friends, but then why was he here with her? She thought she'd addressed the issue of potential misunderstandings the day before, but why was he helping her if he didn't expect anything in return? They might have decided to be friends, but she still couldn't help feeling a little suspicious. Not to mention alarmed when just the sight of him made her stomach start fluttering as if there were a swarm of butterflies inside looking for a way out.

'So where next? Your brother's house?' He uncrossed his ankles and pushed himself upright to greet her.

'Yes, although I've no idea what I'm going to say.' She felt instantly anxious again. 'I want to help him get better, but I feel so powerless.'

'Maybe just tell him that.' He looked sympathetic. 'Is it far?'

'Just a few streets away.'

'Then let's go.' He bent his elbow and she curled her hand around it, without hesitation and without mistaking it for a wild creature this time either, which was definitely progress, she thought ironically as they made their way through the backstreets. His arm felt just as big and solid as it had the day before, although there was something reassuring and supportive about it now, too. Reassuring *with* butterflies. She wouldn't have thought it possible to feel tense in two such different ways at the same time and yet she did, her concern for David vying with a new sense of repressed excitement with Sebastian.

'Here we are.' She stopped outside a small two-storey wooden building, squeezed between two equally ramshackle others. 'Would you mind—?'

'Waiting outside? Of course not.'

'I don't know how long I'll be.'

'Take all the time you need.' Sebastian squeezed her arm gently before releasing her. 'I'll be right here.'

'Thank you.' She opened the door without knocking and stepped inside, only to find the room just as she'd left it. Messy, freezing and apparently deserted.

'David?' she called softly as she made her way through the downstairs, but there was no answer, not as much as a murmur of acknowledgement. Carefully, she climbed the steps up into the loft space, but that was empty, too, rumpled bedsheets the only evidence that her brother had ever been there. Everything else was eerily still and quiet and forbidding somehow. A lump of dread started to form in her stomach, apprehension getting the better of her nerves. If David hadn't gone to work, then where was he? Surely he couldn't have started drinking again already?

'Henrietta?' Sebastian's shout summoned her back down the steps.

'What is it?' She hurried towards the front door, flinging it open and then stopping dead at the sight of her brother's neighbour confronting Sebastian. 'Oh! Is everything all right?'

'So he *is* with you then?' Mrs Roper's belligerent expression bore a strong resemblance to Nancy's. 'He said he was, but you can't be too careful.'

'No, I suppose you can't.' Henrietta closed the door behind her, unable to mask her disappointment. 'Mrs Roper, do you have any idea where my brother is?'

'Not exactly.' The neighbour looked as if she were suddenly keen to leave again. 'My boy came back this morning saying David was awake and feeling a bit worse for wear, but sober enough.'

'Oh.'

'He was muttering some strange things though, my

boy said, all about going away and making a fresh start.'

'Going away?' Henrietta felt as though she'd just been slapped in the face.

''Course we thought it was just the headache talking so I made him some tea and bacon, but by the time I brought it over, he was gone. So, I checked in his coffer, I hope you don't mind, and it was empty.'

'Empty…' Henrietta swallowed, trying to maintain an outward appearance of calm when her insides felt like a butter churn. 'But… I don't understand—what about his sons?'

'He *did* ask where they were, my boy says, so he told him they was with you and…well, David said something about it being for the best.'

'What?'

'But I'm sure he didn't mean it like that. He loves his boys, there's no doubting that. No matter how much he drinks, he won't abandon them…not for ever, anyways.'

'Didn't he give *any* clue about where he was going?'

'No, but if I hear anything I'll send word straight to the shop. In the meantime, you take care of 'em boys and I'll keep an eye on the house. I'll give it a good clean up, too. Ready for when he comes back again. It's the least I can do for Alice.' Mrs Roper gave a loud sniff. 'She was a lovely girl.'

'She was.' Henrietta found herself blinking furiously. 'Thank you, Mrs Roper. I'm grateful for everything you've done.'

'And you take care of *her*—' Mrs Roper turned fierce eyes on Sebastian '—whoever you are.'

'Oh, forgive me, this is Anna's brother,' Henrietta

murmured, having forgotten about introductions until that moment. 'Mr Sebastian Fortini.'

'The *Countess's* brother?' Mrs Roper's expression turned instantly to one of dismay. 'I do beg your pardon, sir.'

'Don't mention it.' He inclined his head. 'You were absolutely right to be suspicious. I'm sure Mr Gardiner would be most obliged.'

Henrietta reached for his arm before he could offer it, glad of the support as he led her back towards Belles. Now that the initial shock had passed, she felt as though she were walking through a cold fog, unable to see what was going on around her and feeling numb all over. It was taking all of her energy just to put one foot in front of the other. As for her mind… The same questions kept swirling around her head. Where was David? How could he have got up that morning and just left? Or had he been planning to do it for weeks, simply waiting for an opportunity to leave the boys with her? No, surely he wouldn't have done anything so calculating? *Surely* he wouldn't have done this deliberately to her, to his sons, to all of them?

'Can you think of any place he's likely to go?' Sebastian's voice jolted her back to the present and thankfully out of the fog. They were already turning the corner on to Swainswick Crescent, she noticed, though she had no memory of even crossing Pulteney Bridge. 'Do you have any other family?'

'No, it's been just the two of us, and then Alice, for years.'

'It still might be worth paying a visit to Ashley.' He looked thoughtful. 'With your permission, I'll take a ride out there and see. If he's walking that way, then

I'll likely pass him on the road. If not, I can leave word at the local tavern to contact you if he makes an appearance.'

'No.' She shook her head. 'There's no need to involve yourself any more in my troubles. I've put you out enough.'

'Not at all. I want to help and it's a nice day for a ride.'

'You don't have a horse!'

'But I *do* have friends with horses.'

'Mr Fortini—'

'Sebastian.'

'Sebastian… I'm very grateful for your help, but you said that you were staying in Bath to catch up with old friends. How can you do that if you're chasing after my brother?'

'There's plenty of time for both.'

'Is there? Because I don't want to inconvenience you or to keep you from your family either. They don't even know that you're back in England. They'll still be worried about you.'

'Ah, but not for much longer. I wrote to both Staunton Manor and Feversham Hall this morning. That should put Anna and my mother's minds at rest.'

'Good.' She let out a heartfelt sigh of relief. 'I'm sure it will.'

'Although I admit it felt slightly absurd to be writing to such addresses, never mind to a countess.'

'But why should it? Your grandfather was a duke, wasn't he?'

'He was.' His steps faltered briefly as his brows snapped together. 'Did Anna tell you that? We hardly ever spoke about it growing up.'

'Ye-es.' She was faintly perturbed by the stern change in his demeanour. 'She told me just before her wedding to the Earl. All about your mother eloping with a footman, too. It sounded very romantic.'

'I suppose it was, until her family cut her off without a penny. Or has she forgotten that part?' He clenched his jaw, his throat working silently for a few seconds. 'Now, what time do your nephews finish at school?'

'Midday.'

'Then I'd better hurry if I'm going to get to Ashley and back in time. With your permission, I thought I'd take them to Sydney Gardens this afternoon. They need to start cadet training in earnest if they're going to be captains by the time they're twenty.'

She hesitated, still uncertain about accepting his help, but they were friends now, weren't they? And if it helped to find David… The thought decided her.

'I think they'd enjoy Sydney Gardens very much. Definitely more than whatever jobs Nancy has planned, but I'd like to come, too, if she doesn't mind looking after the shop. I need to tell them that they'll be staying with me for a little while and they're bound to have questions.'

'Good point.'

'I was actually wondering whether it might be better to tell them that David's unwell? Then if—*when*—he changes his mind and comes back, they'll never know that he left.' She paused. 'What do you think?'

'I can see why you might want to, given the circumstances…' Sebastian made a face.

'But?'

'But if he doesn't come back and they think that you deceived them… It might make things worse in the long run. They seem like bright boys and you don't want to lose their trust.'

'So, you think that honesty is the best policy?' She chewed her bottom lip thoughtfully. 'Maybe you're right. I just can't bear the thought of them being hurt any more or feeling they're not wanted.'

'But they have an aunt who loves them.' He stopped outside Belles and turned to face her, his dark gaze boring into hers so intently that she could almost feel it like a touch on her skin. 'Don't underestimate that.'

She felt her breath catch, her legs feeling slightly unsteady all of a sudden, unable to think of a response. There it was again, that temptation to lay her head on his shoulder, only not to cry this time, just to be close, to wrap her arms around him and feel his arms around her. What would his shoulders feel like beneath her fingertips? What would it be like simply to be held?

'Now, if you'll excuse me.' His gaze dropped to her lips for a fleeting moment before he moved away. 'I need to go and see a man about a horse. I'll see you this afternoon.'

She nodded, feeling oddly disorientated as he bowed and walked away. She still wasn't entirely sure why he was helping her, but at that moment she was extremely, possibly foolishly, glad that he was.

Chapter Nine

'So, he's just abandoned them?' James summarised, holding on to the horse's bridle while Sebastian climbed the mounting block.

'That's what it looks like. He left sometime this morning.'

'Poor Miss Gardiner, but if he doesn't want to be found then he's not likely to go anywhere familiar, is he?'

'Probably not,' Sebastian conceded, throwing one leg over the saddle. 'But it's still worth a try. Thanks for the horse, by the way.'

'Don't mention it. Dulcie's a docile old creature, but she'll get you there all right.'

'Docile is good.' Sebastian picked up the reins with a grimace. 'It's been five years since I last did this. Where are the oars again?'

'The same place as the mast.' James looked mildly concerned. 'Are you sure you wouldn't prefer to take the cart?'

'I'd *much* rather take the cart, but it'll take too long. I said I'd be back by early afternoon.'

'I'm sure she'd prefer to have you back in one piece, but it's up to you. Good luck.' James gave him a pointed look. 'Try not to fall off.'

'I'll do my best.' Sebastian nudged his legs and set off. It was approximately six miles to Ashley, just over an hour's ride if he took it steady, which between him and Dulcie was probably the only way he *could* take it. Then he'd need an hour in the village to look around and make friends with the local innkeeper, followed by another hour to ride back. He wouldn't get back to Bath in time to collect the boys from school, but they'd still have plenty of time to spend in Sydney Gardens.

He rubbed a hand over the mare's neck, vaguely wondering what on earth he was doing. He was *supposed* to be visiting his family and enjoying his newfound freedom, not volunteering to ride around the countryside on behalf of a woman who'd asked him to treat her like a sister, in search of a man he'd never met. It couldn't *just* be because it was what Anna would want him to do, could it? He didn't know, but then he was finding it hard to think clearly about anything involving Henrietta.

In truth, his mind was still preoccupied with the smile she'd given him that morning. He hadn't been certain how she'd react to seeing him again, but the way her face had come to life when she had, as if she were genuinely happy, had turned her from beautiful into...what? He couldn't even think of a word to do her justice. Radiant, exquisite, ravishing, *pulchritudinous*? It had started with a gleam in her eyes and then the rest of her features had followed suit and before he'd known it, her whole face had lit up as if she were glowing from within.

The sight had stolen his breath away and apparently addled his senses, too, because he'd volunteered to ride out to Ashley without even asking what her brother looked like! But it was too late to turn back, even if doing so wouldn't have made him feel just a little bit foolish. All he had to do was keep his eyes open for a man who looked as though he might have a hangover—and probably one with fair hair, too, if Henrietta and the boys were any indication.

On a more positive note, at least the weather was co-operating. It wasn't particularly sunny, but the roads were dry and navigable. The views were like a balm to his soul, too, the rolling hills and arable valleys familiar and comforting. They made him want to start quoting poetry or break out into song. He'd missed these views over the past five years, he realised. In all of his travels, he'd never ever seen anywhere to compare, not because the landscape was particularly dramatic or spectacular, but because it was home.

Not that he'd waxed quite so lyrical two days ago during the interminable stagecoach ride from Plymouth, but now he seemed to be viewing the world in a whole different light and there was only one reason he could think of to account for it. A reason with golden hair and a willowy figure that, despite the unfortunate circumstances, had struck him as even more attractive on the second day of their acquaintance. He wondered how she would look on the third and fourth and fifth…and fiftieth.

It was tempting to remain in Bath to find out, but they were *just* friends, he reminded himself sternly, just friends who exchanged long and intense looks on the street—or had he imagined that? Not that it mattered.

He was only staying a few more days, no matter how attractive she looked or how poetically inclined he found himself. Hopefully her brother would have turned up by then. Because after that, he really *had* to go.

It was three hours precisely before Sebastian opened the back door of Belles and raised his hand to his forehead in a salute. Henrietta's nephews were all sitting fidgeting around the kitchen table, looking ready to burst out of their seats at any moment.

'Who's ready for some naval training?'

'I am!' Peter was the first to his feet.

'Not so fast.' Henrietta came through from the shop, wiping her hands on her apron as she looked at him enquiringly. 'I need to speak to Mr Fortini in the parlour first. You can be getting your shoes and coats on in the meantime.'

'I won't be long.' Sebastian threw Peter an encouraging smile before following her up the stairs. He wished he had better news to impart, but unfortunately all he could do was shake his head the moment they were alone. 'I'm afraid there was no sign of him.'

'Oh...' Her eyelashes dipped as she pressed her lips together. 'I told myself not to hope, but I still wondered...' She put a hand to her throat and rubbed gently. 'Thank you for trying.'

'He might just want to lie low for a while.' He couldn't resist the impulse to reassure her. 'I doubt that he's gone far.'

'Then he's probably still in Bath.' She looked hopeful again. 'Maybe I ought to go and look for him? I could visit a few of the taverns.'

'Absolutely not.' He closed the distance between

them in two strides, putting his hands on her shoulders without thinking. The very idea of her visiting a tavern made him feel suddenly, fiercely protective. 'It could be dangerous.'

'I have to try.'

'You can let me do it.'

'No. You've done enough.'

'Visiting a few taverns isn't exactly a hardship. I can be more discreet and I'm a lot less likely to be groped.' He slid his hands over her upper arms, vaguely appreciating the irony as his fingers skimmed across bare skin. 'Only I forgot to ask what your brother looks like. It would be useful to know.'

'Oh, I never told you that, did I?' Her voice caught as she glanced down at one of his hands, as if she were uncertain what to make of its presence. 'Just like Michael, only a larger version. They're almost identical.'

'Well, that should make life a bit easier.' He smiled and released her, his fingers still tingling with her body heat. 'I'll go tonight with James. If your brother's still in Bath, then we'll find him, I promise, but first you and I have an expedition to the park to enjoy.'

'Yes, but please don't feel obliged. You must be tired after your ride...'

'Any more objections and I'll make you join in cadet training, too,' he interrupted sternly. 'I keep telling you, I *want* to help.'

'But *why*?' Her eyes flashed with a look of suspicion. 'It can't just be because of Anna.'

'Actually it can, although not just because it's what she would want me to do.' He paused. It was the same question he'd asked himself earlier, but suddenly the answer seemed a lot clearer. 'The truth is, I wasn't here when Anna needed me after our father died and I've always felt guilty about that. She had to run the shop almost single-handedly. And now she's married, she doesn't need me at all and there's no way I can make it up to her. But I still *want* to make it up to her. I thought perhaps I could help you and your nephews instead, if you'll let me?'

'I see.' Her brows knotted, as if she were thinking the idea through. 'So, you want to help me to make amends to Anna?'

'Yes.' He nodded. It was the truth, too, or at least the part of it he understood. 'And because there was a time in my life when I felt utterly futile and helpless. It was a horrible feeling and I hated it. Now that I *can* help, I want to. You'd be doing me a favour, giving me a chance to redeem myself, if that makes any sense?'

'It does.' Her gaze softened again. 'In that case, I'd be honoured by your help, Sebastian.'

'As I am to give it.' He bowed his head, feeling a flicker of heat in his chest at the words, a flicker that built into a glow, then flared into a blaze, until he felt hot all over.

'Well then…' She turned towards the stairs, mercifully oblivious to the inferno now raging inside him. 'I'd better fetch my bonnet.'

Sebastian took a few deep, though not particularly cooling, breaths before following and they were on their way in a matter of minutes, Peter and Michael walking on either side of him, chattering excitedly, while Henrietta walked hand in hand with Oliver. It was a strange feeling, Sebastian thought, to be jealous of a five-year-old, but he was, especially when said five-year-old was also hugged and kissed on numerous occasions. Just *one* hug would have sufficed for *him*, he thought, watching covertly, although perhaps he was deluding himself and keeping his hands away from Henrietta was the wiser course of action… Truthfully, there was no *perhaps* about it.

He insisted on paying their entry to Sydney Gardens and led them inside, past the maze and faux castle to a secluded corner that was more woodland than manicured lawn. At this time of year there were hardly any people on the paths and none at all after the first few minutes, which was exactly what he wanted.

'How are we going to train as sailors here?' Peter looked confused. 'The lake's over that way.'

'Yes, but the oak trees are here.'

'What do oak trees have to do with ships?'

'Aside from the fact that most ships are made from oak?' Sebastian put his hands on his hips and craned his neck backwards. 'Ever climbed a mast?'

'Oh!' Henrietta let out a worried exclamation. 'That doesn't sound very safe.'

'Children ought to climb trees. I always did. So did Anna for that matter.' He grinned as Peter and Michael's faces lit up with excitement. 'I'll look after them, don't worry. As a matter of fact…' He tossed his hat carelessly to one side. 'I think I'll join in.'

'I'm exhausted!'

Sebastian threw himself on to the ground beside Henrietta. Fortunately, she'd brought a blanket to sit on, although one corner of it was covered with a collection of pine cones that Oliver had obviously gathered for her. The young boy had tired of climbing after only a few minutes.

'I'm not surprised.' She smiled down at Sebastian, the winter sunshine catching the hair beneath her wide-brimmed bonnet so that it shone like spun gold. 'I feel exhausted from just watching you. That was nerve-racking.'

'I didn't let them go so high, although they're pretty good climbers already.' He lifted his head and looked around. 'Where's Oliver?'

She gestured to a nearby shrub. 'Building a den inside that. You're invited to visit, but apparently girls are forbidden.'

'How ungentlemanly.'

'I thought so.'

'That was fun!' Michael and Peter came running over to join them. 'What next?'

'Next you need to give an old man a rest.' Sebastian laid his head back down again.

'You're not old. Nancy says you're younger than Papa.' Michael dropped down on to the blanket and crossed his legs. 'Where *is* Papa anyway?'

'About that...' Henrietta threw Sebastian a swift glance before continuing. 'How would you feel about staying with me for a bit longer?'

'Why?' Peter sounded suspicious.

'Well...the truth is that your father's gone away for a little while.'

'You mean, he's left us?' Peter's voice hardened.

'He doesn't want us.' It was Michael who spoke this time. 'He loved Mama, but now she's gone he doesn't want us any more.'

'No, it's nothing like that.' Henrietta put her arm

around the little boy's shoulders. 'He loves you very much.'

'He doesn't if he's left us.' Peter answered belligerently, turning on his heel and stalking away.

'Does he really love us, Aunt?' Michael's eyes were suspiciously bright.

'Of course he does. I promise.'

Sebastian waited a few moments before giving her a single nod and getting up to follow Peter. The boy was standing off to one side, his back turned and shoulders hunched, obviously trying not to cry.

'Permission to join you?' Sebastian came to a halt beside him, looking out over the park.

'You don't have to ask. You outrank me.'

'But you were here first. I don't want to intrude.' He paused, but there was no answer. 'You know, I used to come and climb here with my friend James when we were boys. The park attendants used to yell and chase us.'

'He's not coming back, is he?'

Sebastian turned his head. It was obvious the boy wasn't talking about James. 'I don't know.'

'Michael's right. He doesn't want us any more.'

'It's not as simple as that.'

'Why not?'

Sebastian rubbed a hand over his chin, trying to think of a way to explain. 'You know, in the navy each man is given a single tot of rum a day. Just one, mind, so that they don't fall off the rigging.'

Peter looked at him strangely. 'What does that have to do with Papa?'

'Nothing directly. I suppose what I'm trying to say is that too much drink is dangerous. It makes men forgetful and encourages them to take risks, but sometimes, when a man *wants* to forget something, it can be a means of escape, too. Then he can come to prefer that feeling to real life. It becomes an illness and he doesn't know how to stop drinking.'

'So, Papa is sick?'

'I think so, but I know that he hasn't left because of you. It's more likely because he loves you and he doesn't want you to see him the way he is now. Sometimes people need to go away in order to get better. And he made sure to leave you in good hands, didn't he?'

'Aunt Henrietta needs to run the shop. I heard her and Nancy talking. She doesn't know how she's going to manage.'

'But she will.' Sebastian glanced over his shoulder to where Henrietta was now holding a crying child in each arm. 'I haven't known your aunt long, but if there's one thing I'm certain of it's that she won't let you down.'

Peter looked pensive for a moment. 'Are you going to marry her?'

'What?' He let out a startled cough. Suddenly the solid ground beneath his feet felt ten times more precarious than the branches he'd just been swinging from.

'Is that why you're helping Aunt Henrietta to take care of us?'

'No-o.' He cleared his throat. 'We're friends, that's all.'

'But you won't leave, too?'

Sebastian tensed. Staying beyond the end of the week wasn't what he'd intended, but something about Peter's anguished expression at that moment reached inside him and pulled at his heart strings… He'd seen was exactly the sort of thing she ought *not* to think about a friend!

'Look, Aunt Henrietta!' Michael scrambled to his feet when he saw her, holding aloft a piece of string with a triumphant expression. 'It's called a cat's paw.'

'What a lovely name.' She bent over to admire it. 'That looks tricky.'

'*This* is the most important knot!' Peter held up his own piece of string. 'A bowline.'

'They're both very good.'

'And wait until you see this...' Sebastian gave Oliver a nudge. 'It's an overhand knot. One of the best I've ever seen.'

'Goodness me.' She made a show of examining each in turn. 'I hope you aren't planning to tie my feet together.'

'Umm...' Michael and Peter exchanged looks as if that was exactly what they'd been planning.

'Oh, dear.' She shook her head, looking around the gazebo at each of them in turn before her gaze settled on Sebastian and she smiled. It was a smile that seemed to come from deep within, as if her very heartstrings were tugging at the corners of her mouth. Maybe it was contagious, she thought, all this smiling. Despite her worries about David, at that moment she couldn't have stopped if she'd tried. She was aware, too, of a strangely dizzy feeling, as if the gazebo itself were spinning around. She actually had the bizarre impression that all her thoughts and feelings were up in the air, rearranging themselves somehow, and that when she stopped spinning and they settled down again, as they eventually had to, then nothing would ever be the same again.

that look on other boys' faces before, but at least this time he could do something about it.

He put a hand on his shoulder and squeezed. 'I'll stay for as long as your aunt needs me. How about that?'

'Thank you.' Peter nodded stiffly.

'Now, do you know what we need?'

'No.'

'A cricket bat. You need to vent those feelings.'

'We don't have a cricket bat.'

'But we do have branches and pine cones.' He looked around, searching the ground for suitable candidates. 'That's another trick you learn in the navy. Improvisation.'

And that, Sebastian realised, was that. He'd just made a promise to a ten-year-old boy that he wasn't going anywhere. Oddly enough, he couldn't even bring himself to regret it.

Chapter Ten

Knots.

Henrietta wandered slowly around the gazebo, listening with amusement as her nephews were tutored on the apparently ancient art of knot-tying inside. Overhand knots, square knots, granny knots, bowline knots, oyster knots, reef knots, thief knots, figure-eight knots... So many that she'd quickly forgotten the names of the rest. She'd declined the offer of instruction herself, preferring to enjoy the winter sunshine than play with bits of string—a choice of words that had earned her a stern look and lecture from Sebastian.

She laughed softly to herself at the memory of his outraged expression, though he'd been unable to maintain it for more than a few seconds. He seemed almost incapable of *not* smiling for long, as if his sense of humour were irrepressible. Somehow, it suited his general air of dishevelment, the way he never tightened his cravat or fastened his coat, as if he were too busy being cheerful to notice or care about such details.

Now they'd reached a clear understanding about his reasons for staying in Bath to help her, it was surpris-

ing how much she enjoyed his company. She'd known he'd felt guilty about leaving Anna to run Belles alone, but she hadn't realised quite *how* much, and his honesty endeared him to her more than she would have expected. As did his behaviour generally. They'd come to the park together with the boys for a couple of hours every afternoon that week, after which she took over the running of the shop and gave Nancy the rest of the day off, and his good nature had never once wavered.

After a week, there was still no sign or word of David, but Sebastian seemed determined to stop her from worrying, distracting both her and the boys with his so-called nautical training. Overall, it was surprisingly pleasant to have him as a friend. She felt as relaxed with him now as she had on the first night they'd met, so much that she was even wearing her blue dress today, having eventually decided that Nancy was right and it wasn't her fault or responsibility how anyone chose to interpret her clothes or behaviour. So why *shouldn't* she wear her favourite dress if she wanted? As for Mr Fortini specifically, she felt safe with him. She trusted him. Which meant that she could wear her best bonnet, too, for good measure!

She propped her shoulder against one of the gaze
columns and peered in through the archway. The b
were all sitting cross-legged on the floor while Se
tian crouched beside them, making corrections
smiling encouragement—*of course smiling*! He
classically handsome by any means. His feature
far too rough hewn and irregular for that, yet
sided smile made his face a thousand times mo
tive than that of any other man she'd ever m

It was outlandish and unexpected and alarming. And yet here she was, *still* smiling. And so was Sebastian. They were both smiling at each other. For almost a whole minute before Michael asked what they were doing.

'I enjoyed that.' Sebastian chuckled to himself as they walked home an hour later, the boys scampering ahead, still comparing and competing over who'd tied the strongest knots. 'It was just like old times.'

'They enjoyed it, too.' Henrietta turned her head to smile at him, that genuine smile that made him feel as if his lungs couldn't draw in enough air. She was looking exceptionally pulchritudinous today, he thought, like a rare and precious orchid escaped from a hothouse. She was dressed far less sombrely than on any of their previous excursions, too, in a blue-green gown the exact same shade as her eyes, not that he'd said so. Or allowed anything even remotely resembling a compliment to pass his lips, though it was getting harder and harder to stop himself. He must have thought at least a hundred complimentary things since he'd collected her a couple of hours before. Frankly, he was starting to wonder if he had masochistic tendencies, agreeing to simply be her friend.

'I'm afraid you're making life at sea sound far too appealing,' she went on, *still* smiling. 'No offence to the navy, but I'd rather keep the boys closer to home.'

'I recall my mother once saying something similar.'

'I'm not surprised. It must have been very hard for her when you left.' She winced. 'Sorry. I'm not trying to make you feel any guiltier.'

'I know. I suppose I just hoped she'd get used to the

idea eventually. They say sailors' wives do.' He blinked at his own words. What on earth had made him say that? They'd been talking about mothers, not wives.

'Really?' She gave him a sideways look, so quickly that he couldn't catch her eye.

'They say it gets easier anyway.'

'I suppose it's just a different way of life.'

'Yes.'

'But it must still be lonely.' She seemed determined to look straight ahead now.

'I suppose so. Of course the men miss their wives, too.'

'Of course.'

'So it's hard for both of them.' He paused. 'I'm not sure it's the kind of marriage that I'd want for myself…' And why was he telling her that? 'Although my naval days are behind me.'

'They are?' This time, she *did* look at him. 'Have you decided for certain?'

'Yes.' He nodded firmly. 'I don't know what I'm going to do next, but it won't be the navy.'

'Oh.' There was a faint crease between her brows. 'I see.'

'You sound disappointed.'

'No, just surprised. Anna said you were so desperate to join.'

'When I was seventeen, yes, as soon as I could convince my father to let me go.'

'And you're an acting lieutenant already? You must be good at what you do.'

'It's easier to be promoted in wartime. My captain thought I had a talent for navigation so he made me a midshipman. Then, when we were short of officers, he promoted me to lieutenant.'

'Why were you short of officers?'

'Enemy action.'

'You mean in a battle?'

'Not quite. We were set on by a French Squadron a couple of years ago. Fortunately Captain Marlow hid us in a fog bank, but we sustained a lot of damage.'

'How frightening.' She shuddered. 'Is that why you were out of contact with the Admiralty for so long?'

'Not because of that, no.' He hesitated, tempted to tell her the truth, the things he hadn't told anyone, even James, but it was hard to find the words to begin…

'Forgive me.' She seemed to notice his expression. 'It's none of my business.'

'No, it's not that…' He slowed his pace, suddenly *wanting* to tell her. 'The reason we were out of contact started a few months later when we were sent in pursuit of a Spanish frigate. She led us across the Atlantic and down the coast of South America.'

'Around Cape Horn? I remember you said you were stuck in the Pacific for the past year.'

He grimaced, swallowing against a sudden constricting sensation in his throat. 'That wasn't *quite* true, I'm afraid. That is, we did round Cape Horn, but then the frigate turned around again. We never did find out why.'

'Oh.' She looked faintly puzzled.

'Forgive the deception. Only the truth is difficult to talk about.'

'Then you don't have to.'

'But I think I'd like to. You see, our Captain fell ill just off the coast of Brazil not long afterwards and we were forced to berth in the West Indies for him to get medical treatment. He was a good captain: honourable, strict, but fair, too. Unfortunately, his replacement, Captain Belton, was the opposite. He had no honour at all. He was a bully and a fool, determined to find the lost frigate and prove himself no matter what the cost. He got information that it had gone north so we followed, all the way up to Lower Canada, never mind that it was nearly winter and we were all practically freezing to the masts.'

'Couldn't you object?'

He made a face. 'Objecting isn't really an option in the navy. Naval vessels have a strict hierarchy. Obeying the chain of command is everything, even when the commands in question don't make any sense. There's only one punishment for mutiny.'

'But surely if he was endangering your lives…?'

'That's not something for the crew to decide. A ship's doctor can diagnose madness, but stupidity isn't the same thing, not in the Admiralty's eyes anyway.' He shook his head. 'We were off the coast of Newfoundland when a blizzard set in. We were blown off course into a bay and trapped. *Literally* trapped. When the storm abated, the ship was held fast by ice.'

'How terrifying.'

'As I recall, I was too cold to feel a great deal of anything except numb. Fortunately, at that point our worthy captain decided to barricade himself in his cabin.'

'Fortunately?'

'It left smarter men in charge. We'd restocked on provisions in the West Indies so we had enough food to wait for a thaw and we all stayed below deck together, trying to keep warm and desperately hoping the ice wouldn't crush the ship. It wasn't easy. Some of the men came close to despair. Most of the boys, too. They tried to act like men, but they were frightened.'

'Like Peter is now?' She tightened her grip on his arm. 'No wonder you're so good with him. I think those boys were lucky to have someone like you with them.'

'I don't know. I tried my best to keep their hopes up, but I felt so powerless, as if I were failing them. But we were lucky and survived. Any further north and we'd have been done for. A few men lost fingers and toes to frostbite, but after a few months, we were able to escape.'

'So that's why Anna didn't hear from you for so long?'

'Yes. We made it back to the West Indies eventually, but needless to say, the Admiralty wasn't impressed. We were forbidden from sending messages home while there was an investigation, but in the end the whole thing was hushed up.'

'But wasn't your captain punished?'

'Retired.' He gave her a pointed look. 'His brother is a marquess.'

'Ah… So then you came home?'

'*Then* we had to wait for the ship to be repaired, but, yes, then I came home.'

'Well, that explains it.'

'Explains what?'

'Why you always dress as though it's the middle of summer.'

He chuckled. 'I believe there are parts of my body now permanently immune to the cold.'

'You still shouldn't be careless about it,' she scolded him. 'I'm going to knit you a scarf.'

'Really?' He felt both surprised and pleased by the idea. 'I'd like that.'

'Yes. What's your favourite colour?'

'Blue,' he answered without hesitation. Which was funny because up until that moment he'd always thought it was red. And they were standing outside Belles, he realised suddenly. He hadn't even noticed that they'd reached it, although he'd seen the boys go inside.

'Blue it is.' She moved closer to him, so close that every inch of his body seemed to tingle with awareness. He was vividly aware of the heavy thud of his own heartbeat. Any closer and she would be, too. 'I'm glad you made it back to England safely.'

'So am I.' He made a conscious effort to keep his voice steady. 'Although I'd rather not share the details with my family, at least not yet. Since I wasn't here to help them, I'd rather they thought I was away doing something useful. I don't want them feeling sorry for me either.'

'I understand.' She smiled softly. 'Thank you for telling me.'

'Well… I ought to be going.' He inclined his head, reluctant to leave after sharing something so personal, although he hated saying goodbye to her in general, he realised, even when it was only for an hour or two. If the past week was any indication, he'd be craving her company again in a few minutes, but she had a business to run and he had more taverns to visit and they were *just friends*, dammit. All of which meant that he ought to be going.

Gently, he untucked her hand from the crook of his arm and lifted it to his lips. He did it every time he left, but this time he did it more slowly than usual, half expecting her to pull away, but she didn't. Instead her eyes widened and flickered with a distinctly *un*friend-like expression, the pupils swelling slightly as his lips touched the back of her glove. And why kissing fabric felt so damnably erotic at that moment, he had no idea.

'Yes.' Her voice sounded breathy. 'Until tomorrow then.'

He took a step backwards and nearly ran down the street.

Chapter Eleven

Henrietta watched Sebastian through the glass pane of the shop door as he walked, surprisingly quickly, down the street. The dizzy, disorientated sensation she'd felt in the gazebo was back and stronger than ever. When he'd kissed her hand she'd actually felt as if her insides were trembling, a rush of heat coursing wildly through her veins straight to her abdomen. It felt new and exciting and shockingly wanton. As wanton as she'd once been accused of being. As wanton as…no, she'd never been wanton with Mr Hoxley. As wanton as she imagined a woman might feel for a man she cared about. Whatever she'd felt in the past was nothing compared to this. She didn't even know what *this* was, but she had a suspicion it might be desire…

She placed her forehead against the glass to cool down. Even now, her pulse was still racing, hard and fast, and her legs were shaking, as if she'd been sitting on them for too long and they'd gone numb. She only hoped that Sebastian hadn't noticed the effect he'd had on her limbs. It would be too mortifyingly ironic after the way she'd behaved towards him on that first day. It already *was* too ironic. She'd condemned him because she'd thought he'd been trying to flirt with her and now here she was tempted to flirt with him!

She didn't know which was worse, the irony itself or the fact that she'd been wrong about his intentions and he was only helping her to make amends to his sister and because of the boys he thought that he'd failed on his ship. Both of which were even more reasons to like him! It was all such a tangle…

'Nancy?' she called out, unable to unravel the skein at that moment. Maybe she'd try later, when she was in bed and had time to think, although thinking about him in bed probably wasn't such a good idea either… 'Are you in the kitchen?'

'I'm here.' Nancy came hurrying through from the hallway abruptly, marching up to the shop door and turning over the *Closed* sign before drawing one of the bolts. 'But we need to close for a while.'

'Why? Are you all right?'

'I'm fine. Only somebody else isn't.'

'David!' Henrietta gasped and started towards the kitchen.

'Not him.' Nancy caught at her arm, lowering her voice to an undertone. 'Remember the woman from the street?'

'Ye-es.'

'She says you offered her help.'

'I suppose so, but she ran away.'

'Well, apparently she's changed her mind.'

'Oh.' Henrietta took a deep breath. Her meeting with the woman seemed like such a long time ago now, but an offer was an offer… 'Where are the boys?'

'I sent them upstairs to play.'

'Right.' She straightened her spine. 'Well, hopefully it won't be anything too difficult.'

'Oh, I don't know. I thought we could do with some fresh challenges.'

Nancy threw her a speaking look before striding back through to the kitchen. The woman was sitting at the table, twisting her fingers together and looking more than a little nervous, although she'd removed her cloak and bonnet, Henrietta noticed, which at least suggested she wasn't about to run away again.

'Hello.' She gave a warm smile as she sat down opposite. 'I understand that you'd like to take up my offer of help?'

'Yes.' The woman bobbed her head so vigorously that a couple of sable-coloured tendrils escaped from her bun. 'If you're still willing, that is?'

'Of course. Might I ask your name?'

'Bel...' the woman hesitated '...linda. *Belinda.* It's not my real name, but...'

'But it's the one we'll use. I understand. I'm Henrietta and you've already met Nancy. Now, why don't you tell us what we can do to help?'

'Well...' The woman put her hands flat on the table as if she were bracing herself. 'I'm looking for a lady who lives in the boarding house opposite, a Miss Foster. She's a former governess, *my* former governess, and this is the last address I have for her. I've been waiting outside, hoping to catch her one day on the street, but it's been almost two weeks and I haven't had as much as a glimpse. I waited for five hours yesterday.' She paused for breath. 'Do you know her?'

'I'm afraid not.' Henrietta threw a quick glance at

Nancy, who also shook her head. 'Forgive me, but why don't you simply ask the proprietor?'

'Because I can't.' The woman dropped her gaze to her hands. 'There's a chance that they've been told to look out for a woman like me asking questions and if they were to report back on my whereabouts…' She swallowed and looked up again. 'I haven't done anything criminal, I promise, but I can't take the risk of being seen. It's hazardous enough waiting on the street. Now I don't know what to do. I had it all planned out when I…' She stopped and bit her lip.

'When you ran away?' Nancy prodded her.

'Yes,' she admitted, rubbing a palm over her cheek as tears trickled down her face. 'I made my way here by stagecoach, but I only had enough money for a couple of weeks. Now it's almost run out and there's still no sign of Miss Foster.'

'Right then.' Nancy clapped her hands together. 'Give me five minutes.'

'What?' Belinda got halfway up from the table. 'Where are you going?'

'To find out if she's still there.'

'But if you ask questions they might get suspicious.'

'Not of me they won't. I'll take a basket so it looks as though I'm making a delivery and it's not as if they'll mistake my description for yours.' Nancy tugged at her copper-red curls. 'Don't worry.'

'It'll be all right.' Henrietta gestured for Belinda to sit down again as Nancy tramped out through the back door. 'She's one of the cleverest people I know and she doesn't take no for an answer. Now let's have some tea while we wait, shall we?'

'Thank you.' Belinda gave her a tremulous smile,

her cheeks still damp, when Henrietta came back with two cups. 'I truly am sorry to involve you.'

'There's no need to be sorry.' She shook her head reassuringly, recalling something similar she'd said to Sebastian. 'We all have our burdens. It helps to share them if we can.'

'I don't want to get you into any trouble.'

'You mean with your family?'

'No.' Belinda gave a short laugh. 'I doubt my family care where I am. They won't want to see me again, not now.'

'Then who?'

'I...' She sounded hesitant. 'I'm afraid I can't say. All I can tell you is that I did something foolish.'

'Ah.' Henrietta slid a hand across the table. 'Well, we all make mistakes sometimes.'

'Yes, but this was a very big one.' Belinda sobbed and then hiccupped. 'I'm sorry. I'm not usually so emotional. It's just been such a worry, waiting and watching and—'

'She's not there!' Nancy flung the back door open dramatically.

'What do you mean?' Henrietta squeezed their new companion's hand, alarmed by the way all the blood seemed to have drained from her face.

'I mean that she left a month ago, only not as Miss Foster. She's Mrs Sheridan now, and who knows where on her honeymoon.'

'Oh, no!' Belinda's face turned positively ashen. 'She was my last hope. What will I do now?'

'Don't panic for a start.' Nancy deposited her basket on one of the counters. 'That never does any good at all.'

'But how can I not?'

'Where are you staying?' Henrietta tried a more sensitive approach.

'At another boarding house on Tibberton Street. I've told the proprietor that I'm a governess between jobs, looking for a new position, but I think he's suspicious about me.'

'Of course he's suspicious.' Nancy gave a snort. 'Your cloak alone must be worth twenty pounds.'

'Is it so obvious?'

'Yes. Everything you're wearing is much too expensive for a governess.'

'Oh, dear.' Belinda looked crestfallen. 'I've never run away before.'

'Obviously.'

'Nancy.' Henrietta gave her a chiding look. 'It's not Belinda's fault.'

'I never said that it was, but it's obvious she's not going to survive on her own—and I'm not saying that's her fault either.' She held her hands up as she flopped down into a chair. 'Ladies aren't taught how to survive because men don't want them to find out the truth: that they can live perfectly happy and independent lives without them. *That's* why they're taught embroidery and opera instead of anything useful. I mean, what use is piano playing in the real world?'

'Nancy, this might not be the best time…'

'So, as far as I can see, there's only one thing we can do.'

'What?' Henrietta and Belinda asked together.

'We can give her a job here in the afternoons.' Nancy spoke as if the answer ought to be obvious. 'It's actually the perfect solution now you have the boys to take care of. Then I won't be working on my own and she'll have the money to pay her rent until…well, until she learns how to stand on her own two feet.'

'But she's a lady! Sorry.' Henrietta threw Belinda an apologetic look. 'But a lady like most of our customers. What if one of them recognises her?'

'They won't,' Belinda chimed in eagerly. 'I don't know anyone.'

'Anyone?'

'*Hardly* anyone.'

'There you go.' Nancy folded her arms with a look of satisfaction. '*Problem* solved.'

'Can I really have a job?' Belinda's expression was pleading.

Henrietta opened her mouth, closed it again, considered and then gave an exasperated laugh. 'Oh, very well, the more the merrier. Welcome to Belles.'

Chapter Twelve

'And *that's* how Nelson escaped the polar bear!' Sebastian concluded his story with a bow in the middle of the street.

'That *can't* be true.' Michael turned to Henrietta for support. 'He just made that story up, didn't he?'

'Upon my honour as a sailor, it's all true.' He put a hand on his heart. 'Or at least that's what I've heard.'

'So his musket misfired and he fought it with the other end like a club?'

'Exactly! I'm not saying it was one of his better ideas, but he was only fourteen so we ought to make allowances.'

'It seems very convenient that the ice broke up and he was able to escape.' Henrietta looked somewhat sceptical, too. 'Are you certain Nelson didn't make that story up himself?'

'Embellished, maybe. Who knows, but he was certainly brave enough for it. Ask anyone who served with him at the Battle of the Nile. *Or* Copenhagen. *Or* Trafalgar. He was wounded in combat three times.'

'Did he really lose an eye?' Michael's expression turned slightly bloodthirsty.

'No, just the sight in it, but he did lose most of one arm. That's enough, don't you think?'

'I want to be just like him,' Peter announced, somewhat incongruously. 'But I have to hurry. He was a captain before he was twenty-one.'

'You have ten years.' Henrietta laughed. 'That sounds like plenty of time to me.'

'But we'll accelerate your training anyway. This afternoon's subject: map-reading!' Sebastian winked and then grinned at the boy's happy expression. A week and a day into his new routine, he was surprised to discover that despite his *friend* status, he was actually enjoying himself. Being a nursemaid wasn't a career he'd ever contemplated before, but it felt good to be doing something useful again.

In the mornings he picked up the boys from Belles, escorted them across the city to school, then collected them again for excursions in the afternoons, usually accompanied by Henrietta. In his spare time, he visited old acquaintances, helped James in his store and continued to make enquiries about David, so far without any success. Although he hadn't yet told Henrietta, it seemed increasingly likely that her brother had left Bath altogether.

'Will you teach us to row?' Peter asked as they approached the school yard.

'Yes, as soon as you've learned how to swim. Unfortunately, November's a little cold for that.'

'Then will you teach us in the spring?'

'Mr Fortini has other places he needs to visit.' Henrietta leaned forward. She'd joined them that morning to do some shopping and was walking on Sebastian's other side with Oliver holding on to each of their hands and swinging between.

'But he said he'd stay as long as you needed him!'

'He *did*?'

'I did,' Sebastian confirmed, trying to sound casual despite her obvious surprise.

'Oh...well...here we are.' She gestured towards the front door of the school. 'Have a good morning.'

'Yes, Aunt.'

'Goodbye!'

'Sorry about that.' Henrietta looked apologetically at Sebastian after they'd all scurried inside. 'You know, you mustn't feel obliged to stay and help us.'

'So you keep saying.'

'But surely you want to go and visit your family soon?'

'Ye-es.' He felt a stab of guilt at the words. He really ought to be heading north, but somehow he couldn't bring himself to leave Bath either. 'I've had a letter from my mother, as it happens.'

'Oh? How is she?'

'Very well. Only it seems that Anna isn't in Derbyshire at all. The Earl's grandfather is ill and they've gone to stay with him.'

'Oh, dear. I'm afraid that sounds serious. He seemed very frail the last time I saw him.'

'Apparently it is. So Anna is in Retford, although my mother still urges me to visit her and my...' he clenched his jaw, steeling himself to say the words '...my grandmother and uncle in Yorkshire.'

'Don't you want to?' She looked at him curiously.

'I suppose so.' He pressed two fingers against the

bridge of his nose and squeezed. 'It's just that I never imagined a reconciliation was even possible. It's hard to accept a family I've never met before, especially given the circumstances.'

'From what Anna told me, your grandmother never wanted the estrangement in the first place, but your grandfather was very proud.' She placed a hand on his arm with a sympathetic expression. 'There may be more to the story than you think.'

'Perhaps.' He resisted the urge to put his own hand on top of hers. 'But it's still hard to feel enthusiastic, especially when…' he paused, trying to think of a way to finish the sentence that didn't involve mentioning her '…when Bath is my home. I feel as though I'm just settling back in.'

'I'm sure— Oh!' She came to a halt abruptly.

'Henrietta?' He turned to her in alarm. Her expression looked strained all of a sudden, as if her skin was pulled too tightly across her cheekbones. 'Are you all right?'

'Yes. No. I just didn't realise we were walking this way.'

'I thought it would make a nice change.'

'Yes, but…' She looked up at him and then quickly away. 'Can we take another route?'

'Of course, but what's the matter?' He looked up and down the street, trying to work out what had upset her. Everything looked perfectly normal to him.

'The shop where I used to work is over there.' Her voice sounded noticeably smaller than before.

'Ah.' He followed the direction of her gaze. 'I understand. In that case, we'll go another way.'

'Thank you.'

'So...what do you need to buy?' Sebastian asked, discreetly changing the subject after a few minutes of walking in silence. 'Now that we're out shopping.'

'Hmm?' She sounded preoccupied. 'Oh, new stockings for the boys. I've given up on Oliver's.'

'Redbourne's, then?'

'Yes. I thought I might buy us something nice for tea, too. You're obviously invited, only...'

'James isn't?'

'I'm afraid I wouldn't dare.' She made an apologetic face. 'Once Nancy makes up her mind about a person, there's not much anyone else can do about it.'

'It's strange. I've tried asking what she's got against him, but he won't say a word.'

'I'm sure it's all a big misunderstanding. I can't imagine him doing anything hurtful.'

'Neither can I. And speaking of James...' Sebastian raised a hand as they entered the shop.

'You again?' His old friend looked up from a ledger book and grinned. 'I thought you were out for the day?'

'Stockings.'

'I beg your pardon?'

'I need them for the boys,' Henrietta interjected. 'I'll just be a moment.'

'So...' James gave Sebastian a subtle nudge in the ribs as Henrietta walked across to a different counter. 'Still *just* friends?'

'Trying to be. It's not easy, but it's all she wants.'

'Ah. Well, I'm not the man to give advice about unrequited affection, I'm afraid, although spending so much time with her might not be the best thing for your sanity.'

'I know. Only I'm not sure leaving would do me any good either. *And* I made a promise.'

'To her?'

'To one of her nephews. So…' He spread his hands out in a futile gesture. 'I can't go anywhere, sane or not.'

'All done.' Henrietta came back with a full basket and a smile. 'I'm glad we bumped into you, Mr Redbourne. Sebastian told me you've been helping him look for David.'

'Yes. I only wish we'd had more success.'

'You still tried and I'm grateful.'

'Well then…' Sebastian found himself offering his arm, vaguely irritated by the way she was smiling at his friend. 'We'd better get back to Belles.'

'And I'd better get back to work.' James lifted an eyebrow before smiling at Henrietta. 'Good day, Miss Gardiner.'

'Mr Redbourne.'

Henrietta gave Sebastian a quizzical look as they stepped back on to the pavement. 'Are you in a hurry?'

'Me? No, but I thought you might want to check up on your new assistant. What does she call herself again? Belinda?'

'Yes… Wait! How do you know that's not her real name?'

'Bel-linda?'

'Oh… All right, it's not.'

'Belinda Smith, by any chance?'

'No.' Her lips twitched. 'Belinda Carr. And she's doing very well in the shop. As for the baking…she's learning.'

'As bad as that?'

She lifted her shoulders as if she were trying to be charitable. 'She's doing her best, but it might take a while. Nancy and I are taking turns to give her lessons, but we haven't had much success so far. I don't think she's ever set foot in a kitchen before, let alone prepared any food.' A small giggle escaped her. 'You should have seen her face the first time she saw the rolling pin. I think she thought Nancy was about to attack her.'

'Knowing Miss MacQueen, that's surely a reasonable assumption?'

'Nancy wouldn't hurt a fly.'

'I beg to differ. She tipped me off a sofa, remember?'

'Only because she thought you were a burglar.'

'A burglar who takes a nap on the job?'

'She probably didn't have time to consider that. What I mean is that Nancy wouldn't hurt a fly unless the fly deserved it. Which she thought you did at the time.'

'True.' He chuckled. 'Fortunately Belinda seems to have got off to a better start. I suppose there's no point in my telling you she might be a fugitive?'

'She's not a fugitive. She says she hasn't broken any laws.'

'And you believe her?'

'Yes. She's obviously in some kind of trouble, but if she doesn't want to tell us the details then I'm sure she has good reasons and I know Anna would think the same. Everyone deserves a second chance.'

'That's very trusting of you.' He gave her a sidelong glance as they approached Belles. 'But then I suppose you'd understand more than most.'

'What do you mean?' She froze mid-step.

'About second chances...' He could have kicked himself for the words. 'I mean because Anna trusted you.'

'Why *wouldn't* Anna have trusted me?' She pulled her hand away from his arm, twisting sharply to face him.

'No reason.' He cleared his throat when she continued to stare. 'Just a turn of phrase.'

'A turn of phrase...' She seemed to go very still as she repeated the words. Which was curious because she was already still, but there seemed to be a new tension about her, too, suddenly, as if she were suppressing some powerful emotion. 'Then tell me this...' Her voice was clipped now. 'What did you mean about *understanding*?'

'Pardon?' He had an urgent desire to escape from the conversation.

'Ten minutes ago when I didn't want to walk past my old shop, you said that you understood, but I never told you why I left. So *what* do you understand?'

'I heard a rumour, that's all.'

'What *kind* of rumour?'

Sebastian glanced at the pavement, vaguely wishing a chasm might open up beneath his feet, big enough for him to hide in. 'Something about you and the owner's son.'

'Something such as?'

He groaned inwardly. Really, it didn't have to be a chasm. A reasonable-sized hole would suffice. 'All right. I heard that you were caught in some kind of indiscretion and that his mother accused you of being a fortune hunter and threw you out without references. Which is what I meant about Anna giving you a second chance, but I wasn't condemning you. I'm sure it wasn't as bad as it sounded and you must have been very young when it happened.'

'So you're *not* condemning me?' She lifted a finger and poked him hard in the chest, her whole body shaking as if she were cold. 'How *generous* of you, especially in the light of such overwhelming evidence as gossip and speculation.'

'I didn't say—'

'You've said quite enough! Forgive me if I don't care to listen to any more. Good day!'

'Hen—'

'I said good day!'

'Damn it.' He took a few seconds to vent his feelings before following inside, but there was already no sign of her. He judged by the sound of stomping footsteps, however, that she was already halfway up the stairs.

'Where do you think you're going?' Nancy jumped out from behind the counter, blocking his way as he went in pursuit.

'I need to talk to Henrietta.'

'Why? What did you do?'

'I said the wrong thing, obviously.'

'About?'

'About what happened, what she was accused of doing at the dressmaker's.'

'You mentioned *that*?' Nancy looked appalled. 'Why?'

'I didn't intend to mention it. We just happened to walk that way by accident and it came up and… please—' he gestured towards the staircase '—let me talk to her.'

'No. In case it isn't already obvious, she doesn't want to talk to you.'

'I need to apologise.'

'You need to do more than that.' Nancy's eyes flashed. 'Didn't it ever occur to you that the rumours you've heard *weren't* true?'

'I told her I was sure it wasn't as bad as it sounded and—' He stopped talking, struck with the distinct impression that Miss MacQueen was about to throw a fist at his head.

'If that's the best you can do, then you should turn around and leave right now.' From the sound of it, her teeth were gritted. 'If you weren't Anna's brother, I'd throw you out myself. Henrietta never set her cap at Roy Willerby. He was besotted with her! Only she wasn't good enough for his mother so once the old bat found out, she gave Henrietta her marching orders. Without references, too, just to make it look as though it was all her fault.

'And do you know what else?' Nancy advanced a few steps towards him, standing on her tiptoes to speak into his face. 'Even after his mother threw her out, Mr Willerby *still* wanted to marry her. She could have married him just to spite his mother and to have a place to live, too! But she didn't because she didn't care about him that way. Instead, she searched and searched for a job until finally your sister was smart enough to give her the benefit of the doubt. Unlike *some* people I could mention.'

'I see.' Sebastian felt his gut clench at the accusation. It was a fair one. He hadn't necessarily assumed that Henrietta was guilty, just that there had been some grain of truth in the rumours…

'Look...' Nancy's expression relented a tiny bit. 'You seem—*seemed*—different. You've been a lot of help with the boys and as far as I can tell you've behaved decently, too. Most men take one look at her and their minds go straight to one thing, and because she's a shop girl they think they can get it, too. That's why she doesn't like compliments, in case you were still wondering. She's learnt her lesson about men the hard way. So if that's all you're after—'

'It's not,' he interrupted her. 'We're friends.'

'Are you sure? Because I've seen the way you two look at each other. You may be helping her with the boys, but maybe it's time you started thinking about your intentions, too.'

'My intentions?' Sebastian ran a hand over his jaw. The whole situation struck him as ludicrous. Here he was, standing in his own family's shop, being challenged by a woman younger than him, barring his way with an expression as ferocious as Boudicca herself. As for the matter of intentions, Henrietta had made it very clear that anything besides friendship was out of the question, so unless she'd changed her mind... And what had Miss MacQueen just said? *The way you two look at each other*, not the way *he* looked at *her*...

'In any case...' Nancy continued as the shop door opened to admit an elderly couple '...you can go and do your thinking elsewhere. She doesn't want to speak with you at the moment.'

Sebastian bowed his head, feigning agreement before darting past the counter and up the stairs before Nancy could let out as much as a squeak of protest. He wouldn't have long, he knew, but if he could just find Henrietta before Miss MacQueen found him...

Had she changed her mind? His pulse quickened at the thought. Because if she had, then he'd be more than happy to oblige. And he couldn't wait another minute to find out…

Chapter Thirteen

Sebastian reached the landing in less than three seconds. Unfortunately, there was no sign of Henrietta in the parlour so he carried on up to the next floor, the one he was least acquainted with. Despite growing up above the shop, he'd never spent a great deal of time in either of the two bedrooms—his own sleeping arrangements being a truckle bed in the parlour—but the staircase was still familiar enough for him not to feel strange about going there. Which, in retrospect, was probably a mistake, but then discretion had never been one of his strong suits.

'I'm sor—'

He skidded to a halt, stopped in his tracks by the sight of Henrietta standing just inside her bedroom door, the grey gown she'd been wearing that morning draped over a chair while her yellow shop dress was only halfway over her hips.

'What—?' She jerked her head up at the sound of his voice, her expression turning swiftly from anger to shock to anger again before she reached a hand out and slammed the door in his face. Fortunately, his nose was far enough away this time *not* to suffer injury, although he had a feeling she wouldn't have hesitated if it hadn't been. She might actually have preferred it.

Double damn. He closed his eyes and pressed his forehead against the wood. That hadn't been supposed to happen. He'd come to apologise, not to ogle, to tell her he wasn't like the other men Miss MacQueen had mentioned, but he had a horrible sinking feeling that he'd just lost the moral high ground on that one. Still, since it *had* happened, he couldn't quite bring himself to regret it either—and he definitely wasn't going to forget it any time soon.

Not only had she been half dressed, but her undergarments had been in a state of considerable disarray, in all the right places in his opinion. The way her breasts had been popping out of her chemise as she'd bent over had made the view nothing short of mesmerising. It was probably fortunate that he'd had only a few short seconds to appreciate it since his body had come dangerously close to combusting as it was. He had a feeling the memory alone was going to heat his blood for some time to come.

He was still leaning against the door, wondering what to do next, when it opened again abruptly, sending him toppling forwards into the room and on top of a now fully clad Henrietta, knocking her off balance like a domino and sending them both stumbling towards the bed.

'Wait!' It was a foolish thing for him to say, Sebastian thought, even as the word left his mouth. *Wait?* It wasn't as if there was anything she—or he—could do to arrest their fall, though he made a valiant attempt to minimise injury none the less, curling one arm behind her back and managing to twist them both sideways so that they landed side by side rather than with his full weight on top of her.

'Sorry.' It was his second useless word in a row, he realised, staring into her eyes, which he couldn't help but do since their noses were only an inch apart and their bodies were even closer, pressed intimately together with his arm squashed between her breast and the mattress. 'I was leaning against the door.'

'I noticed.' She skewered him with a look though her cheeks were flaming red.

'I didn't know you were changing your clothes.' He felt an additional need to explain. 'Are you all right?'

'It's a mattress.'

'Good point. Here, let me...' He shuffled his body backwards, trying not to notice the soft weight of her breast against his arm, and stood up, offering her a hand which she pointedly ignored.

He coughed, racking his brains to remember why he'd gone up there in the first place. 'I really am sorry.'

'So you said.' She rolled herself to a sitting position.

'Not just about that—about all of it. That's why I'm here, to apologise. Don't blame Nancy.' He held a hand up as she opened her mouth. 'I waited until she was distracted. She'll probably be here to throw books at me any second.'

'I would never blame Nancy.' She didn't smile at the joke. 'You shouldn't have followed me.'

'You're right, but I wanted to explain. I should never have listened to gossip.'

'No, you shouldn't have.' She turned her face away with quiet dignity. 'I trusted you. I *thought* we were friends.'

'We are.'

'Friends don't think things like that about each other. They're supposed to know each other better!'

'I didn't think about it, not really. It didn't matter to me what happened.'

'It matters to me!'

'I know. I'm not explaining myself well. What I mean is that I knew it wasn't who you were. *Are.*' He paused. 'Nancy says it was the other way round and Mr Willerby was in love with you.'

She gave a short laugh. 'No, he only thought that he was.'

'What makes you so sure?'

'Because we never had a single real conversation. All he ever did was stare at me and tell me how pretty I was. He never asked me a single question about where I came from or what I liked to do. It was as though I was just another mannequin in the shop window.'

'If his mother was the owner, then she ought to have done something to stop him.'

'She blamed me.' Henrietta pressed her lips together tight and then sighed. 'And maybe I wasn't entirely blameless. Maybe I was friendlier than I ought to have been, but I thought I was being polite. No one ever told me that smiling was a bad thing!'

'It's not. It wasn't your fault.' He reached for her hand, but she stood up, stalking across the room away from him.

'Yes, it was! Because I didn't learn my lesson even then. I kept on smiling because I was young and foolish and flattered by compliments. Anna tried to warn me it could get me into more trouble, but I didn't listen. I didn't understand that my appearance was all most men ever saw or cared about. I didn't realise that they'd take a smile for a promise either.'

He tensed. 'What do you mean?'

She looked back at him, her jaw muscles clenched tight. 'Do you remember what I told you about the Earl's friend, Mr Hoxley? He came to the shop a few times to see me. He was handsome and charming and I liked him better than any man I'd ever met before. I knew he was a gentleman, but I was still naive enough to believe in daydreams and I thought he truly liked me, too.'

'What happened?' Sebastian heard his voice darken. Hearing another man described as handsome and charming was bad enough, but he had a feeling he was about to get even angrier.

'One day he invited me to meet him alone. He said he had something important to ask me and stupidly I believed him. I even lied to Anna about where I was going. I felt terrible about it, but I was so excited. I thought that he wanted to marry me like Mr Willerby, only it turned out he had much baser motives. It never occurred to me that he meant to seduce me, but fortunately a lady, the Earl's grandmother, in fact, intervened. She made his intentions *very* clear.'

'I see.' He was clenching his fists, Sebastian realised, so hard he could feel his fingernails digging into his palms.

'So there it is. Yes, I've been foolish and naive in the past, but I changed on that day with Mr Hoxley. I *stopped* smiling at men. I stopped doing anything that could be taken for flirtation or encouragement. I've done everything I can to prove I'm not the woman the rumours paint me as and yet people still want to believe the worst! I'm not a flirt and I would *never* try to seduce a man into marriage.'

'I know.' Several aspects of her behaviour all made sense at once. 'That's why you objected to me calling you beautiful that first day, wasn't it? You were afraid I was trying to flirt with you?'

'Yes.' Her chin jutted upwards a notch. 'I thought that maybe I'd given you the wrong impression during the night and that was why you'd invited me to walk with you.'

'And the clothes?'

Another notch. 'They weren't so bad.'

'They weren't good either.'

'That was the whole point!' She glared at him. 'I didn't want to look good. I didn't want to be flattered. Sometimes it feels as though I'm wearing a mask that no one wants to take off because they don't care what's underneath. As if there isn't anything underneath.' Her eyes glinted, but with pain, not anger. 'You know, when enough people treat you like that, you start to wonder if they're right and you *are* empty inside. But I'm not. I'm more than my face. I've made myself more than that and I won't be treated like an ornament to be possessed or used ever again. I want to be seen for my whole self.'

'I *can* see you.' He moved towards her, but she swayed backwards. 'Henrietta, I'm not like those other men, I promise. I don't want to possess or to use you.'

She shook her head sadly. 'When we became friends I thought that maybe I'd been too suspicious and you really were an honourable man, but now it turns out you've been thinking the worst about me this whole time!' Her eyelashes quivered. 'Tell me the truth. Is *that* the real reason you're still here?'

'You know that's not true.'

'Do I? Or did you think that if you helped with my nephews then I'd repay you somehow?'

'No! I've told you why I want to help.'

'So you *don't* want anything else?'

'No.' He stopped and frowned, compelled to be honest. 'Yes, but not like that. Truthfully, I've wanted to kiss you from the first moment I saw you, but you made it clear that you only wanted friendship and I would never abuse that, but it doesn't stop me from finding you attractive. *You*, that is, not just your face. Yes, you're beautiful. That night when we first met, I thought you were the most perfect-looking woman I'd ever seen. I thought that it was impossible to imagine anyone more beautiful, but none of that would matter a damn if it wasn't for who you are inside. Your beauty is in your heart and soul. It's in the way you care for your nephews, the way you let Nancy rant whenever she wants to, the way you help strangers who stand outside your shop looking hungry. *That's* the real you. That's why you're even more beautiful to me now.' He paused. 'But you're not perfect.'

She blinked and then stared at him, her eyes wide with a look that he couldn't interpret. 'I'm not?'

'No, I only thought so at first.' He took a cautious step forward, only this time she didn't move away. 'The fact is, one of your eyes is a slightly greener shade than the other, your laugh can be a little too high-pitched and you smooth your hair much too often.'

'What's wrong with smoothing my hair? I like to be neat.'

'I've noticed, but some people could argue that you're a little *too* neat, especially when you're standing next to a ruffian with a bruised nose. It's enough to make a man feel self-conscious.'

'Oh.' Her lips parted slowly. 'And you're not just saying all this to make me feel better?'

'Yes and no. I can want to make you feel better and mean it, too, can't I?'

She frowned as if the idea had never struck her before. 'I suppose so.'

'Just like I can think that you're beautiful and see more than your face?'

'Ye-es.' Her breathing sounded erratic now, almost as ragged as his own. 'Then you really want me? The real me?'

'Yes. Quite a lot, in fact, but I thought you only wanted friendship?'

'I did.' She swallowed, drawing her tongue lightly across her top lip. 'Before…'

'Before?' His pulse thudded at the word.

'Before I got to know you.' Her eyes widened even further, as if she were trying to hypnotise him again. 'But how do I know you're telling the truth? I couldn't bear to make another mistake.'

'Then I won't be a mistake.' He lifted his hands to her face, cradling her cheeks between his fingers. 'I promise you, Henrietta, but I won't kiss you unless you want me to…'

Henrietta caught her breath, trying to get her swirling thoughts into some kind of coherent order, though it seemed impossible when Sebastian was standing so close, his lips within a hair's breadth of hers, his gaze smouldering with desire and the promise he'd just made her. The feeling of his hands on her cheeks raised gooseflesh on her skin, making her mouth feel dry and her heart skip one, if not several, beats. He'd just said that he liked her. He'd just said that he wanted to kiss her, too. The words ought to have sent her running and yet, for the first time in what felt like a long time, they didn't. Because she trusted him. She knew that in as much as she knew anything at that moment—so much that the whisper was past her lips before she even realised she was speaking.

'I want you, too.'

She didn't have to wait long for his response. The words were barely out of her mouth before his lips brushed against hers, soft and warm and gentle, as if he half expected her to pull away. Instead she kissed him back and it was more, much more, than the moderately pleasant feeling she'd experienced the one time she'd kissed Mr Hoxley. She felt as though her body had just come to life, as though she really were an ice queen and her frozen limbs were melting to liquid.

Her heart was racing a mile to the minute, too, making her feel vulnerable and strangely powerful at the same time, and she was aware of a strange mewling sound in the back of her throat as Sebastian's hand moved to the small of her back, drawing her body against his and kissing her even more deeply… It was bliss, it was perfect, it was how she'd always imagined being kissed…

They both jumped, his arm tightening protectively around her waist at the sound of a thud, followed by a splash and two loud squeals from below.

'What—?'

They both exclaimed in unison, exchanging startled glances before rushing down the stairs and through the hallway to find Nancy and Belinda standing side by side in the middle of the kitchen, the former soaking wet and the latter covered from head to toe in white powder.

'Oh!' Henrietta slapped a hand over her mouth in surprise. 'Oh, dear.'

'I dropped the flour,' Belinda explained, unnecessarily, putting her hands to her cheeks and making them look even worse. 'I didn't notice Nancy come in and I turned around and we bumped into one another and…' Flour-covered hands moved to her forehead. 'I'll clear it up, I promise, every last speck.'

'Don't worry. There's no point in crying over spilt… you know.' Henrietta gave a reassuring smile, though unfortunately Sebastian was less charitable, his laughter clearly audible behind her.

'You.' Nancy pointed a finger accusingly. 'This is all your fault.'

'Me? How?' He sounded faintly aggrieved.

'Because I was rushing to get a bucket of water to hurl over *you*! You had no right to run past me!'

'Then this serves you right, doesn't it?' He chuckled again. 'I'd call that poetic justice.'

'Do you know what else you can call it?' Nancy started forward, arms pumping as if she were about to throw more than a bucket.

'Wait! You'd better go and change.' Henrietta stepped swiftly between them. 'And Belinda should go outside and brush herself down. I'll start to clean up.'

'While I watch the shop,' Sebastian volunteered.

'No!' Nancy stopped and folded her soggy arms. 'This is the last straw. We can't go on like this, what with looking after the boys and teaching Belinda to bake and *him* visiting every five minutes.' She threw another belligerent look at Sebastian. 'The shop isn't big enough for all of us.'

'I know.' Henrietta sighed. 'But what's the alternative?'

'You can come north with me.'

'What?' She spun towards Sebastian, uncertain about which of them had just gasped the loudest, her or Belinda or even Nancy, as they all stared at him in amazement. It would have been a surprising enough offer even before what had just happened upstairs, but now…

'Come with me,' he repeated, more firmly this time. 'Anna might be away, but my mother's in Yorkshire. You can bring the boys, too. It'll be a holiday for them.'

'What about David? What if he comes back?'

'Then he'll come here and Miss MacQueen will tell him where you are.'

'But I can't just go to Yorkshire with you!'

'Why not?'

'Because…' She gaped at him. There were almost too many reasons to name! The first and most obvious being, 'It wouldn't be seemly!'

'We'll be staying with my mother, grandmother and uncle. It won't exactly be sordid.'

'But your grandmother was a duchess!'

'And?'

'I can't stay in the same house as a duchess!'

'A dowager duchess.'

'That's not the point. What will she think if you turn up with a shop girl and three children in tow? It could ruin your chances of a reconciliation.'

'If it does, then I don't believe she's someone I want to reconcile with.'

'I won't fit in!'

'Neither will I, most likely. I'm a sailor whose father was a footman-turned-baker, remember?'

'It's different and you know it. You're a blood relation. I'm just...'

'Don't.' He lifted a hand, his dark eyes flashing so brightly it was as though lightning had just streaked across them. 'Whatever you were about to say, don't. You're not *just* anything. If other members of my family have a problem with you, then we'll turn straight around and come back.'

Henrietta swallowed. Ten minutes ago she'd resolved to throw him out of her life for believing gossip about her. Five minutes ago she'd been clasped in his arms, kissing him with a quite shameless amount of enthusiasm. *Now* he was asking her to go away with him. She felt as though time were accelerating. She'd only just accepted the possibility of their being more than friends...

'This is ridiculous.' She shook her head against the temptation to say yes. 'Nancy, tell him how ridiculous he's being.'

'Personally, I think it's the most sensible thing I've ever heard him say.' Nancy unfolded her arms. 'I presume he's apologised?'

'What?' Henrietta looked between the two of them in consternation. 'You wanted to throw a bucket of water at him a few moments ago!'

'Yes, well, the cold water's given me a chance to reconsider and now I think it's the perfect answer. You could do with a rest after the past couple of months and it would take the boys' minds off their father.'

'What about the shop?'

'Belinda can move in.'

'Oh! Can I?' Belinda clapped her hands so enthusiastically that a cloud of white dust billowed into the air, making them all cough.

'Yes,' Nancy spluttered as she waved her arms around. 'I'll make a baker of you if it's the last thing I do. Which will be *much* easier without so many people under my feet.'

'But what will people say?' Henrietta drew her brows together at her own question. The gossips would no doubt say that she was up to her old tricks again, trying to seduce yet *another* employer's son. She might as well confirm everything bad they'd ever said about her. Mrs Willerby would be particularly delighted. And the worst of it was that this time there'd be some truth in the accusations. She'd kissed Sebastian. If it hadn't been for the interruption, she would have kissed him some more. Given the opportunity, it was entirely likely she'd kiss him again. Which made travelling north with him probably the worst idea in the world. And yet, insane as it sounded, she wanted to go.

I won't be a mistake... She didn't know what the future held, but she knew those words at least were true. If she trusted any man, it was him.

'I'll go a day ahead and meet you in Bristol,' Sebastian offered. 'Then no one in Bath will know that we're travelling together. You can say that you're going to visit Anna.'

'No.' She pulled her shoulders back. 'I've wasted enough time caring about what people say about me.

They'll never change their minds anyway. In their eyes, I'll always be either a fortune hunter or an ice queen and I don't want to be either. From now on, I'm going to be myself and let people interpret that however they please.'

Sebastian's gaze warmed. 'Then you'll come to Yorkshire with me?'

She sucked in a deep breath, struck with the feeling that the whole of her future depended on this one moment. 'Yes. We'll go together.'

Chapter Fourteen

'Are we there yet?' Michael flung his head back against the seat with a loud sigh. 'We've been in this stagecoach *for ever*! It must be time to stop soon.'

'I told you the journey would take a few days.' Henrietta gritted her teeth, trying to sound sympathetic, although if he asked the question one more time, she thought she might open the door and jump out from sheer exasperation. It wasn't as if she was any more comfortable than he was! In fact, she was undoubtedly a lot *less* comfortable. Oliver and Peter had both fallen asleep, one on her knee, the other leaning against her shoulder, making it impossible for her to move for the last hour. Belles in biscuit tins were treated better than this, she thought, ironically. At least *they* came individually wrapped in tissue paper, something she might have used to make the headrest more comfortable. Every part of her ached or was numb with fatigue, but at least Michael was right about one thing. *Surely* it had to be time to stop soon… 'Are you warm enough?'

'Yes.' Michael scowled at the blanket tucked over his lap. 'But I'd rather ride up top like Sebastian.'

'It's far too cold for that.'

'It's not too cold for *him*!'

'Yes, well…he's a grown man.' Henrietta pursed her lips. She wasn't particularly happy about Sebastian riding on the roof of a violently swaying stagecoach in the middle of winter either, but unlike her three charges, she had no right to tell him what to do—besides, there hadn't been any alternative. Between her and the boys squeezed on to one side and a middle-aged couple and their teenage daughter on the other, the carriage was already bursting at the seams.

'Sebastian said a good sailor doesn't complain.' Peter mumbled sleepily across her. 'I bet he was talking to you.'

'He was not!'

'No arguing!' Henrietta felt as though her temper were hanging by a single, extremely frayed thread. 'Or we'll get off at the next inn and go straight back to Bath.'

'But…'

'Not *one more word* until we stop again!'

Incredibly, the threat worked, allowing her twenty minutes of rare, comparative peace, listening to the sound of Oliver's snoring and looking out at the darkness encroaching over the landscape outside. From what she could see through the carriage windows, Derbyshire had a wild, untamed kind of beauty, filled with wild-looking moors and jagged rock formations. Unfortunately for them, however, it *wasn't* Yorkshire, which meant that they still had another day of cramped conditions and moaning ahead before they reached Feversham. Which also meant another day of gradually building trepidation and dread.

It had seemed like a good idea at the time, leaving Nancy and Belinda in peace and giving herself and the boys a holiday, but now she was starting to wonder if she'd taken leave of her senses by agreeing to come. It wasn't just that she was going to stay in a manor—*a manor*! She knew Sebastian's mother well enough to know that she wouldn't be turned away, no matter what his uncle and grandmother might think of her. It wasn't even that she was afraid of being in the same company as a dowager duchess. Anna was a countess, after all, and one of her best friends.

It was that she'd kissed Sebastian! Right after she'd told him that she wouldn't be used or possessed by any man ever again! She'd kissed him and now she had no idea what it meant. In all the commotion of packing and organising, there hadn't been any chance to discuss it and it wasn't as if they could talk in front of her nephews. Which had left her with three days, trapped inside a carriage, with little to do except think.

What did it mean? More to the point, what did his invitation to come north mean? She knew that he wasn't the kind of man who would act dishonourably, but that didn't mean he'd thought their situation through. In fact, he *definitely* hadn't, considering that he'd both kissed and invited her on impulse. And even if he *had* felt serious about her at the time—serious enough to invite her to meet his family—surely he'd change his mind once he had time to reflect?

For a start, and no matter what he said, they were too far apart socially. For another thing, there were the boys. It was one thing to *help* her look after them, but to take responsibility and become a surrogate father if David didn't come back, which she was starting to accept as a real possibility, was a different matter entirely. In which case, it was foolish to even contemplate a future together and better to remain as *just friends*... wasn't it?

The situation wasn't helped by the fact that they were sharing a chamber at night. It had actually been her idea to pretend they were a man and wife travelling with their sons. In her defence, she'd had a sneaking suspicion that Sebastian had charged her only a fraction of the real price of stagecoach tickets, despite her own insistence on paying, and she hadn't wanted him to spend any more money on her and her nephews than necessary. Besides which, as she'd explained with increasingly red cheeks, it was safer for them all to be in one room and it would save the bother of explaining the situation to every innkeeper they met.

She must have had children at a very young age, Sebastian had teased her, but he'd agreed readily enough, telling the boys that it was all part of a game. Consequently, every evening after dinner, he left the chamber to allow them to wash and change into their nightclothes before coming back and settling himself into either a spare truckle bed or an armchair by the fire. It was an eminently practical arrangement, but one that had left no opportunity to talk privately, something she really wanted to do *before* they reached Feversham, if only to work out how they ought to behave.

And all this thinking was giving her a headache...

She was just attempting to adjust her position when the carriage swung sideways abruptly, lurching to a halt in front of a small coaching inn and jolting Peter and Oliver awake at the same moment.

'Here we are.' Henrietta gave them both a squeeze,

letting the middle-aged couple and their daughter descend first before climbing out of the carriage and stretching her arms above her head with relief.

'I'm hungry,' Michael grumbled beside her.

'We're all hungry.'

'I don't know about you, but I could eat a cow.' Sebastian jumped down from the roof, landing with a heavy thud beside them. 'Only let's start with something smaller, shall we? Some stew, perhaps?'

'I like stew.' Oliver grinned.

'Excellent!' He reached down, scooping her youngest nephew up under one arm before grabbing hold of their travelling bag with the other. 'Now let's go and find a room, shall we? You boys can carry that chest between you, I hope?'

'Yes, sir.'

Henrietta watched with amazement as Michael and Peter transformed into young cadets before her eyes, trotting behind Sebastian as he led them first into the taproom and then up a creaking staircase into a cosy, wood-panelled bedchamber.

'I'll order some dinner before it gets too busy.' Sebastian dropped a giggling Oliver on to the bed and the bag on to the floor alongside.

'Let me do it.' Henrietta showed the boys where to put the chest. 'You should warm yourself by the fire. You must have been frozen on that roof.'

'I've felt worse, believe me, although I have to admit the wind was bracing. I have no cobwebs left, but at least we're done with stagecoaches now. Feversham's only a few miles from here. If it wasn't so late, I'd hire a cart to take us there tonight.'

'Just a few miles?' Henrietta's voice emerged as

a croak. Suddenly she wished they had a week of cramped carriages ahead of them. 'But I thought we were still in Derbyshire?'

'Only just. Yorkshire's over the next hill.'

'So we'll arrive tomorrow?'

'Before lunch, I should think.' His smile faltered briefly. 'Now, I'll be back in a few minutes. Stew all round!'

'Wait...!' Henrietta hastened into the corridor after him, pulling the door half closed behind her to block out the chorus of cheers from within.

'What's the matter?' Sebastian turned around at once. 'Would you prefer something else?'

'No, it's not the food, it's about tomorrow. I've been thinking—perhaps it isn't such a good idea our coming with you to Feversham, after all. Maybe we could just stay here for a few days? Or somewhere close by? I don't want us to be in the way.'

Sebastian's brow furrowed. 'If you think I'm just going to abandon you here, then you're very mistaken. We've come this far together and that means we stay together.'

'But it's not your house. It's your uncle's. He might think that you've taken a liberty by inviting us.'

'He might. In which case, our visit will be a short one.'

'Sebastian.' She adopted the stern voice she used occasionally with the boys, exasperated by his refusal to see any problems. 'What I'm trying to say is that if you're having any second thoughts about any of this then I would understand. I don't want you to feel any obligation.'

'Obligation?' He mused over the word. 'No, I can't say that I do.'

'*Especially* considering what your family might think of us travelling together. I wouldn't want them to get the wrong impression.' She was starting to think that she might need to hit him over the head with a stick to make him understand. 'They might think there's more between us than friendship.'

'Probably.'

'*Probably?*' She blinked.

'It's the likely conclusion.' He looked remarkably unbothered by the idea. 'And it's the truth, isn't it?'

'I...' She hesitated. 'I don't know. We haven't talked about what happened. We've been so busy...'

'Ah.' He looked faintly relieved, reaching for her hands and twining their fingers together in a way that made goose pimples rise on her skin. 'The truth is, I was afraid you might change your mind if we talked too much. And I suppose I've been preoccupied, too. I'm not thrilled about the idea of meeting my family. Seeing my mother, yes, but *her* mother and my uncle?' His brows contracted. 'I can't help but feel as though I'm betraying my father.'

'Oh, Sebastian.' She slid her thumbs around so that they were on top of his hands. 'Surely if your mother can forgive them...?'

'Then I should, too, I know. Even Anna seems to have made peace with it all, but if it wasn't for them...' A muscle tightened in his jaw. 'My father spent his whole life trying to make up for what my mother lost by marrying him. He never wanted her to regret their elopement. She didn't and she told him so often enough, but the worry was always there underneath. I think it's part of the reason he worked so hard. I'm not saying that her family were responsible for his death, but it's hard not to resent them. And now it's as though my mother's gone backwards, as if my father never even existed. I know that's not fair, but all of this has happened so quickly.' He shook his head as if to clear it of unpleasant thoughts. 'But I'm glad that you're with me. I can't think of anyone I'd rather be with. Truly, Henrietta.'

'Then I'm glad to be here, too.' She caught her breath, her chest feeling too tight all of a sudden.

'But I don't want you to feel any obligation either.' He looked serious again. 'If you're not happy or you want to leave for any reason, just say the word and I'll take you back to Bath. You have my word on it.'

'Thank you.' She jumped at the sound of a loud thud from the chamber behind her. 'In that case, while we're staying with your family, I think that we ought to remain as just friends. I might not care what the shopkeepers of Bath think of me any more, but I do care about your mother.'

'*Just* while we're staying there?' He quirked an eyebrow.

'Until we can talk about things…properly.'

'Ah.' He glanced at the partially open door behind them, his expression inscrutable. 'As you wish. Now I'd better let you go. It sounds like a herd of cattle in there.'

Chapter Fifteen

It was a perfect winter morning, Sebastian thought, the kind you might get only once or twice in a season. The December sun was blindingly low, gleaming off the river that ran behind the inn and bathing the trees alongside in bright yellow light. Aside from their bare branches, however, there were almost no signs of winter, just a light frost gilding the scattering of stones beneath. He stood by the window, admiring the scene for a few moments before turning around and clapping his hands together enthusiastically.

'Shall we go for a stroll?'

'Right now?' Henrietta gave him a surprised look. They'd eaten breakfast and she'd just finished repacking their chest. 'I thought you wanted to go and hire a cart?'

'I do, but it's such a lovely morning and the boys could do with some exercise.'

'Of course, if you like.' She appeared to bite her tongue as she wrapped a shawl around her shoulders. 'That would be very pleasant.'

He watched as she bundled her nephews into their

caps and jackets. *Just friends.* The words had rankled and rattled around his brain all night. They weren't exactly what he'd been hoping to hear, though perhaps she had a point about not scandalising his family. Still, he was starting to regret his *friendly* behaviour over the past few days.

After what she'd told him about her previous romantic experiences, he hadn't wanted her to feel under any pressure, especially when they were sharing a chamber, or to change her mind about accompanying him, but now it appeared, ironically, that he'd been *too* well behaved. She'd got used to them being just friends again. His only consolation was that she hadn't said she *never* wanted to kiss him again...only while they were in Yorkshire, until they could find some time to talk...which made him want to get this visit over with quicker than ever.

They were halfway down the staircase when Michael let out a yelp and a small tin fell from his fingers, spilling marbles all over the corridor below.

'Oh, no!' Michael and Peter immediately sprang after them.

'Careful!' Henrietta kept a firm grip on Oliver's hand. 'Don't slip!'

'Do you know how many you had?' Sebastian went to help, crouching on his haunches.

'Twenty altogether.'

'All right. Where's the tin?' Quickly, he scooped up a handful of marbles and dropped them in one by one. 'That's eight.'

'I have another five!'

'I've only got two.'

'Keep looking.'

'I can't find them!' Michael wailed after a few minutes. 'Maybe they rolled outside?'

'Are these what you're looking for?' A grey-haired gentleman with a round, friendly face and wispy hair appeared in the taproom doorway, holding the last five marbles. 'Wouldn't do to lose them.'

'Thank you, sir.' Michael darted forward with a grin.

'Here. I'll carry them in my pocket from now on.' Sebastian gave a nod of thanks and reached for the tin. 'So that we don't have any more accidents.'

'Sorry, Sebastian.'

'Come on.' He ruffled Michael's hair. 'Let's go for that walk. Good morning.'

He tipped his hat to the gentleman, surprised when the man only stared quizzically back, and went outside. The stagecoach had already departed and the courtyard was relatively peaceful now, most people preferring to stand in the sunshine of the main street. That was wider than he'd given it credit for the previous evening, with several shops interspersed with neat-looking grey houses. A number of shoppers were out and about, too, milling around and chattering. Altogether it was a pleasant place for a stroll, he thought, made even pleasanter by the touch of Henrietta's hand on his arm.

He couldn't help but watch her out of the corner of his eye, wondering whether she was having regrets about kissing him at all. Her words the previous evening implied it. Or maybe she was simply having more doubts about whether or not she could trust him. Or maybe she was genuinely worried about what his family might think? Or was it about his intentions in general? And what were they anyway?

He tipped his hat to a group of ladies as they walked

by, considering the question. He probably ought to have thought about it sooner, especially after the way Miss MacQueen had chided him, but everything had happened so quickly. What *were* his intentions? Honourable, yes, but *how* honourable? Marriage? Was he really prepared to tie himself down just when he'd become a free man?

He sighed. Whatever his intentions, he was back in *friends* territory just when he wanted to kiss her more than ever.

They had made their way through the town and along a path to the river. The water was fast, but not particularly deep, and there had been stones to throw, branches to race under the bridge and stepping stones to jump across, after which the boys had been so hungry that Henrietta had had to pop into a bakery for some bread for them to share. All of which meant that it was past noon by the time they headed back to the inn to collect their bags.

'Sebastian?' Henrietta lowered her voice as they wandered back.

'Mmm?' He liked the way she said his name. *Sebastian*...with an emphasis on the *B*. Nobody else said it like that.

'You know it might just be better to get it over with?'

He gave her arm a small nudge. 'Are you suggesting that I'm delaying the last leg of our journey on purpose?'

'It crossed my mind.' She nudged him back. 'Although I wouldn't blame you if you were.'

'I'm not saying you're wrong, but I've run out of

excuses anyway. I'll go and ask the innkeeper about that cart n—'

'Sebastian!'

He stopped mid-stride at the sound of his name, looking up to see two women emerging from an apothecary's just ahead of them. Quickly, he let go of Henrietta, opening his arms just in time for one of the women to launch herself at him, moving faster than he'd ever seen her move in, well—*ever*. If he hadn't taken a moment to brace himself, they would surely both have been sent sprawling into a puddle.

'Sebastian!' the woman repeated, pummelling him in the face with her bonnet as she tightened her grip on his neck. 'I thought you were still in Bath. Why didn't you tell me you were coming?'

'It was a last-minute decision.' He tipped his head back with some difficulty and smiled. His mother had a few more wrinkles and grey hairs than the last time he'd seen her, but her face was just as kind and loving as he remembered. 'It's good to see you again, Mama.'

'You've no idea how good it is to see you.' There were tears in her eyes now. 'It's been so long!'

'I know, but I'm here to make up for it now.'

'Yes, you are. I can hardly believe it. Oh!' She noticed his companion finally, a surprised expression passing over her face. 'Henrietta? How lovely to see you, my dear.'

'Miss Gardiner and her nephews accompanied me,' Sebastian announced, deciding to dive straight in before anyone could start asking questions. 'We decided we were all in need of a holiday. Mama, meet Peter, Michael and Oliver.'

'What fine-looking young men.' His mother gave

them all a wide smile. 'Now, let me introduce you to my mother, Her Grace the Dowager Duchess of Messingham.'

Sebastian tensed as he looked towards that formidably titled personage. Small and white-haired as she was, it was impossible to doubt the family relation. She looked so much like his mother they might as well have had mother and daughter stamped across their foreheads.

'My friends call me Ottoline.' The woman smiled. 'I'm so pleased to finally meet you.'

'Your Grace.' He bowed politely, unable to agree with anything resembling honesty, though fortunately he was saved by the arrival of the gentleman from the inn.

'Tobias!' His mother waved. 'Look who we found.'

'My nephew, I presume?' The man beamed as he shook his hand. 'I wondered when I heard your name, but I couldn't be sure. It's a pleasure to meet you.'

Sebastian exchanged a quick glance with Henrietta. She and the boys were standing off to one side, huddled together and looking faintly bewildered by the number of greetings being exchanged. He was experiencing a similar feeling himself. As first meetings after long estrangements went, it was frankly bizarre. Everyone seemed so...*happy.*

'Would you do me the honour of introducing your companions?' His uncle turned towards Henrietta, still beaming.

'Of course, forgive me. Lord Tobias, this is Miss Henrietta Gardiner.' He paused, rebelling at the thought of referring to her as *just* a friend. 'She's the current manager of Belles.'

'Miss Gardiner, I'm delighted.' His uncle bowed over her hand. 'I hope that you're coming to visit us at Feversham Hall, too? And I presume these young marble-players belong to you?'

'Yes, they're my nephews.'

'Then you must all come to stay. How jolly!'

'I...' She looked somewhat overwhelmed. 'Thank you. If it's not an inconvenience?'

'Balderdash! Where are your bags?'

'At the inn.'

'Then let's go and fetch them! Ah.' Lord Tobias took a few steps before stopping and clucking his tongue. 'It occurs to me, we're not going to fit everyone in one carriage.'

'Sebastian was going to hire a cart.' Michael found his voice again.

'What a splendid idea!' Lord Tobias snapped his fingers. 'In that case, why don't we fellows go and organise that while the ladies go ahead?'

'If that's all right with Henrietta?' Sebastian threw her a questioning look.

'Ye-es...' She looked from him to her nephews and back again. 'If you think it is?'

'I'll collect the bags and keep an eye on the boys.' He gave her a reassuring smile. 'And I'll see you soon. *Very* soon.'

'Well, that's settled. Come along, my dear.' His mother slid her hand through Henrietta's arm. 'The carriage is just over here.'

It was the first time Henrietta had ever been in a private carriage, but despite the cosy leather interior and silk cushions, she fervently wished that she might have got out and walked—or at least travelled in a cart with Sebastian and the boys. Mrs Fortini and her mother were both perfectly pleasant, but she found herself answering their questions in awkward monosyllables, far too aware of the questions *behind* the questions. They were both much too polite to ask outright, but they *had* to be wondering what on earth she was doing there, never mind her nephews! They had to be wondering about her relationship with Sebastian, too, but it wasn't as if she had any answers to give them, not yet anyway. It was a huge relief when the carriage finally drew to a stop, less so when she climbed out and saw a grey brick manor house roughly twice the size of the Bath Assembly Rooms.

'This way.' Sebastian's mother took hold of her arm again, leading her up the steps as a footman came to escort the Dowager Duchess. 'Let's get you settled.'

'I'm so sorry to intrude, Mrs Fortini…' Henrietta glanced over her shoulder, already hoping for a glimpse of the cart following behind. 'It was all such a rush and there was no time to send a message ahead. If we're causing you any inconvenience, then please say so.'

'It's nothing of the sort.' Mrs Fortini smiled benignly. 'And you used to call me Elizabeth, remember?'

'Ye-es, but it's been several months and so much has changed.'

'But not *me*, I hope.' Mrs Fortini—*Elizabeth*—squeezed her arm. 'Do you remember when you made that beautiful evening gown for Anna to wear at Lady Jarrow's party? And then you fixed up one of my old ones so that it looked as good as new? Well, if memory serves, I said that I was indebted that day. Now I'm thrilled to be able to repay you.'

'Thank you, but I would never have dreamed of intruding if… Well, if things hadn't been so difficult recently.'

'At Belles?'

'Oh, no, the shop's in good hands. It's just a situation involving my brother. You see, his wife died and now he's run away and I've no idea where's he's gone and there's nobody else to look after my nephews and—' She stopped short, feeling horribly short of breath and as though she were about to start crying.

'Oh, my dear.' Elizabeth led her in through the great doors. 'How terrible.'

'But Sebastian's been a great help. Honestly, I don't know what I would have done without him.'

'Good! Now let's go into the sitting room and you can tell me all about it.'

Chapter Sixteen

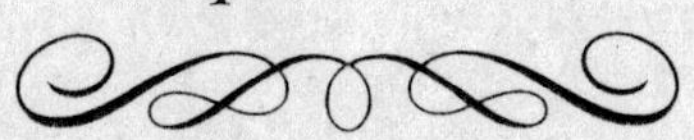

'There's a lake!' Michael bounced to his feet with excitement.

'Careful!' Sebastian swung around, grabbing hold of his waist. 'If you break your leg falling off this cart, then I won't let you go anywhere near it.'

'Sorry.' Michael settled back down again. 'But it's huge!'

'Full of trout, too.' Lord Tobias grinned. 'Excellent for young boys to fish in.'

'We don't know how to fish.'

'You don't? Good gracious. Well, I'd be happy to teach you. A boy ought to know how to fish.'

'Sailors need to know, too.' Peter spoke up this time. 'Don't they, Sebastian?'

'It can definitely come in handy.'

'And there's Feversham.' Lord Tobias pointed ahead towards a large grey house.

'That's huge, too!' Michael sounded thunderstruck.

'I built it myself. Not brick by brick, of course, but I designed it with an architect friend of mine about fifteen years ago. My father wanted to keep the bulk of the estate together for my older brother, but he gave me enough money to be independent so I decided to build this. It gives me plenty of room to indulge my interests.'

'It's a fine-looking house,' Sebastian answered honestly. The building was large, but not imposing, blending discreetly into the landscape instead of fighting against it. 'Is the Messingham estate close by?'

'Don't you know?' Lord Tobias looked surprised.

'No. I made a point of never being interested.'

'Ah. Well, there are properties all over the country, of course, but the bulk of the estate is in Kent.'

'Kent?' Sebastian looked at his uncle properly for the first time. 'That's a long way from Yorkshire.'

'Exactly. Far enough away that I'm not required to visit too often.' Lord Tobias shrugged. 'It's not that I don't love my brother. I do, but we get along much better at a distance. Besides, I always loved this part of the world.'

'What about your mother? Wasn't there a dower house in Kent for her?'

'Yes, but she preferred to come and live here with me. We were always very close.'

'Really?' Sebastian couldn't keep the sarcasm out of his voice.

'Forgive me, I didn't mean to be tactless. I know that she and Elizabeth were close, too, before…well…'

'Before she cut her off without a penny.'

'That was our father's doing.' His uncle's voice took on a harder edge. 'Our mother had nothing to do with it.'

'She still went along with it.' Sebastian threw a cautious glance over his shoulder, but the boys were too busy chattering to be paying any attention to their conversation at that moment.

'Actually I don't believe that she did.' Lord Tobias's knuckles tightened over the reins. 'I was only thirteen and away at school when it happened, but the next time I came home I could see that everything was different. My mother was deeply unhappy, but she was also powerless to defy my father. He was a controlling man at the best of times, but his temper was worse than ever after Elizabeth ran away. I was terrified of him.'

'You were?' Sebastian lifted his eyebrows.

'I'm not saying that we were blameless, my mother and I. Maybe we should have done more, but at the time there didn't seem to be anything we could do. Then, after my father died, we thought of contacting Elizabeth, but it had been so long and we assumed she wouldn't want to hear from us. I thought about visiting Bath and Belles several times, but I never summoned up the courage. Now I wish that I had. I know this situation must be very disconcerting for you and I wouldn't blame you for being angry, but I can't tell you how pleased I am to meet you finally. You're welcome to stay as long as you wish, all of you.'

'You know that I'm a sailor, Henrietta's a shopkeeper and the boys' father is a stable hand?'

'I do now.'

'Then are you *sure* that you want to invite us? Some people might say we're not fit company for a dowager duchess.'

'Some people might. *I* wouldn't. I stopped caring about what society thought a long time ago, around the same time as I lost my sister, as it happens.'

'We might be a handful.'

'I'll enjoy it. I'm an old bachelor myself, but it'll be nice to hear children's voices about the place.' Lord Tobias pulled on the reins, bringing them to a halt in front of the house. 'You can keep trying to deter me as much as you like, but you won't dampen my enthusiasm.'

'What about the Duke?' Sebastian lifted an eyebrow. 'The new Duke, I mean? Has *he* reconciled with my mother, too?'

'No.' A shadow crossed his uncle's face. 'I'm afraid that my brother takes after my father in that regard.'

'Meaning he doesn't approve of her living here?'

'I'm afraid not. He's written to me about it in no uncertain terms.'

'And?'

'And I've replied in a similar vein.'

Sebastian smiled his approval. 'I'd like to have been a fly on the wall when he opened that letter.'

'Nobody should be told who they can or can't share their lives with, or who they can love either.'

'I agree.' Sebastian looked up at the house and rubbed his chin thoughtfully. 'If you were away at school when my mother ran away, then I don't suppose you ever met my father.'

'No, although I wish that I had. From what Elizabeth tells me, he was a very special man.'

'He was.' Sebastian nodded, starting to suspect that his uncle might be, too. 'Now, I ought to go and find Henrietta.'

Pouring her heart out to Elizabeth had been soothing, Henrietta realised, as Sebastian walked into the drawing room half an hour later alongside his uncle and her nephews. Now that her tears had dried, her mind felt ten times easier than it had that morning. Surprisingly, *he* looked more relaxed, too, albeit a little confused, as if he were trying to make sense of something.

'We're going to learn fishing!' Michael announced, already hurtling across the room.

'Are you?' She gave him a pointed look that only just stopped him from leaping on to the sofa beside her.

'Oh!' He skidded to a halt and sat down gingerly. 'Yes, Lord Tobias said that he'll teach us.'

'With your permission?' Sebastian's uncle looked towards her with a smile.

'Of course.' She smiled back. 'That's very kind.'

'And we're allowed to call him Uncle Toby!' Michael blinked. 'Only I just forgot to.'

'I see.' She glanced uncertainly at Sebastian, who only lifted his shoulders.

'We decided it would be easier, didn't we, young man?' His uncle's smile grew even wider. 'Lord Tobias sounds much too formal.'

'I've asked Mrs Lancaster to prepare the nursery,' Elizabeth commented, speaking to her brother, though her gaze was focused on Sebastian, Henrietta noticed.

'The nursery?' His uncle chuckled. 'You know, my architect insisted on calling it that, but I never thought I'd have a use for it. The rooms will need a good airing.'

'I'm sure Mrs Lancaster is seeing to it now.'

'In the meantime…' His uncle caught his sister's eye and took a tactful step backwards. 'Perhaps I could take the boys into the library and have a marble tournament? I'll send for some refreshments, too.'

'What a good idea.' The Dowager Duchess reached for her walking stick. 'I think I'll join you.'

'Maybe I should, too...' Henrietta started out of her seat.

'No. You stay.' Sebastian turned sharply towards her. 'If you don't mind,' he added more gently.

'If that's what you want...' She sat down again, looking between him and his mother anxiously.

'Henrietta's just been telling me about Belles.' His mother spoke first. 'I'm glad that the shop's doing so well, although I never doubted she'd do a good job.'

'Yes. Has she told you her idea about selling tea?'

Henrietta shook her head quickly. 'It's still just an idea.'

'But it sounds like a very interesting one.' Elizabeth smiled. 'I'm sure Anna would love to discuss it when she comes back from Retford, but I'm afraid that may not be for a while. The Earl's grandfather died last week and they don't want to leave his grandmother. I doubt we'll be seeing her before the new year.'

'Oh, how sad.' Henrietta felt genuinely sorrowful. 'He was such a kind man. He used to talk to me about bees.'

'I remember. Anna was very fond of him.' Elizabeth turned to her son as he sat down in the chair just vacated by the Dowager Duchess. 'And how was your ride with Tobias?'

'Fine... Enlightening... Good.'

'Good,' his mother repeated, leaning forward to place a hand on his knee. 'I can't tell you how wonderful it is to see you again. When I got your letter from Bath, I thought that my heart would burst. I've been so worried.'

'It's good to see you again, too.' His slightly perplexed expression turned to one of affection.

'But tell me, what happened? Why didn't we hear from you for so long?'

'It's a long story, one for another time. The main thing is that I'm here now.'

'Well, I can't argue with that. And will you stay?' Mrs Fortini looked between the two of them. 'Oh, do say you will, at least until after Christmas.'

'We'll need to talk about it.'

Sebastian caught Henrietta's eye and she bit her lip. Christmas was still several weeks away. Nancy had told her to take as long as she needed, promising to send word if there was any sign of David or any problems, and she knew that Sebastian would insist on accompanying her and the boys if they left any sooner. And how could she do that when Mrs Fortini was looking at her with large, distinctly moist eyes? But Sebastian was giving her a way out, she realised, giving her the power to say yes or no, as if her desires and comfort mattered more than his. In which case…how *could* she say no?

'I'd be delighted to stay.'

Until after Christmas… Henrietta sat on the edge of a large four-poster bed, looking around a bedroom larger than any she'd slept in in her life. And it was hers—*until after Christmas*!

She'd agreed to stay. *Of course* she'd agreed to stay. It would have felt cruel to Mrs Fortini not to, but what was she supposed to do for the next month? Especially now that the boys had been appointed a pair of house-maids to tend to their every need as if they were little dukes themselves! She'd insisted on reading them a bedtime story that evening, but she had no doubt that they were still wide awake up in the nursery, wonder-

Chapter Seventeen

'What a beautiful day.' Elizabeth Fortini sighed happily as she walked arm in arm with Sebastian through Feversham's frost-covered garden. 'It looks as though the world is covered in sugar.'

'That sounds like something Father would have said.'

'It probably was.' She smiled nostalgically. 'He always made me look at the world in new ways and he saw the beauty in everything. It was one of the things I loved most about him, that optimism. You remind me so much of him, you know, even more than when you left, although I think you might be even more handsome.'

Sebastian bent to press a kiss on her cheek. After four days in his uncle's house, he was finally starting to relax, enough to talk about his father. It was the first time that he and his mother had done so since his arrival.

'Did you have any doubts when you ran away with him? He always said it was love at first sight, but it was a big risk.'

ing what on earth had happened to their lives. She was wondering the same thing. It was as if her whole existence had been turned upside down from the moment she'd rammed her kitchen door into Sebastian's face.

Speaking of doors... She heard a light tap on hers and hurried across the room to open it.

'Ready for dinner?' Sebastian stood in the hallway, dressed in his regular clothes instead of the dinner suit she might have expected. Which was a relief. She'd been afraid that her best evening gown, a pink muslin with a lacy trim around the neckline, wasn't formal enough.

'I think so.' She smoothed a hand nervously over her hair. 'Do I look all right?'

'Am I allowed to give compliments now?' He leaned closer, his dark eyes twinkling. 'Because if I am, then I'd say you look as beautiful as always.'

'I meant, do I look smart enough? This is my best dress.'

'And it looks gorgeous on you.'

'Sebastian...'

'I mean it. You have absolutely nothing to worry about.'

'What should I talk about at dinner?'

'Damned if I know. I'm just glad that you're with me.'

She glanced at his profile as they made their way to the staircase, surprised by the apparent depth of feeling behind the words. He sounded as if he genuinely meant them, as if he were relying on her as much as she'd come to rely on him over the past couple of weeks.

'Your family seem very pleasant.'

'Yes. They're not what I expected.'

'They've been very welcoming. I don't think the Dowager Duchess has stopped smiling since she set eyes on you.'

'Does that mean you really don't mind staying?' He gave her a searching look, smiling when she nodded. 'Well then, I'm grateful to them for that. I couldn't tell from your expression earlier. I was afraid I might have to sleep outside your door to stop you running away in the night.'

'I promise that if I run away then I'll do it broad daylight.'

'Good. Because I have a very comfortable-looking bed down the hall and I'd like to make the most of it. Not that I didn't appreciate all the sofas and chairs I've been sleeping on recently, but a real bed makes a pleasant change.'

'Mmm.' She stared straight ahead, feeling her cheeks start to flush. It didn't feel quite right to be discussing beds with him. Or to be thinking about him in one either...especially when her imagination seemed determined to place her in the scene, too. 'Your mother seems very happy.' She changed the subject hastily.

'Yes. I'm pleased about that. As for the rest... I don't know quite how to feel yet.' He turned to face her as they reached the bottom of the staircase. 'All I *do* know is that I'm hungry. Ravenous actually.'

'Me, too. I was too nervous to eat earlier.'

'Then will you do me the honour of accompanying me into the drawing room, my lady?' He made a bow, sweeping his hand so low that it skimmed lightly across the floor. 'Although I doubt that we'll be able to find the dining room on our own without a map.'

'I'd be most obliged, my lord.' She laughed, sinking into an equally low curtsy before tucking her arm into his elbow and then immediately trying to extract it again as they entered the drawing room to find Mrs Fortini, Lord Tobias and the Dowager Duchess all waiting. Sebastian was faster, however, raising his other hand and clamping it down on top of hers.

'Good evening.' Lord Tobias stood up to welcome them. 'The boys are all settled, I trust?'

'Yes.' Henrietta dipped into a slightly less effusive curtsy. 'Thank you, Lord Tobias. They like the nursery very much.'

'Call me Tobias, please. Now, dinner's ready if we are?' His smile looked almost in danger of splitting his face. 'I never would have thought when I got up this morning that by tonight I'd be welcoming my own long-lost nephew into my home. I honestly couldn't be any happier.'

Henrietta nudged Sebastian lightly in the ribs when he didn't respond. Instead, his expression looked oddly tense for a few seconds before he let her go and reached an arm out. 'Here you are, Uncle. I didn't shake your hand properly before. It's a pleasure to meet you and, for the record, I'm happy, too.'

'Thank you. And Miss Gardiner...' his uncle continued. 'I do hope your nephews will be happy here, as well.' His laugh positively boomed around the room. 'There appear to be nephews everywhere these days!'

'It was both. I remember the first time I saw him, standing outside the drawing room at Messingham Hall. Footmen weren't supposed to look directly at us, but he was never very good at following the rules. I was eighteen years old and thought he was the most handsome man I'd ever laid eyes on. He quite took my breath away.'

'But how did you know that you loved him? You can't have spent much time together before you eloped.'

'No. We met in the gardens a few times, but never for long.'

'Then how could you be sure that he was the right man for you?'

'I'm not sure. I just *knew*.' Her brow creased slightly. 'I suppose you could say I had anxieties more than doubts. I was afraid of upsetting my mother, but I was young and impetuous and I hoped that my family would forgive me and accept him eventually. Deep down, I suppose I knew that would never happen, but I also knew that I'd never be happy with any other man. So we eloped. It was the only way. If my father had got even the slightest inkling of how we felt, then he would have made sure we never saw each other again.'

'So you never regretted it?'

'Being estranged from my family? Very much. Marrying your father? Never.' She stopped to smile up at him. 'I consider myself a very lucky woman. I miss him every day, but we had seventeen happy years and two wonderful children together.'

'And now you're happy here? Even with your ailments?'

'Yes.' She nodded emphatically. 'I still feel stiff most days, but I feel as though I can finally put the past behind me. Mainly because I know your father would have been happy for me. I've no doubts at all about that.'

'Then I'm glad, too. As much as it pains me to admit it, I like them, your mother and Tobias.'

'They like you, too. I can tell.'

'Which means that they would probably have liked Father.'

'Yes, but there's no point in regretting that now. When you get to my age, you realise life is too short to harbour ill will.' Her expression shifted as they started walking again. 'You know, they like Henrietta and her nephews, too.'

'Do they?' Sebastian fixed his gaze on the lake.

'Yes.' Her arm tightened perceptibly. 'As for myself, I understand your reasons for bringing her, but you must know how it looks.'

'What if that were the truth?'

'Then I'd be delighted. I've always liked Henrietta, but I'd also want to be sure that you have the right motives for pursuing her. She's a very beautiful woman.'

'Meaning?'

'Just that it can be hard not to be blinded by beauty. Some people might mistake that for love.'

'I know. So does she.'

'You haven't known her for very long.'

'How many times did you say you met Father before you eloped?'

'*Touché.* Then you truly care for her?'

'I do.' He didn't even need to think about the answer. 'Maybe I was dazzled by her beauty at first, but now she's just…' he gave an exaggerated shrug '… Henrietta.'

'Do you love her?'

'Love...' he hesitated '...is a big word, but I like her a great deal. She's caring and intelligent and much more than a beautiful face.'

'She's always been a great deal more than that.' His mother smiled her agreement. 'And if you can see that, too, then I wish you both joy. So...?'

'So?'

'Don't be obtuse. What are you going to do about it?'

'Oh, I don't know.' He lifted his eyes to the sky and whistled. 'There's no rush.'

'Sebastian Fortini!'

'I'm going to propose, obviously.'

'Good, although if her brother doesn't come back—'

'He's not going to.'

'What?' She put a hand over her mouth in surprise. 'How do you know?'

'Because of a letter I received yesterday.' He glanced over his shoulder, making sure there were no small boys around to overhear them. 'I asked James Redbourne to listen out for any news of Henrietta's brother and he finally heard some. Apparently David Gardiner didn't run away on his own. He went to Bristol with one of his friends, only when the friend sobered up he changed his mind about their plans and came home again. Her brother didn't. He took a ship for America instead.'

'So he's really gone and left his sons?'

'Yes. He knew that Henrietta would take care of them, probably *better* care of them, but, yes, he's gone.'

'Have you told her?'

'Not yet.' He shook his head. 'She needs a holiday and I don't want to spoil it. I thought maybe I could tell her after Christmas.'

'Absolutely not.' His mother lifted her chin. 'She's not a child and she won't thank you for keeping it from her. She has more of a right to know than you do.'

'Yes, but...'

'You *know* you have to.'

Sebastian gritted his teeth. 'I suppose so. I just don't want her getting hurt.'

'I think that's unavoidable at this point.' His mother quirked an eyebrow. 'But I hope you understand what this means. Henrietta will be their mother from now on, so if you marry her...'

'Then I'll be their father.' He nodded. 'It had occurred to me.'

'It's a lot to take on.'

'I know, but I want to.'

His mother reached a hand to his cheek. 'You really have grown up.'

'I suppose so. A little sooner than I'd hoped, but I don't seem to be able to do anything about it.' He grinned. 'You know, this will make you a grandmother.'

The caress turned into a light pat. 'I think I might enjoy that.'

'You'll be wonderful at it. You were a wonderful mother, after all.'

'Come on, let's go inside.' His mother gave a suspicious-sounding sniff. 'You need to speak to Henrietta and then comfort her. The sooner that's done, the sooner you can propose.'

'Don't tell me...' Sebastian leaned against the doorframe of the nursery, rubbing his chin thoughtfully. 'You're a snowman?'

'A polar bear!' Oliver peered up at him through two holes in a white sheet.

'Ah.' He clicked his fingers. 'Of course, silly me. Might I enquire why?'

'We're rehearsing a play.' Michael jumped down from a chair, wielding a wooden sword. 'It's all about Nelson fighting the polar bear.' He straightened his shoulders proudly. '*I'm* Nelson.'

'Naturally.' Sebastian inclined his head and then looked across the room towards Peter. 'And you are...?'

'A pirate.'

'In the North Pole?'

'I challenge Nelson to a duel after the polar bear escapes.'

'Well, that all sounds excellent. I'm looking forward to it already.' Sebastian nodded approvingly. 'Now I don't suppose you happen to know where your aunt is?'

'In there.' Michael gestured towards a door in the opposite wall. 'She's making up our beds. So we don't make any more work for the maids, she says.'

'Ah.' Sebastian looked pensively towards the door. After dragging his feet up three staircases, he'd been hoping for an excuse to postpone the task for another day or a few weeks, but his mother was right, Henrietta had a right to the truth.

'I tell you what...' he jerked his head at the boys '...why don't you run down to the kitchens for something to eat?'

'We just had breakfast.'

'Then it must be time for a snack.'

'Biscuits?'

'Naturally.'

He stepped aside, letting them scurry past before making his way reluctantly to the bedroom.

'You know you don't have to do that.' He gestured to the coverlet Henrietta was smoothing over the furthest of the three beds.

'I know.' She straightened up with a smile. 'But it makes me feel better.'

'I'm glad I found you anyway. I have some news.'

'Oh.' A hand crept to her throat. 'About David?'

'Ye-es.' He pulled the letter from his coat pocket. 'My friend James heard a rumour and went to investigate.'

'And?'

'And...' He cleared his throat, unable to find any way of softening the blow. 'It seems that when your brother left he went to Bristol and...well, according to what James has heard, he took a ship for America.'

There were several moments of absolute silence as she stared at him, so pale and motionless that it was hard to tell if she were still breathing. She looked frozen.

'Henrietta?' He moved back towards her, alarmed by the silence, but she held a hand out, holding him back.

'He's gone to America?' Her voice was different, high-pitched and laced with hurt. The sound of it made his heart wrench.

'Apparently so.'

'America...' Her expression seemed to waver between shock and hurt. 'I don't understand.'

'Maybe you ought to sit down?'

'Why?' She stared at him as if he'd just told her to go for a swim. 'What good will that do? How could he just go to America? How could he abandon his sons?'

'I don't know. He must have thought he had no choice.'

'I can't... I don't... Argh!' She swung around, wrenching the quilt and pillows off the nearest bed and stomping on top of them. 'If he were here, this is what I'd do to him!' She moved to the next bed, punching her fist into the pillow before hurling it across the room. 'And this!'

'And he'd deserve it, only...'

'His own sons!' She dropped heavily on to the bare mattress behind her. 'What am I supposed to tell them?'

Sebastian sat on the adjacent bed, facing her. 'Maybe nothing for now.'

'*Nothing?* You were the one who told me to be honest with them before.'

'I know, but you need time to come to terms with this first.'

'Maybe you're right.' She dropped her head into her hands, golden hair spilling over her fingers. 'You know, I wondered, but I kept telling myself that he'd come back. I really thought it was just a matter of time.'

'I know.'

'Thank you for telling me.' She sat upright again after a few seconds, dragging the palms of her hands across her cheeks.

He made a face. 'To be honest, I didn't want to. My mother said you had a right to know, but I didn't want to upset you.'

'It's not your fault I'm upset.' Her jaw tightened. 'But at least now I can make plans.'

'What do you mean?'

'Plans for the boys. I have to be their mother from

now on. That means I need to be practical and find a job that works around their schooling.'

'What? No, you don't have to leave Belles.'

'Yes, I do. It wouldn't be fair on Nancy to carry on as we've been doing. The shop demands a lot of time, you know that as well as anyone.'

'There's Belinda now, too. *And* me.'

'You?' Her whole body seemed to tense. 'But I thought you wanted to enjoy your freedom? You said you didn't know what you wanted to do next.'

'I think I've decided. Now that I'm back on dry land, I want to stay. More than that, I want to stay with you and help to take care of the boys properly.' He hesitated, the next words hovering on the tip of his tongue. This probably wasn't a good idea. It wasn't the time or place for a proposal. She'd just had a shock and he'd planned to wait for a few days. It wasn't the least bit romantic, but suddenly he couldn't stop himself from dropping down on to one knee. 'Henrietta Gardiner, I'd consider it a great honour if you'd consent to be my wife.'

Chapter Eighteen

'What did you just say?' Henrietta stared at Sebastian open-mouthed. It sounded as though he'd just proposed to her.

'It was a bit long-winded, to be honest.' He looked faintly abashed. 'Not like something I'd usually say at all.'

'But what *was* it?'

'Ahem…' He cleared his throat and tipped his head to one side, almost apologetically. 'I asked if you'd marry me.'

'That's what I thought you said…' If she hadn't been sitting already, she was quite certain her legs would have collapsed beneath her. Her knees already felt as if they were trembling and her ankles…well, they'd surely have twisted from shock. 'Are you mad?'

'I don't think so, although I've wondered occasionally.' Sebastian rubbed his chin. 'But I don't *feel* mad. Not at the moment anyway.'

'You must be.' She leaned forward to put her hands on his shoulders, ready to talk some sense into him. '*Think* about it. I'm a shopkeeper.'

'As was my father. As I would have been if I hadn't joined the navy.'

'You're the grandson of a duke.'

'This again?' He rolled his eyes. 'Haven't we been through this enough times? I don't care who my grandfather was or wasn't.'

'But the world will. Sebastian, I have no family and no money. Nothing in the world except three little boys to take care of. You should be marrying up, not down. Look at Anna. She's a countess now.'

'Anna married for love, or so you and my mother keep telling me. Rank had nothing to do with it.'

'Yes, but...' She gulped, feeling an almost electric jolt at the mention of love. Was he saying that he *loved* her? No, he was comparing them to Anna and the Earl, but not in that way...

'And since my grandfather disowned my parents and by extension me, I don't see what his vaunted position has to do with anything.'

'All I'm saying is that you could marry a lady if you wanted.'

'*If* being the operative word.' He sounded almost angry at the suggestion. 'Or are you saying that I should marry a lady on some kind of principle?'

'No-o, I just think...'

'I think you are.' He tore himself free from her hands and stood up, pacing the room as he spoke. 'You're suggesting that I ought to make up for my mother's so-called "mistake"! That I ought to act as if my father never existed and take up some kind of position in society.'

'Not necessarily, but maybe you ought to meet a few more ladies before deciding against them.'

'I've met ladies. I've served them in the shop enough times and trust me, there's no difference between them and any other woman except for clipped vowels and expensive clothes. I told you the first day, that's not my definition of a lady.'

'It's not just about vowels and clothes! It's about all of this!' She waved her arms around in a circle. 'This house. This estate. This is the world your family lives in now! That makes it part of your life, too, and how could I ever be a part of it? I don't belong here.'

'And you think that *I* do? Henrietta, I may have a tenuous connection to this place by birth, but in case you hadn't noticed, this isn't my world either. I'm glad to be here with my family again, but as a guest. I'm not a gentleman.'

'But you *could* be.'

'I doubt it. Honestly, I can't think of anything more boring. People expect you to make calls and wear damned dinner jackets every day!'

'Sebastian.' She couldn't help a burble of laughter from escaping her lips.

'I'm not saying that there wouldn't be compensations. Good food, a feather-filled bed, servants catering to my every whim and cigars after dinner, but none of that's who I am. I could never live in a place like this. Whereas a house in Bath, close to Swainswick Crescent, maybe next to the park where the boys could play, with a woman who knows how to work for a living, a friend and an equal, someone I like and respect...well, that sounds pretty close to perfect to me.'

She swallowed again, staring into his eyes as they bored into hers, unable to think of a single thing to say. He was right, it *did* sound pretty close to perfect...

'Henrietta...' He crouched down, his knees touching against hers. 'I know who I am and who I want to be. There have been moments in my life when I've felt guilty and helpless, but I finally feel as though I'm making up for those times now. I feel as though I'm doing something useful and worthwhile again. Most of all I want to do the right thing.'

The right thing? She blinked at the words. He was talking as if she were a lady and he'd compromised her. Which, if she *had* been a lady, she supposed would be true. He'd kissed her and slept in the same room, albeit chastely, on several occasions over the past week. But she wasn't a lady and there was no need for him to do the right thing. Neither she nor the boys were his responsibility. Besides, what about love? she wanted to ask, but somehow she couldn't bring herself to do it. How could she expect him to answer a question she didn't know the answer to herself? She liked him, she enjoyed his company far more than she'd ever expected to enjoy any man's company, but surely it was too soon for love? And wasn't what he was offering her enough? Friendship, mutual respect and a home, not just for herself, but for her nephews, too. It would have sounded greedy to ask for more.

'I'm not saying I can afford a house immediately.' He looked faintly sheepish. 'In fact, I'm not even sure where we'll live, but I'll work something out. I have some savings and I'll earn the rest. I was thinking about your idea of serving tea at Belles. Maybe we could expand the premises? Or better still, find somewhere new and call it *Henrietta's*. What do you think?'

'I don't know.' She closed her eyes and then opened

them again, trying to stop the room from spinning around her. 'I'm speechless.'

'Then just nod your head. Or shake it, but I'd prefer a nod.'

'Sebastian...'

'Wait.' He reached for her hands, clasping them firmly between his. 'If you're going to say no, then let me say one more thing first. I know this is a bad time to ask. In fact, it's a terrible time, probably the worst I could possibly have chosen, but I want you to know that you don't have to face the future alone. I want to be there for you—all of you.'

'But you don't *have* to.' She shook her head. 'You don't have to marry me just to be useful and make amends for the past.'

'It's not just that. Yes, I still feel guilty about Anna, but not enough to propose, I promise you.' He lifted one of her hands and kissed the pulse at the base of her wrist. 'It's not *just* a question of feeling guilty. It's you, too.'

Her breath stalled. 'What about your freedom?'

'I'll still be free. So will you. We'll make our own decisions together and with our own crew. Me, you and the boys.' He grinned. 'I'm happy. Right here and now, I'm happy and a large part of that is due to you. I think we could be happy building a life together.'

'Oh.' She felt her lips part, though for the life of her she had no idea how to close them again. Or how to form words for that matter.

'We're friends, aren't we? Maybe even a little more than that? You kissed me once.' His dark eyes glinted. 'It wasn't *such* a painful experience, was it?'

'No.' She let out something between a laugh and a

hiccup, the joke unlocking her tongue. 'No, it wasn't painful.'

'Damning with faint praise...' The top half of his body swayed forward. 'In that case, maybe you'd let me try to persuade you again?'

He brought his face slowly to hers and she moved to greet him until they met somewhere in the middle. It wasn't that she'd intended to move, she thought with a vague sense of surprise, just that she couldn't help it, as if there were an invisible rope tied around them, drawing her closer and binding them together. It was a perfect moment, tender and serene and somehow just *right*, lasting for several heart-stopping seconds before something seemed to catch fire between them and she found herself moving again, trying to press even closer towards him.

Sebastian gave a low, surprised-sounding murmur before curling his arms around her waist, his lips clinging to hers as if he felt the same fire, too. She reached her own arms around his neck, absorbing the heat of his chest with her breasts in a way that made her stomach clench and contract with tingles of pleasure. She felt as though she had one of his knots inside her, being pulled tighter and tighter, although surely it had to stop at some point? If you pulled on a knot hard enough, then eventually, surely *eventually* it had to unravel. Or the string would snap. Or...well, *something* would happen! Only she had no idea what.

'I must be mad, too.' She panted as they came apart finally, foreheads pressed together as they each struggled to regain their breath.

'Does that mean you're considering my proposal?'

He laughed huskily, one of his hands sliding across the small of her back and up to her shoulder blades.

'No.' She shook her head, smiling back. 'I've already considered. Yes. Yes, I'll marry you. I still think it's madness, but I—'

She didn't get any further as his lips seized upon hers again, kissing her so deeply that she felt a wave of heat rush all the way from the top of her head to the tips of her toes in a cascade of sensation. If this was madness, she decided in the split second before coherent thought abandoned her, then sanity was vastly overrated.

Sebastian had always thought of kissing with ambivalence. It wasn't that he didn't enjoy it, just that there were other, similar and yet slightly more energetic activities that he preferred. Kissing Henrietta, however, was different. Words like 'new' and 'exciting' were far too mild to describe what they were doing. It was an utterly engrossing, nerve-tinglingly heady sensation, unlike any kiss he'd ever experienced before. It was, quite simply, bliss. He could have happily done it all day. Two days. A whole week if he could have gone that long without food and water. Her lips were the smoothest he'd ever felt, the sweetest he'd ever tasted, the most exquisitely shaped…

'Wait!' She pulled back abruptly. 'The boys! They're next door.'

'No, they're not.' He trailed his mouth over her cheek, across her jaw and down the delicate column of her throat. 'I sent them to the kitchens.'

'They might come back.'

'We'll hear them coming, believe me.'

'But I might not have time to straighten up.' She lifted her hands to his chest. 'You've unfastened my hair.'

'Have I?' He lifted his head, surprised to find that she was right. Somehow he'd managed to unpin and unravel her hair without even noticing. Now it was lying over her shoulders in a pale golden torrent. And if she thought that drawing attention to it was the way to convince him to let her go then she was extremely deluded… He gave a low moan and buried his face in the tresses.

'Mmm.'

'What are you doing?'

'Breathing you in.' He inhaled deeply as her body sagged against him. 'It smells different from usual.'

'It does?' Her voice sounded breathless.

'Just a little. Usually it smells of sugar and baking. Now it smells of…' He drew in another deep breath. 'Apricots?'

'The maids gave me a soap.'

'I like it. I like both. Have you ever considered making an apricot-flavoured Belle?'

'I think we have enough to deal with at the moment.' She laughed huskily. 'But we really should stop.'

'All right.' He pressed one last kiss to the tip of her nose before moving away. Truth be told, it *would* look somewhat incriminating if they were disturbed now and not just by the boys. Both his uncle and grandmother had paid visits to the nursery over the past couple of days and if they discovered him and Henrietta together like this…well, it wasn't just her loose hair that would give them away. He was going to need a few minutes to recover himself.

Henrietta pressed her lips together, watching him through her lashes as she coiled her hair up and then looked around for the pins.

'Here.' He reached down, picking a handful off the floor.

'Thank you.' She fixed the roll into place and folded her hands in her lap. 'Just so you know, it wasn't that I didn't like it. Kissing you, I mean.'

'Glad to hear it.' He grinned. Her pose reminded him of the first time they'd met, when she'd clasped her hands so primly in front of her. 'Because if you didn't, then I'm afraid you'll find marriage to me somewhat tedious.'

'Really?' Her eyelashes fluttered. 'Do you intend to kiss me a lot, then?'

'If you mean do I intend to wake you up with kisses every morning then, yes, yes, I do. For the record, I also intend to lull you to sleep the same way.'

'I don't think that will work.' The corners of her lips tugged upwards, her dimple more pronounced than ever. 'It doesn't seem to have made me very sleepy.'

'Wait and see.' He winked, barely resisting the urge to pull her into his lap. 'In the meantime, let's go and share the good news.'

'Right now?' She looked startled.

'No time like the present. Then we'd better start packing.'

'You mean you want to go back to Bath?'

'No. The other direction, actually.'

'What? Sebastian, what are you talking about?' She shook her head at him. 'Where are we going?'

'Gretna Green. *Today.* I'm not giving you a chance to change your mind.'

Chapter Nineteen

'Are you sure you've got enough blankets?'

'Yes, as well two hot bricks and five layers of clothing. If we take any more, the horses won't be able to pull us.' Sebastian chuckled as his mother peered anxiously inside the carriage. 'We'll be fine.'

'I still think it's a ridiculous time of year to be heading to Scotland. What if it snows when you're up on the hills?'

'If it looks like bad weather, then we'll stop somewhere, I promise. It's not as though we're in the middle of the ocean.'

'Don't even joke about that.' His mother gave him a stern look before surrendering to the inevitable. 'Oh, very well. In that case, travel safely and don't worry about the boys. They'll be perfectly safe here.'

'Are you sure you don't mind me going away for a few days?' Henrietta crouched down in front of her nephews.

'We don't mind,' Peter answered. 'Lord Tobias says he'll carry on our cadet training. He's going to teach us about ich...icthy...'

'Ichthyology?'

'That's it!'

'And we'll have our play ready for when you get back,' Michael added.

'Will you still be our aunt when you're Mrs Sebastian?' Oliver sounded anxious.

'Of course. I'll *always* be your aunt. I'll just be Mrs Fortini, too.'

'Good. In that case you can go.' He grinned as she kissed him on the cheek.

'Now take care of each other and be good.'

'I'm sure they will be.' Elizabeth smiled warmly. 'We're going to have fun, aren't we, boys?'

'And *we'd* better be going.' Sebastian gestured towards the carriage door. 'The sooner we get there, the sooner we can get back again.'

'Try to be a little more romantic, dear.' His mother rolled her eyes. 'It is your wedding, after all.'

'You're right.' He winked and then bowed to Henrietta. 'Your carriage awaits, my lady.'

'Thank you, my lord.'

She gave the boys one last hug each and then climbed inside, burying herself beneath a pile of his mother's blankets.

'Off we go.' He took a seat beside her and banged on the roof. 'No second thoughts?'

'None, but how long will it take to get there?'

'A couple of days, I should think. We'll be back with the boys by the end of the week, don't worry.'

She nodded and then looked anxious again. 'What do your family really think?'

'They're happy for us. They said so.'

'It's just so hard to believe, considering everything.'

'Considering nothing.' He gave her a sharp look. 'You know my mother said something earlier about life being too short to carry ill will. I think my uncle and grandmother know it's too short to judge a person by where they come from, too. At the very least, they know it's foolish to stand between two people who care about each other.' He paused briefly. 'As we do.'

'As we do.' She met his gaze with a smile. 'I wonder what Anna will say?'

'That you're too good for me, I expect.' He slid across the bench, nudging his shoulder against hers. 'Now, are you warm enough?'

'You sound like your mother.'

'I know, but she made some good points. It *is* colder than it was last week. I don't want a frozen bride.' He twisted his head as she laughed. 'What?'

'Some people do call me an ice queen.'

'There's no need to live up to it.'

'Then you'll be glad to hear that I'm feeling quite toasty. Almost too warm, actually.'

'You do look a bit flushed, now that you mention it. Are you feeling all right?'

'Perfectly. It's probably just the hot brick. I'm only worried about the poor coachman.'

'For a start, there are two poor coachmen and I've said they can take turns travelling inside if they want to. For another thing, they're both being paid a small fortune.'

'Good.'

'Then we're all set.' He slid his hand into hers, lacing their fingers together and tipping his head back with a sigh. Maybe his mother was right and it *was* foolish, racing off to Scotland in the middle of December, but now that they were on their way, he couldn't wait to be married.

'We're here.'

'Not yet...' Henrietta shook her head as she felt Sebastian's hand on her shoulder. 'I'm sleeping.'

'I know, but we have an anvil to get married over.'

'Oh!' She prised her eyelids open and looked out. After two days, most of which time she'd spent asleep, both in the carriage and the inn where they'd stayed for the night, it seemed they were finally over the Scottish border and in Gretna. Which was a relief in more ways than one. She'd gone from feeling slightly warm to quite ill the morning after they'd left Feversham. Not *very* ill, just aware of a tightness in her throat and behind her eyes, not to mention an overwhelming sense of exhaustion, all of which suggested she was on the verge of a bad cold.

Naturally, she hadn't shared any of this information with Sebastian. She had a feeling that he would have turned the carriage around if he'd known the truth and now that she'd agreed to marry him, she wanted to do it as quickly as possible. As it was, she could tell that he'd been watching her more closely than usual.

He'd tried not to be too obvious about it when she was awake, but the tilt of his head, facing straight ahead but with his chin turned slightly sideways, gave him away. Every time she'd sniffed, which had started to happen more and more frequently, his fingers had twitched beneath hers. There had been moments when she would have given a large proportion of her meagre savings just to be able to blow her nose without him noticing. Instead, she'd tried to angle her face away from his scrutiny and towards the window, but after a while it had made her neck stiff.

'Are you sure you're not feeling unwell?' He asked, climbing out of the carriage.

'I'm fine.' She stifled the urge to sneeze. 'So what do we do now?'

'Now I'll go and speak to the blacksmith and see if he can marry us.' He paused. 'Are you sure—?'

'I'm *fine*.'

'Hmm.' He sounded unconvinced. 'Come into the inn so you can wait in the warm.'

'Good idea.' She looked around and shivered. The village of Gretna was covered in a thin layer of white. 'Snow!'

'Just a little. It won't stop us from leaving again tomorrow.' He spoke briefly to the coachman and then reached for her hand, leading her into an old and cosy-looking inn.

'Wait here.' He found her a vacant armchair by the fireplace, his expression still full of concern. 'I'll be as quick as I can.'

Henrietta fumbled in her purse for a handkerchief and sank into the armchair with a sense of relief. It was old and tattered and stained in places, but she didn't care. All she wanted was to bury herself in its warmth and close her eyes again. Her nose was running, she was finding it increasingly difficult to swallow and, overall, she was starting to suspect that she was a great deal sicker than she'd initially thought—certainly more than she'd let on. Feverish didn't seem like a strong enough word for the hot tremors now coursing through her body. Even so, if she were going to collapse, she was determined to do it as a married woman. If anything happened to her, then what would become of her nephews? Sebastian would take care of them, but it would be much easier if he was already legally their uncle.

'You are *not* all right.'

She opened her eyes with a jolt to find him leaning over her, looking as though there was a lot more he wanted to say.

'No, I'm not.' She lifted her head with an effort. 'What did the blacksmith say?'

'That he won't marry women who are sick.'

'He did not!'

'He'll probably say something about you needing to be in your right mind.' He placed a hand on her forehead. 'You're burning up.'

'That doesn't mean I'm not in my right mind.'

'You have a fever.'

'I'm just a bit hot.'

'It's more than—'

'No, it's not, not yet.' She pushed his hand away. 'It probably will be, but I can still say *I do* without sneezing. After that, I admit I might require some kind of medicine, but right now I'd like to get on with it.'

It was a good argument, she thought—authoritative, firm and determined—although it would have been a lot more effective if she hadn't decided to add gravitas to the words by standing up and then immediately veering off to one side.

'That's it.' He caught her elbow, stopping her from tumbling over. 'You're going to bed.'

'I'm not. We didn't come all this way to give up now.'

'We're not giving up. We're postponing.'

'No!' She grabbed his shoulder, trying not to lean too heavily against him. 'Did the blacksmith *say* he'd marry us now?'

'Yes.'

'Then we're getting married now or I'll change my mind.'

'Is that so?' He lifted an eyebrow. 'You wouldn't be trying to blackmail me by any chance, would you?'

'Yes,' she lied. 'It's now or never and right now I'm perfectly capable of making my own decisions. You said we were equals, remember?'

'We would be if we could both stand upright.'

'*Please*, Sebastian.'

His jaw set, as if he were still going to refuse, before he muttered something she wasn't sure she wanted to understand. 'All right.' He tightened his grip on her arm as if he were afraid she might topple over again at any moment, which she had to admit was a distinct possibility. 'But I'm summoning a doctor now. Hopefully he'll be here by the time we get back.'

'Fine.'

'And you're going to stop pretending you're not ill and tell me the truth from now on.'

'Whatever you say.'

'Do you need me to carry you?'

'No, thank you.' She lifted her chin, unwilling to make a scene. 'I believe that, traditionally, the bride makes her own way.'

'I'm not feeling very traditional. Let's just make this quick.'

Hardly the most romantic sentiment for the occasion, Henrietta thought, but at that moment exactly what she wanted to hear. Then, after they were married, he could carry her wherever he wanted.

Chapter Twenty

'Here you are, wife.' Sebastian held out a cup of steaming hot tea. 'Drink up.'

'Thank you.' Henrietta lifted a hand and then sneezed.

'Maybe I'll just hold on to it for now.' He sat down on the edge of the bed with a smile. 'Just tell me when you're ready for a sip.'

'Thank you. *Atishoo!* Oh, dear... I'm sorry.'

'What for?'

'Because this is our wedding night and I... I... *Atishoo!*'

He gave her a pointed look. 'Are you *feigning* sickness?'

'What?' She opened her eyes wide. 'No!'

'Exactly. So don't apologise. If anyone should say sorry it's me, for dragging you halfway across the country in the cold.'

'You weren't to know I'd get sick and it was for a good reason.'

'Yes, but the truth is I've always been impulsive.

Once I decide on something, I like to do it as soon as possible.'

'Oh.' She felt a vague sense of alarm. She wasn't sure she liked to be thought of as an impulse, though hopefully that was only an expression...although her head felt much too hazy to think about it now. 'Can I have some of that tea?'

'With pleasure.' He passed the cup over carefully. 'You're still a bit pale. How does your head feel?'

'Like the time I drank the last of the port in the pantry.'

'What?' He looked at her in disbelief. 'You said you poured it away! I thought it must have been because of your brother.'

'No-o.' She screwed up her lips with embarrassment. 'Nancy and I drank it after she had a bad argument with her mother. It happens quite often, I'm afraid.'

'You amaze me.'

'No, it's not like that. I think a lot of Nancy's anger is because of her mother. She doesn't usually drink because of her stepfather, but...well, that night she said she needed to drown her sorrows and I wanted to support her. What? Why are you smiling?'

'It's just unexpected, that's all.'

'Never again.' She shuddered and drank her tea in a few swallows. 'This is much nicer. I didn't realise I was so thirsty.'

'Anything else I can get you?' He put the cup aside.

'I'm a little chilly.'

'Then come here.' He shuffled up the bed, swinging his legs up and reaching an arm around her shoulders before drawing her head back against his chest.

She closed her eyes instinctively. It felt lovely, blissful even, to be lying so close, encircled in his arms. As if she were exactly where she wanted to be.

'This is nice.' He pressed a kiss on to the top of her head.

'Mmm.'

'Now get some more rest,' he murmured into her ear, his breath warming her neck and making her skin tingle. 'I'll be here when you wake up.'

'A bull escaped, trampling several gardens including that of Lord and Lady Pewter. This reporter has it on good authority that a row of prize-winning hydrangeas...'

Henrietta rolled on to her side, surprised to find herself dreaming of escaped bulls and crushed flowerbeds. Only it wasn't a dream, she realised gradually, more of a voice.

She opened her eyes to find her husband—bizarre as it still seemed to call him that—sitting beside her with one leg draped casually over the other, reading aloud from a local newspaper.

'Sebastian?'

'Ah.' He lowered the paper and smiled. 'And how's the patient today?'

'*Much* better.' She smiled back, pushing herself up on to her elbows as she realised it was true. She felt considerably better than she had when she'd last closed her eyes.

'Here.' He tossed the paper aside and leaned forward, rearranging the pillows before helping her sit up against them. 'Let me help.'

'I can manage.'

'You need to build your strength back up. You've barely eaten for two days.'

'Two days?'

'Since you got into this bed, yes.'

'You mean I've been lying here for *two days*?'

'Yes.' He chuckled tenderly. 'You did seem a bit confused.'

She opened her eyes wider, looking at him properly. He had two days' worth of stubble on his chin, enough to qualify as a beard, and his eyes were circled with shadows, making them look even darker than usual. Now that she thought of it, she had a vague memory of drifting in and out of consciousness. There had been someone else in the room occasionally, but Sebastian had always been there, speaking to her in reassuring tones as she'd tossed and turned. When she'd been shivering, his arms had been around her. When she'd been burning up, he'd pulled the covers away and dabbed at her forehead with a damp cloth. When she'd been neither, well…he'd been there then, too.

'Have you been here the whole time?' she asked even though she already knew the answer.

He winked. 'I'm thinking of a new career as a nurse. The doctor thinks I show a lot of promise.'

'I agree. What else did the doctor say?'

'That it was a fever exacerbated by nervous exhaustion.' He leaned over, brushing the backs of his fingers across her cheek and beneath her jaw until his hand cradled the side of her face. 'So no more worrying. Doctor's orders. Your husband's, too.'

'I'll do my best.' She smiled and lifted her hand to cover his, trapping it against her skin. 'I didn't dream it all, then? We really are married?'

'We really are. Notice the ring. It was my mother's.'

'Oh!' She gasped in surprise, holding her other hand out to study it. 'Why didn't you tell me at the blacksmith's?'

'I thought you'd appreciate the gesture more when you weren't about to collapse.'

'I can't believe that she gave you her wedding ring...'

'Actually she gave *you* her wedding ring. She said she knew you'd take care of it.'

'It's beautiful. I don't know what to say.'

'You said yes. That's enough.'

He smiled into her eyes, his own darkening almost to black before he cleared his throat huskily.

'I apologise for the reading material. There wasn't much else, I'm afraid.'

'That's all right.' Her own throat felt somewhat dry, too. 'The bull was captured, I presume?'

'Yes, though at the cost of several prize-winning hydrangeas.'

'Oh, dear.' She started to laugh and then let out a shocked shriek.

'What?' Sebastian looked panicked. 'What's wrong?'

She pointed across the room to a mirror sitting on top of a dresser. 'I just saw my reflection!'

'Your...?' He practically sagged with relief. 'And?'

'I look *terrible*!'

'Actually, you're looking much better.'

'What?' Shock turned to horror. 'How bad did I look before?'

'Not bad, just...sick.'

'Swollen?'

'A little. That reminds me. May I?' He slid his hands

around her throat, prodding gently. 'Good. You can hardly feel any swelling today and you're definitely not green any longer.'

'Green?' Any pleasure she might have found in his touch evaporated instantly.

'It's perfectly normal when you're sick.'

'Yes, but...' She stiffened. 'Wait, if you've been nursing me, what about my...' she closed her eyes, reluctant to even voice the thought aloud '...needs?'

'Ah.' He drew his hands away, rubbing one of them over his bristly-looking chin. 'To be honest, you were sweating so much that you didn't have many of those.'

'None?'

'Well, *some*...' He made a show of picking up the newspaper and folding it neatly. 'But nothing to concern yourself about.'

'Oh!' She flung herself over, burying her face in her pillow.

'Henrietta.' He laid a hand on her back. 'I've seen and dealt with much worse, believe me. Eight hundred men on one ship, some of them seasick...'

'I'm not a sailor!'

'True.' His hand moved in a slow circle over her back, rubbing gently. 'But you know, one of the advantages of *not* marrying a gentleman is that we're not so squeamish. I wouldn't have left you even if the doctor had brought a nurse. I wanted to take care of you. Besides, maybe this is a good thing?'

'How?'

'You were afraid of me seeing you as just a pretty face, weren't you?'

'That doesn't mean I wanted you to see me sweating, swollen and...*green*!' She groaned and pressed her face deeper into the pillow. 'Never mind anything to do with a chamber pot!'

'It doesn't make me look at you any differently.'

'How can it not?'

'Because I don't care about things like that. You were sick and you needed my help so I gave it.' She felt the bed shift as he lay down beside her. 'You're still as beautiful now as the first day I saw you.'

'Liar!'

'I was referring to inner beauty. *That* never dims, not according to the poets anyway.'

'Oh…' She twisted her head to one side. 'Maybe I'm more vain than I realised.'

'I won't tell anyone.'

She sniffed. 'In that case, do you think maybe myself and my inner beauty could have a bath?'

'I think that could be arranged.' He pressed his lips lightly against hers before leaping up and heading for the door. '*Then* you need to eat. It's about time we had our wedding breakfast.'

Chapter Twenty-One

'Just a few more mouthfuls.'

'No more!' Henrietta protested as Sebastian pushed his own, barely touched bowl of soup across the table towards her. 'I've had plenty.'

'Are you sure?' He gave her an appraising look and then relented. She was looking almost like her old self again, he thought, her still-damp hair trailing over the front of her nightgown in silken coils as she sat by the fire in their chamber. Altogether *too much* like her old self, tempting him to forget that she was still weak and recovering. Both his thoughts and eyes already kept straying dangerously close to the bed, which had been stripped and then remade with fresh sheets, but it was much too soon to even consider anything like that.

He couldn't forget how frightened he'd been just two days before, acutely aware of her breathing, of every soft inhalation and whisper of sound that passed her lips. He'd been terrified that the fever might attach to her lungs. His whole world had seemed to contract to that one bedchamber and the woman inside it.

'Sebastian?'

'Mmm?'

'You look tense.'

'Do I?' He shook his head quickly. 'It's been a worrying couple of days, that's all. I'm glad you're feeling better.'

'So am I. We can probably make a start back to Yorkshire tomorrow.'

'No.' He intended to stand firm on this point. 'Not for another day at least. I don't want you falling sick again.'

'I'm sure I won't.'

'I'm still not risking it.'

'Well, I'm not staying in bed *all* day tomorrow. How will I pass the time?' She gave him a pointed look that turned suddenly speculative. 'You know, you look different with a beard.'

'I ought to shave.'

'Do you have to? I quite like it.'

'You *do*?'

'Yes.' Her expression turned faintly mischievous. 'You look like a pirate.'

'You know, that really isn't a compliment for a naval officer.' He rubbed a hand over his jaw with a grimace. 'Have you met many pirates?'

'None that I'm aware of, but it's how I imagine a pirate might look. And I *do* mean it as a compliment.'

She tipped her head to one side and then sat forward, her eyes glittering with an expression he'd never seen in them before. It wasn't one he recognised either, or at least not exactly. It seemed to be playful and inquisitive and sultry all at the same time, each one of which made him feel at least ten degrees hotter.

'Can I touch it?'

'My beard?' He blinked, both at the request and the jolt of excitement that shot through him. 'If you want.'

'Thank you.' She stood up and moved slowly around the table to perch on the edge of his chair. 'Although it's hard to know where to begin...' She leaned close enough for one of her breasts to brush against his shoulder, making his breath catch and then quicken. 'There's just so much of it.'

'If there's one thing I excel at, it's growing hair.' He tried to swallow, but his face muscles felt unusually taut.

'Maybe here.' She skimmed her fingers across his cheekbone and down to his jaw. 'It's softer than I expected.'

'Is it?' Because the touch of her fingers was making another part of him quite the opposite. 'Not scratchy?'

'No.' Her eyelashes fluttered as she bent her head and laid her own cheek against his, rubbing back and forth gently. 'Not at all.'

Sebastian shifted in his chair, ordering himself to get up and go outside to cool down, but his legs seemed unable to move. Apparently only one part of him was still capable of movement and that wasn't obeying his commands either. Meanwhile, Henrietta's fingertips were trailing a path across his chest, making his body temperature soar even higher.

'You know...' she murmured, her cheek still pressed against his, 'you never kissed me after our wedding. Isn't the groom supposed to kiss the bride?'

Sebastian thought about flags. Naval flags. National flags. Any kind of flags... Maybe if he concentrated hard on remembering those then he could ignore the warm caress of her breath against his ear. It made his skin tingle, not just there, but all over, like ripples on a pond spreading outwards. He gritted his teeth to repress a shiver of pleasure, glad that she couldn't see his face. Or vice versa. If she looked at him just one more time with those big blue eyes, then he had a feeling he might lose his resolve completely. He felt as if he might go mad if he didn't touch her soon, but she was sick, she was recovering, she was...*kissing his ear*?

He couldn't have identified a single damned flag if his life depended on it.

'The bride was sick.' Somehow he pushed the words out.

'But she's not any more.' Her tongue touched his earlobe. 'Or are you afraid of catching my fever?'

'No.' He turned his head slightly, catching a glimpse of her pulse at the base of her throat, just above the buttons of her nightgown. It appeared to be pounding almost as fast as his. 'If I were going to catch it, I think I would have done so by now.'

'That's what I thought.'

Her lips curved against his skin as if she were smiling and he swallowed a groan. One of his hands was clenching the arm of his chair so hard he was afraid of snapping the wood, the other was lying in his lap, itching to curl itself around her waist and pull her fully into his lap. He could do it so easily, too. It would only take a second.

'You still need to rest.' It was actually becoming painful to talk.

'I'm not tired.'

'Henrietta...' He tipped his head to one side, dragging his ear away with what surely had to be the last ounce of his self-control. Men had received medals for less. 'We can't do this.'

'Oh.' She sat back on his chair-arm, digging her teeth into her bottom lip.

'It's not that I don't want to.' His heart wrenched at the look of hurt on her face. 'I just don't want you to overexert yourself.'

'I only asked for a kiss.'

'It might become more than a kiss.'

'I know.' She released her lip again. 'But...would that be so bad?'

Every muscle in his body seemed to go into some kind of collective spasm. 'Do you know what that means?'

'Yes.' Her cheeks darkened as she nodded. 'My sister-in-law told me.'

'Ah.' His chest heaved as his mind raced. If she knew what she'd be letting herself in for, then it wouldn't be so bad, would it? But then knowing in theory was very different from knowing in practice...

'You didn't answer my question.' She was holding her bottom lip between her teeth again. 'Would it be so bad?'

'Not bad.' He swallowed. 'In fact, I think it would be very good, but it's just not a good idea at the moment. I think I should go down to the taproom and you should go back to bed.'

'I'm not an invalid!' She jumped up, taking a few steps away before whirling around again, arms folded around her waist. 'You said that the past few days hadn't affected how you saw me.'

'They haven't.'

'The other day you couldn't wait to kiss me and now you can't wait to get away!'

'Not because I don't find you attractive!' The idea was so absurd that it gave him the impetus to stand up. 'I don't want to leave, Henrietta, but I have to! If I start to kiss you, then I won't want to stop.'

'Then you don't have to.'

'Don't say that. We should wait until you're completely recovered and you've got all your strength back. Then we can—'

He didn't get any further as she kissed him. She moved so quickly that he barely had time to react before her lips were pressed against his, and she wasn't gentle about it either. On the contrary, she was rough, as if she were determined to show him just how recovered she was. It was the fiercest, most potent kiss he'd ever experienced, so unexpected and mind-spinning that it rendered him utterly powerless to do anything but kiss her back. And then she pulled away and stared up at him, hands gripping the front of his shirt as her eyes blazed a challenge and that was it, he realised—he was lost.

The next few seconds were a frenzied blur. He was vaguely aware of reaching for her, of catching her up in his arms as her own curved around his neck, until her feet were trailing along the floor and they were both stumbling towards the bed. And then his clothes were being discarded, scattered in all directions at once, and her nightdress was being pulled over her head, and they were lying side by side, only not *quite* side by side. He was lying half on top of her, one of his legs draped across hers while he kept his weight on one arm, trying to keep from crushing her.

'Mmm...' He kissed her again, one of his hands smoothing a path over her stomach and up her ribcage until he found her breast and cradled it. 'Mmm.' He slid his tongue inside her mouth as he drew his thumb across the bud, swallowing her moan of pleasure. She was a perfect handful, he thought, even more perfect than he'd imagined, and if she moaned like that again, she might just unman him before they could get any further...

'Tell me...' He broke the kiss. 'If you change your mind. If you want me to stop...'

'I will...' she arched her back as his hand slid downwards again, curving gently around her hip '...but I won't.'

'But if you do...' He almost growled the words, needing her to know she could trust him, before he moved downwards, placing his mouth where his hand had left off.

'Oh!'

She cried out as his lips closed around her nipple and suckled. It was beyond any shadow of a doubt the most seductive sound he'd ever heard. It made him feel an even greater need to hurry, although he didn't want to rush her or do anything before she was ready. Which meant that he was going to have to think of something powerfully *un*-seductive to hold himself in check, though frankly it was a wonder he could still think at all when all the blood in his body appeared to have sped straight to his groin.

Flags again?

'Sebastian...' She placed her hands on either side of his head, lifting his mouth back to hers, her breathing fast and erratic. 'I want you.'

'I want you, too.' He rolled on top of her, nudging her legs apart and settling his body gently between her thighs. 'But it might hurt at first.'

'I know.'

He smiled. 'You know a lot.'

'I know that I trust you…' her eyes were wide and intense '…and I can't wait any longer.'

There was only one way he could think of to reply, holding her gaze as he pushed inside her. She gave another gasp, one that sounded like pain this time, and he stopped at once, counting to ten as he tried to remain completely still. He was only part way sheathed. Maybe if he pulled back, it would…

'No.' She moved beneath him suddenly, as if she'd sensed his retreat, pushing upwards until he was fully embedded.

'Hen…' He couldn't even finish her name, pressing his face into the curve of her neck and breathing heavily as they both lay completely still for a few seconds.

She felt so, so good, her body moulded against his, her inner muscles clenching around him so tightly he could have groaned aloud. She was his, his wife, his Henrietta, and she fitted him as if they were made for each other. And then they both started moving, pressing together and pulling apart in an awkward and then less awkward and then almost flawless rhythm. He wouldn't have believed the feeling could get any better and yet it did, so close to perfection that he didn't think he could hold on for much longer. He tried stopping, pushing himself up on his arms to cool them both down, but her breasts were slick with a sheen of perspiration and one of her legs was around his hip and there was nothing he could do. He sank back into her, thrusting one last time before he found his release.

'Sebastian?'

It took him a few oblivious moments to realise that she was speaking to him.

'Are you hurt?' He rolled quickly away from her.

'No.' She placed a hand on his chest and gave a low laugh. 'Stop worrying.'

'Says the woman who collapsed due to nervous exhaustion.' He fell on to his back, raking one hand through his hair. He could still feel his own heartbeat, beating so hard it felt like a drum inside his chest. It was no wonder. The last half-hour—he *hoped* he'd at least lasted that long—had been the most intense experience of his life. He had a feeling it might take him the rest of the night and then some to recover.

'Well, I've learned the error of my ways.' Henrietta laid one arm across his chest and rested her chin on top. 'That was as good as any medicine.'

'It didn't hurt at all?'

'A little at first, but then I forgot about it.'

'Good.' He wrapped his arms around her waist, holding her tight. 'Although I still don't think the doctor would have approved.'

'The doctor isn't a newlywed.'

'True.' He laughed. 'And given the circumstances, I think he would have understood. You're hard enough to resist at the best of times, but in a nightdress it's well nigh impossible. I thought that the first night I met you.'

'You did?'

'Yes. I remember being particularly taken with your ankles.'

'These ankles?' She kicked her legs up in the air behind her.

'The very same.' He regarded them thoughtfully. Exhausted as he was, the sight was irresistible. 'I haven't given them nearly enough attention tonight. Here.' He sat up, turning her over until she was lying on her back with her legs draped across his lap. 'I hate to be neglectful.'

'Sebastian...' She giggled as he ran a hand gently across her calf.

'Don't tell me you're ticklish?'

'No, it's just...' She drew the bed sheet across her waist. 'I'm naked.'

'I noticed. So am I.' He bent her knee and pressed kisses all the way down to her ankle. 'You know, I've never been seduced by a woman before.'

Her mouth dropped open. 'I did *not* seduce you!'

'I beg to differ. I offered to go to the taproom and let you recover in peace.'

'All *I* did was kiss you.'

'There was no *all I did* about it. There are kisses and then there are *kisses*.'

'And the way you're kissing my ankle right now would be?'

'Definitely the latter.' He pressed his lips to each of her toes in turn before putting her leg down gently. 'But you're right. It's too soon.'

'I never said...'

'But it is. I'll just have to dream of your ankles. Now close your eyes and I'll tuck you back in.'

'Oh, all right.' She snuggled against him as he lay down beside her again, hoisting the blankets up to cover them both. 'I suppose I did seduce you a bit, but you *were* going to seduce me at some point, weren't you?'

'As soon as possible, yes.'

'That's all right then.' She smiled and yawned. 'I only sped things up a little bit.'

'I hadn't worked out all the details yet, but it was going to be very romantic.'

'How nice.'

'You would have enjoyed it.'

'I'm sure. Did I spoil things, then?'

'What do you think?'

She laughed and snuggled closer. 'Sebastian?'

'Yes?'

'Do I really have to spend the whole day in bed again tomorrow?'

'Absolutely.'

'Good.' She pressed a sleepy kiss against his chest. 'Because I'm looking forward to it now.'

Henrietta lay back against the pillows and stretched her arms above her head, feeling like the cat who'd got the cream and was basking in sunshine to boot. As horrified as she'd been by her sickbed appearance the previous day, she was starting to think that perhaps having Sebastian as a nurse wasn't such a bad thing, after all. All things considered, she would be perfectly content to lie in bed all day long. Not only was he extremely attentive, but his methods of keeping her there were surprisingly pleasurable. She didn't think there was a single square inch of her body that he *hadn't* kissed that morning, though he'd paid particular attention to her ankles, she'd noticed.

She supposed she ought to feel embarrassed by some

of the things they'd done, but instead, every time she looked at him, she felt a fresh flurry of stomach tingles. They were beyond friendship now, quite a long way beyond, and, although neither of them had mentioned love, they had a new kind of relationship. One based on honesty, affection, respect and undeniable mutual attraction. And if that didn't feel like quite enough, a tiny voice at the back of her mind argued, it was still better than a lot of marriages.

No, she had no regrets, she decided, watching the ripple of Sebastian's shoulder blades as he drew a knife across his cheeks and frowned into the mirror on the dresser that had given her such a shock. None except that she hadn't been able to persuade him to keep the beard, but he'd claimed it was too itchy, promising to compensate in ways that made her imagination run riot.

'There.' He put the knife down and rubbed a piece of cloth over his face. 'All done. What do you think?'

'I *think* I miss my husband.'

'Ah, I forgot, you like pirates.' He placed his hands on his hips. 'I'll just have to save that look for special occasions. Now, am I allowed to get undressed and come back to bed?'

'I don't know.' She tapped a finger against her bottom lip. 'I *would* say yes, but I thought I was supposed to be recovering?'

'That was yesterday.' He was already removing his trousers. 'The doctor's given you the all-clear today.'

'Oh, yes.' She giggled. 'He said I looked quite invigorated.'

'I hope you didn't tell him why.'

'No, although he did tell me I was most fortunate in my choice of husband.'

'And you agreed?'

'I might have.' She glanced at the window. 'What's the weather like outside?'

'Wet and cold.'

'No more snow?'

'Not at the moment.' He gave her a quizzical look. 'You sound disappointed.'

'I am a little. Part of me was hoping we'd get snowed in.'

'That sounds blissful.' He jumped on to the bed and climbed on top of her. 'Although I thought you wanted to get back to Feversham as quickly as possible?'

'That was before I discovered what we could do indoors.' She smiled provocatively. 'Besides, if we were snowed in, then it wouldn't be our fault, would it? A delay would be out of our control. And we'd have to fill in the time somehow.'

'I see.' He nuzzled the side of her neck. 'You wouldn't be trying to seduce me again, would you, Mrs Fortini?'

'No. It's your turn.'

'Challenge accepted.' He grinned wickedly and dived under the covers.

'Sebastian?' She let out a squeal of surprise. 'What are you doing?'

'Ankles.'

She laughed at his muffled reply and settled back against the pillows again. Only it wasn't just her ankles he was kissing, she realised quickly. It was her toes, too, and her calves and the backs of her knees, the insides of her thighs…

'Sebastian!' She thrust her hands under the covers, grabbing his shoulders. 'You can't!'

'I can.' His hands wrapped around her waist, pinning her down again.

'But *what* are you doing?'

'It's much better if I show you.' His head appeared from beneath the covers, one eyebrow raised. 'Let me?'

She hesitated briefly and then nodded, squeezing her eyes shut as curiosity battled with modesty. She probably ought to protest some more, she thought, only she couldn't quite bring herself to do it, not when everything he did, every way and place he touched her felt so good, and even better when he slid up the bed and entered her, thrusting gently until she gave a low moan and started to rock against him, too. It was better than the first time, as if they were truly one body, moving together in total harmony.

And then he reversed their positions, holding on to her hips and rolling them both over until she was positioned on top of him, naked and exposed and feeling more powerful than she ever had in her life. For a moment she wasn't quite sure what to do, but then the sensations seemed to intensify until she was moving to her own rhythm, sliding back and forth, faster and faster until at last she felt a trembling, shuddering sensation in her abdomen as if something had burst inside her, leaving her whole body quivering and shaking. It was a few minutes before she rolled over and came back to herself.

'You really do like my ankles.' She stared up at the canopy in wonderment.

He gave a ragged laugh, though she could tell he was staring at the canopy, too. 'You have no idea.'

Chapter Twenty-Two

Mornings had officially become Sebastian's favourite time of the day. He'd woken up in the same room as Henrietta several times while they'd been travelling north, but he'd quickly discovered that waking up *beside* her, with her face next to his on the pillow, was completely different. Just looking at her while she slept, watching her eyelashes flutter and her chest move slowly up and down made his heart clench with a sense of gladness and contentment. And when she woke up, all tousled and wide eyed… It made it phenomenally difficult to get out of bed, though after two days of so-called rest and recuperation, the continued absence of snow left them no choice but to board the carriage again and head south.

On the other hand, being cuddled up together in a carriage beneath a pile of blankets had its own cosy charm. Henrietta seemed happy, too, which made him even happier. With her arm tucked into his and her head resting on his shoulder, the sense of contentment he'd been afraid might end with the honeymoon only seemed to grow deeper and more intense with each passing mile. He insisted they make regular stops to prevent the coachmen from freezing, as well as to make sure she showed no signs of a relapse, so that it was three days before they eventually came within sight of Feversham.

It was clear from the moment they climbed down from the carriage that it was going to be some time before he got Henrietta to himself again. The boys were like a litter of puppies, rushing down the front steps to hurl themselves at her legs and jump about with excitement. His own greeting was only slightly less enthusiastic: hugs from Oliver and Michael and a firm handshake from Peter, and then his mother and Lord Tobias were welcoming them back, too, while the Dowager Duchess stood at the front door, smiling.

After the comparative peace and tranquillity of the journey, it was a frenetic half an hour of excitement, naturally succeeded by tea in the drawing room as everyone clamoured to hear about the wedding.

'Did you really get married in a blacksmith's shop?' As always, Michael was the most voluble.

'We did.' Sebastian tousled his hair. 'The blacksmith hit the anvil with his hammer when we said "I do".'

'So this means you're really my uncle?'

'It really does.' He reached for Henrietta's hand and squeezed it. Even sitting on the chair next to his, she felt too far away. He'd got accustomed to sitting close beside her, to always touching her. Now it felt wrong to be as much as a foot away.

'And are we all going to live at Belles?'

'I think Miss MacQueen might have a few things to say about that.' Sebastian laughed at the boy's persistence. 'We haven't worked out all the details yet, but you'll be the first to know once we come up with a plan. Right now we'd like to know what you've been up to.'

'We've set up a proper stage for our play!' Oliver bounced enthusiastically.

'And we painted some backdrops,' Peter added.

'That sounds very professional.'

'I helped to make curtains,' his mother joined in. 'It's become quite a production. Tobias even has a small part.'

'A good one, I hope?' He lifted an eyebrow at his uncle.

'They needed another villain…' Lord Tobias spread his hands out. 'Sorry to say, I'm fairly quickly despatched.'

'No match for Nelson obviously. Another pirate, then?'

'Napoleon, actually.'

'Indeed? That sounds…original.'

'It's artistic licence.' His mother smiled serenely. 'All great playwrights have to bend the truth a little.'

'Of course.' Henrietta nodded in agreement. 'It sounds as though it's going to be spectacular.'

'I'm certain of it. They've worked very hard, haven't you, boys? But now it's time for you to go and clean up for dinner.'

'Yes, Mrs Fortini.' Michael looked puzzled. 'Or should we call you Great-Aunt Fortini now?'

'How about Aunt Elizabeth? If that's all right with everyone?'

'It is with me.' Henrietta beamed at Sebastian. 'I think it's lovely.'

'Aunt Elizabeth.' Peter threw his brothers a superior look as they trooped out of the room. 'I told you so.'

'I'm so relieved that you're back,' his mother continued once they'd gone. 'We expected you a couple of days ago. Was the weather bad?'

'Not very, but—'

'I caught a bit of a chill.' Henrietta interrupted. 'Not much of one, but I didn't feel up to the journey home straight away, so we stayed in Gretna for a few days. I'm sorry if we caused you concern.'

'Ah, well, I'm just glad you're back safe and sound, especially now. The weather's taken a turn for the worse over the past couple of days.' His mother held on to his gaze for a few moments longer than necessary. 'In any case, I'll let you get cleaned up before dinner, too. We'll eat a bit early since I'm sure you're exhausted after your journey.'

'A little. All that sitting and bumping around is surprisingly wearing. Give me a ship any day. Come on, wife.' Sebastian stood and tugged on Henrietta's hand, pulling her to her feet. 'We'll see you at dinner, Mama.'

He kept hold of her fingers as they climbed the stairs, not saying anything until they were inside their bedchamber—previously *her* bedchamber.

'A *bit* of a chill?' He spun around, catching her by the waist.

'Yes.' She laughed up at him. 'Your mother would only scold if she knew the truth, and that's my job from now on.'

'Scolding me?' He walked her backwards towards the closed door. 'Is that what you intend to do?'

'Among other things. Fortunately for you, I'm in a good mood at the moment.'

'What a coincidence.' He pressed his lips to the side of her neck, smiling as she tipped her head back against the wood, arching her neck to allow him greater access. 'So am I.'

'Sebastian…' Her breath caught in her throat.

'Mmm.' He slid his hands down, pulling slowly on the fabric of her gown until it was bunched up around her hips.

'It's almost time for dinner.'

'No, it's time to get dressed for dinner. I believe that involves a bit of undressing first.'

'Ye-es, but…' She gasped as he pressed his tongue against the hollow at the base of her throat and then blew softly against it. 'I suppose we *are* newlyweds…'

'Exactly.' He grinned. 'Is that going to be your excuse for everything from now on?'

'For a few months definitely. Shouldn't we move to the bed?'

'Not necessarily.' He held her dress up with one hand, unbuttoning his trousers with the other while his mouth drifted back to capture hers. 'Unless you want to?'

'No, but how…?'

'That…' he pressed closer, sliding one hand behind her back '…is what we're about to work out.'

Chapter Twenty-Three

'So, at the risk of sounding like Michael, what *are* your plans?' Lord Tobias leaned back in his chair at the dinner table, peering at Sebastian through a cloud of cigar smoke. 'Your mother told me she's giving you Belles as a wedding present.'

'Yes…' Sebastian drew on his own cigar, knitting his brows together at the reminder. His mother had taken him aside when he and Henrietta had finally come downstairs for dinner, in even better moods thanks to some very effective manoeuvring, although he still hadn't been quite sure what to make of her announcement. It seemed wrong not to at least share Belles with Anna, especially considering the years she'd put into the business, but as his mother had explained, as Countess of Staunton, his sister didn't have any need of the income. In fact, she'd already approved the plan when his mother had drawn up her will.

'Sebastian?' His uncle looked faintly worried.

'Sorry, Uncle, I was wool-gathering. I'm very grateful. I'm just not sure I deserve it.'

'Your mother thinks you do, but if it makes you feel

any better, it's for you *and* Henrietta. You wouldn't say that *she* doesn't deserve it, would you?'

'Good point. The truth is, I want to keep Belles in the family, but I don't want to put anyone else out of work and I'd like to build something of my own, too. I have some money saved and I think a tea room would make Henrietta happy.' He gave a low chuckle. 'That appears to have become my main purpose in life these days.'

'As it should be.' Lord Tobias rested his cigar on an ashtray. 'I'd like to invest.'

'Really?' Sebastian almost dropped his own cigar in surprise. 'You mean like a business partner?'

'A *silent* business partner. The money will be yours one day anyway.'

'It will?'

'Yes. I intend to make you my heir.'

'Your heir?' It was a good thing he'd tightened his grip on the cigar, Sebastian thought, or he would *definitely* have singed his trousers. 'Me?'

'You're my nephew.'

'Yes, but...'

'I've no children and I'm not likely to marry now.'

'Still... I don't know what to say...' Sebastian felt vaguely dumbstruck. 'Did you never want to marry, Uncle?'

'No, I was always more interested in my studies. Of course, I was forced to endure a few London Seasons in my youth, but fortunately my brother married and let me off the hook quite early.'

'But won't he mind if you make me your heir?'

'He won't be happy about it, but if you knew my brother then you'd know he rarely experiences that emotion anyway. For once, however, there'll be nothing he can do.'

'Does my mother know about this?'

'We discussed it while you were in Scotland.' Lord Tobias sat forward. 'Sebastian, I'm not trying—I would never try—to replace your father, but this way you'll have a legacy from both sides of your family. It would make an old man very happy, too. So, what do you say?'

'I can hardly refuse.' Sebastian held a hand out to clasp his uncle's. 'Thank you. I'm honoured.'

'Then it's agreed. With only one condition...' Lord Tobias smiled. 'That you're not allowed to leave before the new year. I'd like a chance to introduce you to my friends and neighbours. I want everyone to know that you're my heir with my blessing.'

'I'll need to speak with Henrietta, but I'm sure we can stay.' Sebastian nodded thoughtfully. 'We're not allowed to go anywhere until after the play anyway and I'm told it needs a few more rehearsals. I'm actually starting to think—'

He didn't finish the sentence as the butler cleared his throat from the dining room doorway.

'Yes, Dennison?' Lord Tobias glanced up expectantly.

'Forgive the intrusion, sir, but there's someone at the servants' entrance asking to see Mrs Fortini. The younger Mrs Fortini, that is.'

'Henrietta?' Sebastian got to his feet in surprise. 'Did they give a name?'

'Yes, sir. I believe he called himself David Gardiner.'

'What?' He made a grab for the back of his chair. 'Are you sure?'

'Perhaps you could invite our guest to join us in

here?' Lord Tobias stood, too, addressing the butler before turning to Sebastian. 'Should I call Henrietta?'

'No.' He was vaguely aware of his fingers tightening around the wood. 'Not yet. I need to be sure he's who he says he is first.'

'Of course.' Lord Tobias agreed, waiting at his side for what felt like an interminable period of time until the butler returned, leading a man with untidy blond hair and such an uncanny resemblance to Michael that it left not the tiniest shred of doubt about his identity.

'Mr Gardiner.' Lord Tobias spoke when Sebastian just stared.

'Yes, sir.' The other man darted a look between them, his expression somehow both defiant and apologetic at the same time. 'I'm looking for my sister and boys. I was told they were here.'

'They are.' Sebastian found his voice at last, though it sounded strange even to him. Harder and confrontational, but then he was feeling remarkably, uncharacteristically, belligerent. Coming so soon after his mother's gift and his uncle's announcement, the unexpected sight of David Gardiner made him feel as if the ground beneath his feet had just shifted, as if he were standing on a deck and a giant wave had just hit the side of his ship. He had the horrible feeling that if he did the wrong thing now then he might topple overboard, as if the life he'd envisaged for himself just a few minutes ago might disappear into thin air. He'd never experienced sea sickness, but at that moment he felt distinctly nauseated.

'Are they all right?'

'Your sons are upstairs in bed, safe and sound.'

'Thank goodness.' The man's mouth contorted before he let out a strangled sob and put his hands over his face.

'Sit down.' Lord Tobias pulled out a chair. 'Port?'

'No.' He shook his head, recoiling as if he'd just been offered poison. 'No, thank you. I'd like to see Henrietta.'

'Not yet.' Sebastian answered heavily. 'Not until you explain yourself and what you're doing here.'

'I'd rather speak to her. *She's* my sister.'

'But under *my* protection.'

'What does that mean? I've never met you before.'

Sebastian drew himself up, deriving a savage sense of satisfaction from the other man's shocked expression. 'I mean that *your* sister is *my* wife. We were married a few days ago in Gretna Green.'

'What?'

'Perhaps you could have a room prepared for Mr Gardiner?' Lord Tobias gestured discreetly to the butler still standing in the doorway.

'As you wish, sir.'

'I looked for you.' Sebastian narrowed his eyes accusingly. 'One of your friends said that you'd boarded a ship for America.'

'I did.' David Gardiner stared heavily at him for a few seconds before continuing. 'Although I did a lot of drinking first. Then I got all the way up the gangplank before I came to my senses. So I got off again.'

'Then where the hell have you been since?'

'I had no money left so I had to walk back to Bath.' David pushed a hand through his hair. 'I went to the biscuit shop and the woman there told me Henrietta had left with you and sent me to Redbourne's store. She said you were friends with the owner and that he'd be able to get a message to you.'

'And he sent you here instead?'

'He paid my coach fare, yes.'

Sebastian scowled. Typical of James to do the *right* thing, sending David to be reconciled with his family. It *was* the right thing to do, but now he was aware of an unreasonable surge of resentment. How dared David come back and just walk into Henrietta's life as if nothing had happened? As if she hadn't spent the past few weeks working and worrying and struggling before finally moving on with her life? How dared he come back and shatter their plans for the future? He'd given up his freedom for those plans and now David's arrival threatened to destroy everything.

All of which made him want to pick up the chair he was still clutching and smash it to pieces.

'Perhaps it's time to fetch my wife?' he said instead, forcing his fists to uncurl as he glanced at Lord Tobias. 'If you don't mind?'

'Of course not.' Lord Tobias looked as if he were eager for an excuse to flee the room. 'I'll send her directly.'

'Henrietta never mentioned you to me before.' David looked up from the table, sounding as combative as Sebastian felt.

'Really?' He folded his arms. Of course, it would have been impossible for Henrietta to have mentioned him since they'd only met at the same time David had left, but damned if he was going to tell him that. *He* wasn't the one with explaining to do… He took a step towards the open doorway to make sure that Henrietta would see him first.

'Sebastian?' She appeared after only a few minutes. 'Tobias said you wanted to see me.' She stopped at the sight of his face. 'What's the matter?'

'Come and see.' He reached a hand out, telling himself that he needed to hold her steady in case she swooned with surprise. Not that she'd ever swooned before, or seemed prone to swooning in general, but there was a first time for everything. It wasn't that he just wanted to hold her. To hold *on to* her…

'David!' Her fingers had barely grazed his before she tore them away again. It was necessary in order for her to run across the room to her brother, but for the life of him, Sebastian didn't think he could have released her if she hadn't pulled away first. It was all he could do not to clamp his fingers around hers in protest. Instead, he stood watching, half of him knowing that he ought to leave and give them privacy, the other half absolutely refusing to budge as much as an inch.

'Oh, David.' Henrietta clamped her arms tight around her brother's neck, though her voice had a definite tremor. 'You're here! You're actually here.' She pulled back after a few seconds, staring hard into his face as if she daren't believe the evidence of her own eyes. 'What happened? Why did you leave?'

'I'll explain it all later.' Her brother tried to take a step back, though she didn't let him go far. 'At the time I felt desperate, but it wasn't fair of me. I'm sorry, Henrietta, truly, but it won't happen again. I'm a different man now.'

'Then that's all that matters.'

She embraced him again, missing Sebastian's snort of disgust. Was that it? No argument, no condemnation, no judgement at all? He wanted her to rail at her brother, but instead she was all smiles, as if he'd only been away on a holiday. As if he'd never abandoned her in the first place!

'Come on.' Hard as it was to stomach, her smile spread even wider. 'I'll take you up to the nursery. The boys are probably asleep by now, but I can still show you they're all right.'

Sebastian stiffened as they passed. He had a horrible feeling that his wife had already forgotten he was there. *I*, she'd just said. *I'll take you up. I can still show you they're all right.* One glimpse of her brother and all of a sudden they'd stopped being *we*.

A horrible sinking sensation told him this was only the start of it.

'They've missed you.' Henrietta whispered, standing shoulder to shoulder with David in the doorway of the boys' bedroom.

'I've missed them.' He sucked in a breath and let it go again slowly. 'I don't know how I'm going to explain to them what I did.'

'I told them you were sick.' She gave him a sidelong look. 'Which was the truth, wasn't it? And now you're better?'

'Better than I was. I've given up alcohol. It wasn't easy, but it was the only way.'

'Good. Then all you need to tell them is that you love them and that you won't leave again.'

He wrapped an arm around her shoulders. 'I should probably say it to you, too.'

'Yes, you probably should.'

'I love you and I won't do it again. I promise.'

'Thank you. Now come away before we wake anyone.' She stepped back into the nursery, closing the door to the bedroom softly behind them.

'Thank you for taking care of them.' David looked sombre again.

'It wasn't just me. Sebastian's been a great help, too.'

'Mmm.' David's face twisted. 'You never told me you had a beau.'

'I didn't before. It all happened very quickly.'

'How quickly?'

'Well… I met him the night before you left actually, but—'

'And you're already married?' David's expression turned into that of an angry big brother. 'Why? Just because you needed his help?' He shook his head. 'If I'd known you'd do something like this…'

'It's not something like anything.'

'It's all my fault.'

'It's nobody's fault!' She blinked at the harshness of his tone. 'That's entirely the wrong word. Your leaving brought us together, I don't deny that, but I'm glad that it did. Sebastian wanted to help me and we became friends and—'

'He didn't have to marry you to be *your friend*.' David's eyebrows snapped together ferociously. 'What else did he want? Are you certain you're really married?'

'Yes!' She put her hands on her hips. 'We decided that marrying was the right thing to do for the boys. We *thought* that you weren't coming back.'

'It still doesn't make sense. Why does a gentleman marry a shop girl just so that he can help raise her nephews? Why would he care?'

'Because he did! And he's not a gentleman. He's a sailor.' She frowned. 'Or he was anyway.'

'A sailor whose family live in a place like this.' David looked around at the nursery. 'My whole house is smaller than this room.'

'I know.' She felt vaguely uncomfortable at the observation. 'But Sebastian and I have decided to build a life together. We care for each other and we're equals.'

David gave her a sceptical look. 'You can't be in love, not after less than a month.'

Henrietta opened her mouth and then closed it again. Why *couldn't* she be in love after less than a month? Because she was, she realised suddenly. She was very much in love. Only she wanted Sebastian to be the first one to hear the words, not her brother.

'Does he treat you well? Is he good to you? Because if he isn't...'

'He treats me very well.' She folded her arms, struck with a sudden sense of foreboding. 'Trust me, in a few days, you'll be the best of friends.'

'All settled?'

Sebastian was standing beside the fireplace, hands clasped behind his back, as Henrietta entered their bedroom. He was wearing an entirely *un*-Sebastian-like expression. The lines of his face looked uncharacteristically tight and rigid.

'Yes. I didn't mean to take so long.' She closed the door and hesitated. She hadn't expected him to be frowning. She'd expected to come back to their room and for him to reassure her, to wrap his arms around her and tell her how happy he was for her and the boys, too, but unfortunately the sense of foreboding she'd felt with her brother grew even worse. 'David wanted to look at the boys for a while and then we talked.'

'Understandable.'

'Have you told the others?'

'Yes. They were very pleased, as no doubt they'll tell you themselves in the morning. They've gone to bed now.'

'Of course. It's late.' She took a few steps closer. 'I'm glad you're still awake.'

'I wanted to wait and see how you were.' He quirked an eyebrow. 'How are you?'

'Happy.' She smiled, though somehow both the word and action felt unconvincing. It wasn't that she was *un*-happy. She *had* been happy, *very* happy just an hour ago. She was thrilled that David was back, but his obvious antipathy towards Sebastian, not to mention all of his questions about her marriage, had left her feeling tense, too. And now that she thought about it, Sebastian had been frowning downstairs, as well…

'What about you?' Something in his face stopped her from touching him. 'Are *you* happy?'

'Of course.' His smile looked just as unconvincing. His eyes were completely dark, without any sparkle at all. 'It's just come out of the blue, that's all.'

'Yes.' She forced her lips wider, though she had a feeling the effect looked more grotesque than genuine. 'The boys will probably think it's all a dream in the morning.'

'Quite.' There was a long pause before Sebastian cleared his throat. 'Did your brother say anything about his plans? Anything at all?'

'No, but it's too soon for all that, isn't it? He's only just arrived.'

'I suppose so.' Another awkward silence descended

before he stepped away from the fireplace. 'Well… I'm tired. It's been an eventful evening.'

She nodded, avoiding his eyes as they both undressed in silence. *We thought you weren't coming back...* Those were the words she'd used to explain to David why she'd married Sebastian—to explain why he'd married her, too. They'd made a conscious decision to raise her nephews together, which meant that now David was back, the very cornerstone of their marriage was gone, knocked down in one fell swoop. Their reason no longer existed.

She still had no regrets about marrying him, especially now that she'd realised just how much she cared, but…did *he* regret it? His cold behaviour implied that she'd tricked or betrayed him somehow, as if he'd never really cared for her or thought of her as anything more than a pretty face, after all. As if making amends for his guilty conscience had been all that had mattered, had ever mattered… Apparently she was just as foolish and naive as she'd always feared, deep down. She'd truly thought their marriage had meant more than that.

She lowered herself on to the stool in front of her dressing table, staring at the reflection of their bed in the mirror with a new sense of bleakness. She felt cold inside, as if her heart had just frozen. Sebastian was already under the covers, lying on his back with his eyes closed. That was different, too. Usually he sat up, waiting until she came to bed before curling up in a spoon shape beside her.

She pressed her eyes shut to stop the tears from seeping out. How could an evening that had brought so much joy end so badly? She'd fallen in love with her husband just at the moment he seemed to have changed his mind about her.

Chapter Twenty-Four

'Will your brother be joining us?'

Sebastian threw his napkin aside, resisting the urge to glare at his mother as she smiled blithely across the breakfast table at his wife.

'Not this morning.' Henrietta shook her head apologetically. 'He went up to the nursery first thing and… well, there was a great deal of excitement.'

'I can imagine. I think I actually heard some of it. Not that I'm complaining—it was a lovely sound.'

'They're all breakfasting up there together, although David sends his thanks for the invitation. I'll go up again shortly, but I thought I should give them some time alone.'

'Harumph.'

'Is something the matter?' Henrietta twisted her head, lifting an eyebrow at the sound Sebastian hadn't intended to make quite so loudly.

'With *me*?' He put a particular stress on the word. 'Nothing at all. *I'm* perfectly fine.'

'Oh.' A look of confusion, mingled with hurt,

flashed across her face. 'I thought the boys might like to show David around the gardens after breakfast.'

'It's a bit cold, isn't it?'

'We'll wrap up.' She paused. 'Will you join us? We could take a walk down to the lake?'

'No.' He didn't intend to be quite so brusque, only for some reason he couldn't seem to help it. 'I promised to take Mother into the village this morning.'

'That can wait.' His mother seemed determined to earn herself a glare. 'This is much more important and it would be nice for you and David to get to know each other. You're brothers-in-law now.'

'Yes... Very well, then. I'll be in the library when you're ready.'

He pushed his chair back and marched out of the breakfast room at a brisk pace. It was the same pace with which he'd marched out of the bedroom that morning and the one he intended to keep using until he got his emotions under control. He was behaving badly, he knew, but he couldn't seem to help himself. Just as he couldn't help the seething resentment he was experiencing towards his new brother-in-law. Even towards Henrietta. Every time she mentioned her brother he felt as if she were plunging a dagger into his heart and then twisting it for good measure.

Scowling, he threw himself into a green leather chair by the fireplace and picked up a book, reading the same page at least half a dozen times without taking a single word in.

'Mr Fortini?' The butler's voice sounded from the doorway in a tone he was starting to resent. 'Mrs Fortini asked me to inform you that she's ready.'

'Thank you, Dennison.'

He sighed and marched back out through the hall, pulling on a coat and hat before walking out of the front door. Henrietta was already outside, standing next to her brother, though she took a step towards him as he approached, her expression one of trepidation.

'Good morning.' He gave David a terse nod and received an equally terse one back.

'I'm so glad you're coming with us.' Henrietta looked relieved that he'd spoken first. 'Although I don't think we'll have long before it rains.'

'Father's home!' Michael bounced up to him, grinning so widely it looked as if his face might actually split in two. Obviously a forgiving type, Sebastian thought, stifling a rush of resentment. Only Peter looked as if he weren't enjoying himself, standing off to one side with his hands shoved deep into his pockets. That was more like it.

'So he is.' He forced himself to sound cheerful. 'You must be very pleased.'

'Now we're one big, happy family!'

'Let's get moving, then…' Henrietta held out her hand when neither he nor David responded '…before we all freeze.'

'So…' David gave him a sidelong look as she walked ahead. 'Peter tells me you've been teaching them about the navy. He says he wants to join when he's old enough.'

'It's not a bad career for a young man.' Sebastian set off at his earlier brisk march, vaguely irritated when David kept pace beside him. 'Although he's still young enough to change his mind.'

'I hope he does. I don't want any of my boys going to sea.'

'Is that so?' Sebastian gritted his teeth. 'Any particular reason?'

'I've just never trusted sailors, that's all.'

'Interesting. Fortunately, I'd say your boys have minds of their own.'

'Oh, look, some starlings!' Henrietta pointed, her voice unnecessarily loud in the crisp morning air.

'They can still be guided by their father, can't they?'

'Or are they blackbirds?'

'They can when their father is around.'

'I'm here now.'

'And there's a robin!'

'For the time being.'

'For good.'

Sebastian made a snorting sound. 'It still seems a little odd to be laying the law down so soon after abandoning them, wouldn't you say?'

'I didn't abandon them. I left them with their aunt.'

'Whom you abandoned, too. And you say that sailors can't be trusted?'

'You don't understand anything about it.' David glared and then veered off the path with a growl. 'Come on, boys. I think I'd rather see those woods than the lake.'

'What was that?' Henrietta stayed where she was, her hands clenched into fists at her sides as the others scurried away across the lawn, although Peter hesitated briefly before joining them, Sebastian noticed. 'How *could* you?'

'How could I what?' He squared his shoulders, feigning ignorance.

'How could you be so cruel? He knows what he

did was wrong. You didn't have to make him feel any worse. This isn't like you.'

He felt a momentary twinge of guilt. The words *had* been cruel and she was right, it wasn't like him. He was rarely cruel, but he'd wanted to hurt David; wanted to hurt him more than he'd ever wanted to hurt anyone, Captain Belton included.

'He said he didn't trust sailors.'

'I heard. I'm not defending him, but—'

'It sounds like it.'

'Sebastian!'

'At least I'm not pretending nothing happened.'

She folded her arms, eyes flashing angrily. 'David and I have talked about it. I don't need to punish him as well.'

'Well, maybe you should!'

'Why? What good will it do?'

He ground his teeth, silently acknowledging the truth of it. What good *would* it do? Nothing, except to make him feel better.

'Henrietta, he abandoned you!'

'You abandoned Anna!'

'That was different. I would have come back if I could have, but there was nothing I could do.'

'And his drinking was a sickness that he couldn't help either. *You* were the one who told me that. Only you were a lot more sympathetic *before* you met him. Now you're just being a hypocrite. You wanted—you got!—a second chance. You abandoned your sister and you had a chance to make up for it by helping me. Well, David's back and he deserves a second chance, too.'

'So you choose him?'

'What? No, Sebastian, you're my husband…'

'A husband you don't need any longer. Now that David's back, you don't need my help any more, do you?'

'Is that why you're angry? Because you think his second chance means that yours doesn't count any more? As if it's all just been a waste of time and effort! As if our marriage is pointless!'

'No, of course not.' He stiffened, shocked by the expression on her face. She looked more than hurt. She looked distraught. And as if she wanted to hurt him back.

'I think that's what you *do* think.' Her eyes narrowed and then blazed suddenly. 'But really you ought to be glad. You *did* the right thing so you don't have to make amends any more. Now you can have your freedom back and without any guilt this time. You can go wherever you want, I won't stop you.'

She stormed up to confront him. 'I'm sorry I married you under false pretences. I didn't know they were false then, but they were. If I could turn the clock back for you then I would, but I can't. We're married now and there's nothing we can do about that. Just know that I won't expect anything from you ever again.' She turned away from him to follow David. 'We'll leave as soon as I can pack.'

Sebastian stared after her in shock, hardly able to take in the words. She was back at her brother's side before he could even rouse himself enough to open his mouth and then he wasn't sure *what* to say. All he could do was repeat her parting words over and over in his head. He could have his freedom back. He could go anywhere he wanted. She'd be leaving as soon as she could pack… She was leaving him! As if nothing they'd shared over the past few weeks meant anything to her at all!

He turned on his heel, marching away across the lawn until he reached the lake. Unfortunately, that didn't seem like far enough so he kept going, storming all the way around it in a large circle until he came to the top of a hill where an ancient oak tree stood like some long-forgotten sentinel all on its own. Then he stopped, relishing the feel of the cold wind biting his face. The sting of it seemed to match his mood. Hypocrite, she'd called him, talking to him as if he were the one in the wrong! *Him!* After he'd given up his freedom to help her! And yet...wasn't he a little in the wrong? Hadn't he just forced her into making a choice? Wasn't he acting like the most boorish, resentful, jealous fool in the world?

Jealous?

His stomach lurched. Damn it all, he *was* jealous. And not just jealous, but terrified, too. It had been David who'd brought them together—more specifically, his departure—and it was David who had the power to tear them apart. *That* was the reason he'd behaved so badly, because he was afraid she might love her brother and nephews more than she loved the idea of being married to him. The very thought of it turned his blood to ice. Because he loved her, he was in love with her, and he was desperately afraid that she didn't feel the same way.

Neither of them had ever said *I love you.* Until that moment, he hadn't even put a great amount of thought into the matter. There hadn't seemed any rush to do so. He'd been happy as they were, but now the realisation of how much he cared was making him lash out, not because he was angry at what David had done, but because he was afraid of what he could do—*was* doing—with his help! He could hardly have made matters any worse if he'd actually pushed Henrietta into her brother's arms!

He slammed his palm hard against the tree trunk, sending a spasm of pain shooting through his hand and up his arm. He ought to go back and talk to her, not least because his mother had been right about the change in weather and dark clouds appeared to be closing in fast. He'd been in too much of a temper to notice before, but now he was aware of snowflakes dancing in the air around him, slowly gathering in strength.

There was a murky-looking bank of cloud on the horizon, too, like a slate-grey wall heading towards Feversham. He *definitely* ought to go back. Then he could tell Henrietta how he really felt and hope that she felt the same, or something similar anyway. That would be the sensible thing to do—what he *would* do—and he was just about to when a voice called out to him suddenly.

'That looked as though it hurt.'

'Peter?' He tipped his head back, peering up through the bare branches of the oak tree until he caught sight of the boy sitting on one of the uppermost boughs, higher than he would have expected. 'What are you doing up there? I thought you were with your father.'

'I ran off.' Peter's tone was petulant. 'I wanted to be on my own.'

'I know how you feel.' Sebastian leaned his shoulder against the trunk. 'Only this might not be the best time or place.'

'Why not?'

'See those dark clouds? They're coming this way.'

'I don't care.'

'Well, I do.' He looked up again. 'Want to come down and talk about it?'

'I can't.' There was a hint of fear behind the defiance now. 'I don't know how to get down.'

'Ah. Well, in that case, I'd better come up.' He tossed his hat to one side and started to climb, moving up the trunk and swinging his legs over a neighbouring branch in a matter of seconds.

'That was fast!' Peter looked impressed.

'I've had a lot of practice.'

'Will you help me to get down?'

'Why do you think I'm here?' He gave a reassuring wink. 'We'll take it slowly, don't worry.'

'Thank you.'

'So… You ran off?'

'Yes. I told my father I hated him.'

'Ah.'

There was a brief pause. 'I don't.'

'I know. I'm sure he knows that, too.'

'I'm just angry.'

'I don't blame you.'

'Really?' The boy looked surprised. 'Then you don't think I ought to forgive him?'

'I didn't say that.' Sebastian feigned an interest in some nearby twigs. 'Sometimes it can be hard to understand what you're feeling. Sometimes a man needs to run away for a while in order to make sense of things.'

'Is that what you're doing?'

He made a wry face. 'Something like that, but perhaps it's better to forgive and forget and concentrate on what matters. You love your father really, don't you?'

Another pause. 'Yes.'

'Then that's what matters.'

'I suppose so… Uncle Sebastian?' Peter sounded anxious again. 'Now that my father's back, does this mean *you'll* go away?'

'I don't know.' He felt a stab of fear in his chest. 'I hope not.'

'I like having you as my uncle.'

'I like it, too. Very much.'

'And you love Aunt Henrietta, don't you?'

He smiled. 'You're a smart boy, but right now we need to get down before that storm hits. Put your foot here.'

He led the way, instructing Peter where to hold on and where to place his feet as they made their way slowly down the trunk. There were plenty of footholds, enough that they would probably have made it to the ground quite safely if it hadn't been for the rain making the bark slippery. Unfortunately for them, however, it had, a large chunk of it peeling away beneath Peter's fingertips and sending them both tumbling through the air to the ground.

'Oof!' Sebastian felt stunned for a few seconds. It wasn't so much the fall that hurt, or the root beneath his back, as the weight of a ten-year-old boy landing on top of his chest.

'Sorry.' Peter wriggled away to one side and then yelped.

'What's the matter?' He tried to sit up, then fell back as his ribs protested.

'My foot hurts.'

'Can you stand?' He rolled on to his right shoulder, using his arm to push himself up to a sitting position.

That felt marginally better, though he was still aware of a searing pain in his side.

'Only on one leg, I think.'

'Damn—I mean, oh, dear.' He looked up at the sky, just in time for a large drop of freezing cold water to fall into his face. Only it wasn't quite rain—or snow either. It was sludge. Thick, wet, thoroughly drenching sludge that made it downright impossible for them to stay where they were. There weren't any leaves and nowhere near enough branches on the tree to provide shelter.

'We need to get back to the house.'

'But we'll get soaked!' Peter protested. 'Maybe we should wait here for somebody to find us.'

'Not in this weather.'

'We could shout for help.'

Sebastian looked around, but there was no one in sight to hear them. No doubt David was already looking for his son, but the Feversham estate was big enough that it could be hours before anyone came this way. Besides, the clouds in the distance looked even more threatening than the ones above them now. The last thing they wanted was to be huddled beneath a tree in a lightning storm.

'No, we need to move.' He held his hands out and they pulled each other up to their feet with an effort.

'Ow.' Peter hopped a few times on his good foot.

'It'll be all right.' Sebastian crouched down, steeling himself for a fresh burst of pain. 'Climb on to my back. Imagine I'm a mast.'

'But you're hurt.'

'Only a little. We'll manage.'

He clamped his teeth together as Peter clambered

on to his back and then staggered forward, concentrating on putting one foot in front of the other and trying to ignore the sound of rolling thunder in the distance. It wasn't elegant and the pain was excruciating, but at least it was progress, albeit of the infinitely slow kind. If they followed the path around the lake, then it would take them back to the main lawn…provided his ribs could make it that far.

'Uncle Sebastian?' Peter sounded frightened.

'Yes?'

'I'm sorry.'

'What did I just tell you?' He twisted his head, managing to grin over his shoulder. 'Sometimes we just need to forgive. Now come on, cadet, we can do this.'

Chapter Twenty-Five

Bother, Henrietta thought. Bother and fiddlesticks and… She screwed up her face and let loose several of the choicest nautical phrases Sebastian had taught her—or said in close proximity to her anyway, usually under his breath. There hadn't been any *deliberate* teaching, but she had a good memory, especially when it came to such colourful metaphors. Under normal circumstances, she would never have dreamed of repeating any of them, but in this particular instance, the words made her feel better.

'Oh!' Mrs Fortini looked startled as she passed her in the hallway. 'Is everything all right?'

'Yes. I'm just going for a lie down.' Henrietta hurried past, attempting a smile, though she was afraid the effort made her look as though she had some kind of digestive problem.

'Of course. Are the boys still out walking?'

'I think so.' She nodded, though in all honesty she wasn't sure. She'd changed her mind about accompanying David and her nephews into the woods, stomping about the herb garden for half an hour by herself instead.

She ran up the staircase, into her room, and flung herself down on the bed. The fire was lit, but she still couldn't stop from shivering, as if the cold were coming from inside her. Which made sense since her argument with Sebastian had left her feeling as if a part of her had frozen. She'd told him to leave, to go back to sea, to go anywhere he wanted.

She folded an arm over her face, trying to blot out what had happened, but it was impossible. Her mind was a raging whirlwind of misery and self-recrimination and her chest felt tight, as if her heart were truly breaking. That was when she knew how stupid she'd been, spinning daydreams. She'd really thought they'd been more than friends, that he cared about her, that he might even love her, but he hadn't. His motives for being with her might have been more honourable than most other men's, but in the end they'd had nothing to do with the *real* her. Anything else he'd said had only been what she'd wanted to hear.

After what might have been ten minutes or an hour, she got up and went to the window. The weather was abysmal now, the pale grey of the morning replaced by a dark and threatening shade of lead. There were no gaps in the clouds any more, only one single dark mass for as far as she could see, blocking out the sun like a vast cloak across the sky. It was beautiful in a dramatic kind of way, the kind of scene she might have enjoyed watching with Sebastian, with her head resting on his shoulder, his arm around her waist, stroking her hip... She touched the ring on her finger, a lump rising in her throat at the realisation they would never stand that way again.

She swallowed and turned away from the window. David and the boys had probably already gone back to the nursery, which meant she ought to go up and tell them to start gathering their things. She wanted to begin packing right away. If she was only Sebastian's wife in name, then she had no right to stay at Feversham any longer. Whatever the weather, they needed to leave.

She started towards the door at the sound of a knock, surprised when it opened before she could reach it.

'Is Peter here?' David didn't pause to exchange greetings.

'No. I thought he was with you.'

'He was, but he ran away!'

'What?' She felt a stab of panic. Peter hadn't seemed in a particularly celebratory mood when he'd seen his father that morning. Instead, he'd looked angry and guarded, but she'd thought some time alone together would help.

'I don't know what happened.' David pushed a hand through his hair. 'I was just trying to talk to him...'

'Which way did he go?' She grabbed hold of his arm. Why it had happened wasn't as important at that moment as finding him.

'I don't know. He charged off through the trees.'

'Tobias!' She ran out of the room and hurtled down the stairs, trying to think clearly and not panic. Despite the storm, there was still plenty of daylight left. It wasn't even time for luncheon. And Peter wouldn't have been foolish enough to go near the lake, not after everything Sebastian had taught him.

The thought of her husband made her heart contract almost painfully. If only he were there to help! If only they hadn't argued—and in front of Peter, too! The boy hadn't been within hearing distance, but it would have been obvious from their body language that they were arguing. He'd probably guessed that it was about his father. Which was probably why he'd gone on to argue with David himself…

'Henrietta?' Lord Tobias emerged from his library just as she reached the bottom step.

'It's Peter. He's run away.' She could hear herself panting, from barely controlled panic as well as her flight down the stairs. 'We need to organise search parties.'

'Of course. Dennison!' Lord Tobias started towards the servants' quarters. 'We'll send some men out at once.'

'Oh, my dear.' Elizabeth emerged from the drawing room and put an arm around her shoulders. 'I'm sure he can't have gone far.'

'I know. It's just that the weather's so terrible…' She winced at a roll of thunder outside. If the rain now lashing against the windows was any indication, the tempest was increasing by the minute. 'I'm going out to look for him.'

'Absolutely not. I'm sure Sebastian and your brother would both want you to stay inside.' Elizabeth looked around. 'Where *is* Sebastian?'

'I don't know. He went off somewhere, too.' Henrietta shook her head. 'But I *need* to go.'

'I really don't think—'

'But I *must*.'

'Very well.' Elizabeth sighed and unravelled her

shawl. 'But at least wear this. I don't want you getting sick again. Now where are Michael and Oliver?'

'Up in the nursery.' David was already opening the front door.

'I'll go and keep an eye on them.'

'Thank you.' Henrietta flung the shawl around her shoulders and then followed her brother, almost blowing back inside the house again as the wind caught her on the front steps. There was no lightning yet, thank goodness, but the clouds were skidding by at a ferocious pace. It wouldn't be long before the centre of the storm was upon them.

'Where do we start?' she called after David, shouting to make herself heard over the roar of the wind. The outside world felt strange, as if she'd fallen into water and was fighting against the current, which, since she was already drenched, seemed an appropriate image. She had to bow her head and hunch over to make any progress at all.

'In the woods! That's where I last saw Peter!'

'Do you think—? *Look!*' She caught her breath, looking past David's shoulder towards a dark shape coming from the direction of the lake. It was roughly the same size as a horse, only it wasn't a horse. It had two heads and two of its legs were dangling in mid-air and it looked like…

'Sebastian!' she shouted, running across the lawn as fast as the wind would allow, which was still slower than David, who darted like a streak of lightning himself. He was already lifting Peter into his arms by the time she arrived.

'What happened?' She stretched her arms out, grabbing hold of Sebastian's shoulders as he sank to one knee, clasping his side with a groan.

'I fell out of a tree and landed on top of him,' Peter answered for them, water streaming down his small face.

'Out of a tree?' She looked between them in horror. 'Are you injured?'

'I hurt my ankle.'

'And I came to my senses.' Sebastian leaned forward, eyes like hot coals though his eyelashes held tiny droplets of water as he rested his forehead against hers. 'I don't want my freedom back, not from you. I don't want to go anywhere or lose you. I should never have expected you to choose. Whatever our reasons for getting married, I want to stay married.'

'Yes!' She pressed her lips to his wet cheeks, then his chin and nose, covering the whole of his face with kisses. 'Yes to all of that. Everything you just said, especially the part about staying married.'

'Good. Because I love you.'

'I lo— *Sebastian?*'

She tried to catch him, but it was too late. She never got to repeat the sentiment as he tumbled to the ground, unconscious.

'I thought she might want a cup of tea.' David hesitated in the doorway, looking surprised to see Sebastian awake and Henrietta sleeping soundly in a chair by the bed. 'I suppose you can have it if you like?'

'Thank you.' Sebastian answered in the same low undertone. 'I could do with one.'

'Well then…' David put the saucer down on the bedside table and took a few steps back. 'How are you feeling?'

'Better now I'm warm and dry. Well enough to know I owe you an apology.'

'You do?' His brother-in-law lifted an eyebrow dubiously.

'Yes. I haven't been particularly welcoming.'

'No, you haven't.' David frowned and then relented. 'But I would probably have behaved the same way if our positions had been reversed. You didn't say anything this morning that wasn't true.'

'It still wasn't my place to say it. I was afraid of what you coming back might mean for me, but I shouldn't have said those things, especially when I know a little something about abandoning sisters.' He shrugged at the other's enquiring expression. 'I'll tell you another time. How's Peter?'

'Lying on a sofa, enjoying the fuss.' David scratched his chin. 'Thank you for bringing him back safely.'

'He's a good boy. They all are. They'll grow into fine men.'

'I hope so. I never meant to hurt them. I just couldn't see past my grief.'

'And now?'

'It's still not easy, but from now on I'm going to behave the way Alice would have wanted me to. I've been as low as a man can go and I won't go back.'

Sebastian nodded sombrely. 'I'd shake your hand, but I'm not sure I can lift my arm.'

'I just need to know one thing. Do you really love my sister?'

'I do.'

'Then we'll shake hands later.' David jerked his head

towards the chair. 'She hasn't moved from your side since they carried you up.'

'I know.'

'How long have you been awake?'

'Only ten minutes or so, but I know her.'

David smiled for the first time, revealing a familiar dimple in his left cheek. 'I'll leave you to drink your tea in peace, then.'

Sebastian leaned back against the bedhead, watching as Henrietta's eyelashes slowly fluttered and then opened.

'I must have fallen asleep.' She seemed surprised by the fact.

'You did.' He smiled. 'Fortunately, it gave your brother and me a chance to talk.'

'Oh.' She looked worried.

'And to make friends.'

'Oh!'

'I meant what I said on the lawn. I acted like a jealous boor before, but I was just so afraid of losing you.'

'I was afraid it was the other way round, that you thought you were stuck with me.' Her chin wobbled. 'I thought that maybe you didn't want the real me, after all.'

'I'll *always* want the real you. I love you, everything about you, but I was terrified you didn't feel the same way. I was afraid you'd want to go with the boys if they went back to live with their father.'

'I love them dearly, but they belong with David and I...well, I belong with you.' She tipped her head to one side, her gaze softening. 'Why didn't you just tell me how you were feeling?'

'I was too busy being righteously indignant. And

I didn't realise how much I loved you until I thought that I'd lost you. That's when I knew the real reason I married you.'

She blinked. 'What do you mean?'

'That I was in love with you before we even left Bath. I already knew I wanted to spend the rest of my life with you.' He clenched his jaw. 'Henrietta, there's something else I should tell you. Something I've never told anyone before. Something I don't even like admitting to myself, about Anna and Belles.'

'What?'

He swallowed, shame-faced. 'When I got the news about my father's death, I was devastated, but a selfish part of me was also relieved that I was already in the navy. I didn't want to go back to Belles, not then anyway. I was relieved that I couldn't go back and help Anna, even though knowing that made me feel ten times worse. It sounds terrible, doesn't it?'

'You can't help your feelings.'

'No, but what I'm trying to say is, part of the reason I proposed to you was that I knew that with you it was different, that if I left you, I *wouldn't* feel relieved.' He reached for her hand and lifted it to his lips, kissing each of her fingers in turn. 'I knew I'd spend the rest of my life regretting it. So what do you think? Could you be happy with just the two of us?'

'Yes...' She turned her hand around so that their fingers were interlaced. 'Apart from David, you're the only man I've ever been able to trust. I was a little in love with you on our wedding day, too.'

His breathing stalled. 'And now?'

'Now, a little seems to have become quite a lot.'

'Just *quite* a lot?' He raised an eyebrow though his

heart soared. 'Remember you're talking to an injured man. I need some motivation to get better.'

'You're bruised, not broken. The doctor said you'll be up and about in no time.'

'So I don't get any compliments, then?'

She leaned forward, smiling tenderly into his eyes. 'I love you, Sebastian Fortini, more than I ever imagined possible.'

'And I love you more than any ship.'

'What?'

'That's a deeply profound compliment from a sailor.' He grinned. 'But you know, this is all wrong. If this is our happily-ever-after, I shouldn't be lying here in bed. If anything, I should be tending to you.'

'You already did that, remember? Besides, wouldn't it be dull if all love stories ended the same way?'

'I still don't feel very heroic lying here.'

'Well, if you're the hero then that makes me the heroine and I don't want to be a damsel in distress. It should have become obvious by now that the women of Belles don't need rescuing. We might need a little help now and again, but we want equals, not knights in shining armour.' She reached up and stroked the side of his face. 'But you'll always be *my* hero.'

'Mmm. I still think there ought to be some kind of peril.'

'Oh, all right then.' She climbed up on to the bed to stretch out beside him. 'There you are.'

'Are you implying that being in a bed with me is perilous? I have bruised ribs, remember?'

'And why would you assume that *I'm* the one in danger? Now lie still and I'll be gentle...'

Chapter Twenty-Six

'How long until the curtain goes up?' Henrietta sat in front of a makeshift stage in the library next to David. 'I'm too excited to wait much longer.'

'Patience.' Her mother-in-law sat down on her brother's other side. 'Although I have to admit I'm quite excited myself. It's all been so secretive.'

'I thought you were involved in the preparations?'

'Only in set design, I'm afraid. I interrupted rehearsals this morning and I was practically thrown out.'

'Quite rightly, too.' Lord Tobias peered out from between two makeshift curtains draped from a wooden frame. 'However, you'll be glad to know that it's almost time. Lights!' He gestured to a footman who dutifully blew out all the candles except for those close to the stage. 'Where's Sebastian?'

'On his way.' The Dowager Duchess sat down next, arranging her skirts regally around her. 'He was late getting back from the village, but he says he only needs a few minutes to change his clothes.'

'I still can't believe this is all real.' David lowered

his voice to whisper in Henrietta's ear. 'The boys seem almost at home here.'

'That's because they're a part of the family now. Just like you are.'

'I'm starting to realise that, unlikely as it seems.' He shook his head slightly. 'I'm grateful, but I'll be a lot more comfortable when we've moved into our new cottage.'

'I understand.' She squeezed his hand. 'Are you certain about staying in Yorkshire?'

'Yes.' He nodded decisively. 'Lord Tobias's offered me a good job in his stables. Head groom. I'd be a fool not to take it. Never mind his offer of tutoring for the boys.'

'I'll miss them, but you know you can visit whenever you want. You'll always have a home with us, too.'

'Who has a home with us?' Sebastian murmured in her ear a second before his lips found her cheek.

'Oh.' She gave a guilty start, then caught her breath at the sight of him dressed in pristine black and white evening clothes. He looked dazzlingly handsome, not to mention *almost* neat and tidy, for once. 'David and the boys. Obviously I would have asked you first…'

'No need.' He waved a hand as he draped himself over the chair on her other side. 'The more the merrier. I've found I rather like big families.'

'What's this?' His mother swayed sideways. 'Is there something you two want to tell me?'

'Not yet, Mama, but we're working on it.'

'Sebastian!' Henrietta dug her elbow into his ribs, eliciting a small chuckle from him and a placid smile from his mother.

'Good. Because it turns out I enjoy being a grandmother. I only wish that Anna was here to share the fun.'

'When is she coming home anyway?'

'Not for a while. Samuel doesn't want to leave his grandmother just yet. Understandably. Poor Georgiana isn't quite as indomitable as she seems.'

'Your attention, please!' Lord Tobias's head poked through the curtain again. 'Allow me to present the Gardiner brothers' production of *Nelson versus the Polar Bear and Other Adventures*!'

'Oh, good.' Mrs Fortini clapped her hands. 'Now hush, everyone.'

It was, Henrietta thought, linking her arm through Sebastian's as the curtains swept back to reveal several large, white-painted boxes obviously intended to represent icebergs, quite the most bizarre, unexpected and inventive dramatical performance she'd ever witnessed. At some point during rehearsals, Oliver the polar bear appeared to have stolen centre stage from Nelson, who was now relegated to a supporting role while a storm whipped up a blue piece of cloth, presumably representing the ocean, Peter the pirate sang a sea shanty, Napoleon, aka Lord Tobias, fell headlong into an icy crevice and, at one particularly surreal point, Michael turned into an octopus, waving eight woollen tentacles around his head before being finally vanquished by the aforementioned polar bear.

'What do you think the moral is?' Sebastian turned his head, pressing his lips into her hair.

'I'm not sure there is one, but the octopus and polar bear appear to have reconciled. They're embracing now.' She smiled happily. 'I do like a happy ending.'

'So do I. And here comes our young pirate, too.' Sebastian leapt to his feet, pulling her with him. 'Bravo! Encore!'

'Wonderful!' Henrietta clapped enthusiastically. 'A triumph!'

'Do you really think so?' Peter pulled his pirate's eyepatch away from his face.

'It's the best play I've ever seen.' David's voice had a crack in it.

'I agree.' Even the Dowager Duchess was beaming. 'I've seen a lot of plays, but that was spellbinding.'

'Does that mean we can have some cocoa now, Aunt Elizabeth?' Michael grinned cheekily. 'And biscuits, too?'

'Of course. You all deserve a reward.'

'You certainly do.' Henrietta bent to kiss each of her nephews in turn. 'But you'll need to have it up in the nursery. The guests will be arriving soon.'

'Can't we stay for the party?'

'It's not for children.' David interceded, putting an arm around Peter's shoulders and earning himself a wide smile. 'But *I'd* like to join you upstairs for cocoa and biscuits.'

'Are you certain?' Elizabeth gave him a kindly look. 'You're more than welcome to stay.'

'No, thank you.' David shook his head. 'I'd rather be with my boys, but I appreciate the invitation.'

'Very well, but if you're going to escape then I suggest that you hurry. I think I can hear the first carriages arriving now.'

'Come along then, the rest of you.' Lord Tobias tore off his French soldier's costume and made sweeping gestures towards the doorway with his arms. 'Let's go and greet them. It's about time I introduced my heir to the neighbourhood.'

'Feeling nervous?' Sebastian slid an arm around Henrietta's waist as they moved obediently towards the door.

'A little, but it's very kind of your uncle to want to introduce us.' She peered up at him. 'What about you?'

'Not nervous exactly, just slightly in shock. A month ago I was a single man heading home to run a biscuit shop with his widowed mother and unwed sister and now…' He shook his head slightly. 'It's hard to accept that all this is real.'

'I know. I still can't believe that Tobias made you his heir. We aren't really going to live here one day, are we?'

'There's no need to look so horrified.' He laughed. 'But who knows? Maybe I'll decide to become a gentleman of leisure eventually. Or we could turn it into a maritime academy?'

'I think it might be a little far from the sea. What about a baking school?'

'It's an interesting idea.' He stopped and tugged her towards him. 'Speaking of baking, I wrote to James a little while ago, asking him to look out for suitable properties for our tea shop.'

'And he's found one?' She stood up on tiptoes, clasping her hands to her chest in delight.

'He might have. Not on Swainswick Crescent, but only a few minutes' walk away. Next door to his store, actually, with rooms upstairs for us to live in.'

'That sounds perfect!'

'Which means there'll be no need to throw Nancy and Bel-whatever-her-name-is out into the street. They can stay and run Belles together if they want, with a wage increase naturally.'

'As if you would ever have thrown them into the street!'

'You're right. Nancy would have thrown me back.'

'At the very least, and you already have bruised ribs.'

'You know…' he slid his hands gently over her hips '…this will make an excellent story for the children one day. I offered your mother a manor, but she wanted a tea shop…'

'Just for now.' She drew in a breath and then smiled it out again, wanting to purr like a cat at his touch. 'But maybe I'll want to be a lady of leisure some day, too. You never know what the future will bring. I certainly never expected to find a sailor in my kitchen in the middle of the night.'

'And I never expected to find anyone as perfect as you.' He grinned. 'Not beautiful perfect, obviously. Inner perfect.'

She clucked her tongue. 'You know, you're allowed to give me compliments now that we're married. I only objected at first.'

'I don't believe you ever *officially* withdrew your objections.'

'Well, I'm doing so now.' She gave him an arch look. 'You haven't even mentioned how I look this evening.'

'Lovely, but I'm used to you now.'

'What difference does that make?'

'Quite a lot actually. When you love someone, you don't really notice what they look like any more. You only see the essence of them. You could be the most beautiful woman in the world—you *might* actually be, come to think of it—and I still wouldn't notice. To me, you're just Henrietta.'

'Thank you… I think.'

'I *did* just say that I loved you.'

'True.'

'And you love me, too?'

'Also true.'

'Excellent. In that case…' He reached into his pocket and pulled out a red velvet box. 'I ordered this for Christmas, but I thought you might like to wear it tonight.'

'Is this why you went into the village?' She opened the lid to reveal a small padlock-shaped locket complete with a tiny key. 'Oh, Sebastian, it's beautiful.'

'It's so you never doubt that I'm yours. My heart belongs to you now, Henrietta.' He grinned her favourite lopsided grin. 'I couldn't have been happy giving up my freedom for anyone else.'

'It's the most wonderful present I've ever received.' She sniffed as he lifted the locket and fastened it around her neck, his fingers lingering briefly. 'Can I have the key?'

'Of course.'

'There…' She opened it up and pressed a kiss to the inside before holding it out for him to do the same.

'You want me to kiss it?' He looked amused. 'Aren't you supposed to put a picture inside? Or a lock of hair?'

'Maybe, but for now, I just want a kiss. Now hurry up before mine escapes.'

He pressed his lips to the metal. 'Will that do?'

'That's perfect.' She closed the lid and turned the key again. 'Only it makes my present seem a little unimpressive.'

'I'm sure I'll love it, whatever it is.'

'Well, it's in a similar vein… Remember how I once offered to knit you a scarf?'

'You've made me one?' His grin seemed to take over his whole face. 'Well, a handmade gift is even better. I'll treasure it for ever.'

'Just as long as you wear it.'

'Every day. Even when I don't go outside…'

'Are the two of you coming?' Lord Tobias poked his head back around the library door.

'Imminently.' Sebastian slid the key back into the box and inclined his head. 'I just need to kiss my wife first.'

'Again?' Lord Tobias rolled his eyes. 'The poor woman never gets a moment's peace. Make it quick, then.'

'Understood.' He gave a mock salute and then cupped her face in his hands. 'I'll take a lot longer about kissing you later, I promise.'

'Paying special attention to my ankles, I hope?'

'Naturally.' He lowered his mouth towards hers. 'Don't I always?'

'Oh!' She gave a start a split second before their lips touched.

'What?' His head spun towards the door. 'What's the matter?'

'I can hear music!'

'And?' He blinked. 'Is that bad?'

'It could be. Your mother said this was going to be an evening party, but I never thought… What if there's dancing?'

'Does it matter?'

'Yes! I don't know any steps. I've never danced before, not properly. I'm not a lady!'

'As it happens, I don't know any either. And I'm not a gentleman, as I believe I've mentioned a couple of times.'

'But people will be watching us!'

'Then we'll make the steps up as we go along...' He rubbed his thumbs tenderly across her cheekbones. 'That approach seems to have worked pretty well for us so far, don't you think?'

'You're right.' She thought about that for a few moments and then laughed, her heart swelling at the thought. 'I suppose it has.'

'Now about that kiss...?'

'No time.' She twisted away, reaching for his hand and dragging him towards the door.

'But...'

'Your family are waiting.'

He shook his head with a mocking sigh. 'Is this what I gave up my freedom for? Not even a single kiss?'

She stopped at the door, blowing a kiss over her shoulder. 'You can't say I didn't warn you. You're mine now, Sebastian Fortini, and I intend to keep you.'

Epilogue

Bath—January 1807

'What did *he* want?' a belligerent voice called from the kitchen as Beatrix Roxbury—more familiarly known to the patrons of Belles as Belinda Carr—bolted the shop door behind the last customer of the day. Not that the man in question had been a customer, more of a friendly, helpful and, in her opinion, extremely handsome fellow shopkeeper, but there was no way on earth that Nancy would *ever* agree with that description.

'Who?' She smiled mischievously.

'You know very well who!' The voice sounded exasperated.

'*Do* I?'

'James Redbourne!'

'Oh, yes, of course.' She allowed herself a small giggle. 'Silly me.'

'Well?' Nancy demanded as she went through to the kitchen.

'He didn't *want* anything, actually, but you might want to brace yourself.'

'I'm always braced, especially where he's concerned.'

'So I've noticed.' Beatrix murmured, drawing her apron over her head and hooking it over a peg in the corner.

'What?'

'Nothing. He just brought a message from Mr and *Mrs* Fortini, that's all.'

'Sebastian and his mother?'

'No. Sebastian and Henrietta. They're married!'

'Married?' For the first time since they'd met, Nancy seemed unable to form an opinion.

'They went to Gretna Green and they'll be back here in a few days.'

'With the boys?'

'No. They're staying in Yorkshire with their father.'

'What's Henrietta's brother doing in Yorkshire?'

'I presume Mr Redbourne told him where to find them.' She paused slyly. 'I wouldn't be surprised if he paid for him to get there, too. It's just the sort of thing he'd do.'

Nancy's lips thinned. 'You seem to have a very high opinion of Mr Redbourne.'

'I do.' Beatrix kept her tone placid. 'I think he's a good man.'

'Harumph.'

'You might have to get used to him. I expect he'll be spending a lot more time here with Mr Fortini. Maybe it's time to—'

'Never!' Nancy glared and then grimaced. 'I suppose we ought to start looking for new positions then, not to mention somewhere else to live.'

'No need. Henrietta says they're starting a tea room

and they're going to live there, too. So they want us to stay and run Belles. Which makes you the new manager!'

'*I'm* the manager?' Nancy looked almost on the verge of tears before she cleared her throat briskly. 'Well, that's very good of them, I will say—*and* a relief. I didn't want to be sharing a house with a pair of newlyweds, thank you very much. Much better for us spinsters to stick together.'

'Mmm...' Beatrix chewed on her bottom lip for a few seconds before coming to a decision. 'About that, being a spinster, I mean... I think it's time that I told you the truth.'

'About who you are?' Nancy looked amazed for the third time that evening.

'Yes. I should have told you from the start, but I was scared and I didn't know who to trust. Now I know I could trust you with anything. My life if it came to it.'

'Well, it's about time you realised that.' Nancy appeared both pleased and embarrassed at the same time.

'I'm sure you must have wondered who I was.'

'Once or twice.'

'Which is why I'm so grateful that you never insisted I tell you. Here.' She pulled out a chair from the table. 'You might want to sit down.'

'This sounds serious.' Nancy made a show of seating herself. 'Let me guess. You're a runaway princess.'

'Nothing so romantic, I'm afraid. However, for a start, my real name isn't Belinda. It's Beatrix.'

'Oh.' Nancy looked disappointed. 'That's not so shocking.'

'That was the easy part. I'm not a spinster either. I was married two months ago.'

'What?' Nancy gave her a look that implied she'd just taken leave of her senses. 'But you've been here for a month! And you said you were in Bath for a while before that.'

'I know. I can't say I have a great deal of experience of married life...or any, in fact. I ran away from my husband.'

'Why?' Nancy's eyebrows shot up, her expression shifting to one of outrage. 'What did he do?'

'Nothing. He never had a chance. I never even got to the wedding breakfast.'

'You mean you ran away on your wedding day?'

'Yes.' She pursed her lips, wondering how to explain. The only way she could think of was to go back to the beginning. 'The truth is that I am—*was*—quite wealthy. My mother died when I was a baby and my father a few years later. He was a merchant, dealing in tea mostly, and after he died, his entire fortune came to me.'

'So you're an heiress?' Nancy's eyes gleamed with excitement. 'How *much* of an heiress?'

'Sixty thousand pounds.'

Nancy's jaw almost hit the table. *'Sixty thousand?* And you're here making biscuits for a living?'

'I like making biscuits. Anyway, my father left me in the care of his brother, my Uncle Benedict, and his wife, Augusta, but neither of them were very pleased about it. All they cared about was the annual payment they received for allowing me a home under their roof. Maybe they'd expected more from my father's will and they considered the money as their due, because they certainly never went out of their way to earn it. They never liked me.'

'Why not?'

Beatrix lifted her shoulders. It was a good question, one that she'd asked herself countless times over the years. As a ten-year-old orphan, she'd wondered if it was because she was simply unlovable. Either that or inherently wicked somehow. Only the arrival of the kind-hearted Miss Foster had saved her from a lifetime of despair and self-loathing. Eventually, however, she'd realised that her family's behaviour had much less to do with her than themselves. Despite following his brother into trade, her uncle had never enjoyed anything close to her father's success and his wife and children never ceased to remind him about it. The whole house had reeked of bitterness, jealousy and ill will, most of it vented on her.

'Bel— Beatrix?' Nancy looked concerned. 'Was it so bad?'

'It was...unpleasant.' She shook her head, reluctant to dwell on the worst of her experiences growing up. 'My cousins were older than me and I was never accepted into the family.'

'But why didn't you just leave and set up your own house? Especially if you had so much money.'

'Because I didn't have the money. My father put my whole fortune into trust until I turned twenty-five. Unless I married, of course, but I could only do that with my uncle's consent. I couldn't do *anything* without his consent, not even leave the house.' She clenched her jaw at the irony. 'My uncle and aunt didn't want me, but they were terrified of me running away. After a few years, they even became afraid of my friendship with Miss Foster so they dismissed her and appointed a maid to guard me instead. Then once I turned twenty-two, they decided to find me a husband, one important and aristocratic enough to help my uncle's business interests, but impoverished enough to need my money.'

'Eurgh.' Nancy leaned across the table. 'Old and smelly?'

'No, actually, although I'm sure my aunt would have preferred that.' Beatrix drew her brows together as an image of her stern, raven-haired husband flickered into her mind. 'Quite handsome really, and only six years older than me.'

'Cold and cruel?'

'Cold, perhaps, but not cruel, I think. It was honestly hard to tell. I only met him twice, once when he proposed and then again at our wedding. I've barely spoken to him except to say *yes* and *I do.*' She shook her head. 'I know it sounds ridiculous that I would marry a man I didn't know, but if I'd refused my uncle, it would have meant another three years living like a prisoner under his roof. Marriage seemed like the only escape. I thought it couldn't possibly be any worse, especially after...well, something else.' She dropped her gaze, unwilling to specify what the other thing had been. It was mortifying enough to think about, let alone to tell anyone else. 'I was upset and confused and it was only after I'd said my marriage vows that I realised I'd made a terrible mistake. We went back to my husband's house for the wedding breakfast and I went up to my new room to freshen up and then...well, for once there was nobody about, nobody watching me. Before I knew it, I was running down the back stairs and out of the servants' entrance.'

'So that's when you came to Bath?'

'Not straight away. There was someone else...someone I thought I could go to, only it turned out I was wrong about them. Then I remembered the last address I had for Miss Foster and I came here. You know the rest.'

'Mmm, I can see why you were afraid to tell the truth.' Nancy leaned back in her chair, folding her arms over her chest.

'But I never lied. I told you I wasn't a criminal and as for hurting anyone, my uncle and aunt only cared about the money and my husband…well, it's not as if he ever had a chance to care about me, though goodness knows what he must think of me now. He probably hates me for humiliating him so badly.'

'Sixty thousand pounds probably softens the blow.' Nancy lifted an eyebrow. 'Still, if he finds out where you are…'

'He hasn't found me yet.' Beatrix glanced towards the back door as if she half expected a man to appear there at that moment. 'There was a time, when I first arrived in Bath, that I thought maybe he *had* tracked me down. I had a funny feeling that someone was following me, but I must have been imagining things and now…' She paused and bit her lip.

'Now?'

'Now I think that I'm safe, but I wonder if I ought to write to him.'

'What?' Nancy's voice was more of a shriek. 'Why?'

'Because I want to ask for a divorce.' Beatrix kept her voice calm. 'And I think it's a reasonable request. He won't want me back as a wife. Running away was scandalous enough, but these past months should have ruined my reputation beyond any repair. I've given him more than enough to divorce me with.'

'Wouldn't a divorce have to go through Parliament?'

'Yes, but he has the money to do it.'

'Only thanks to you.'

'True, but at least he'd be putting it to good use.'

'I don't know. A divorce would cause even more scandal. What if he decides it's easier to lock you up in a dungeon for the rest of your life?'

'I'm not sure he owns a castle, let alone a dungeon.'

'You said he's an aristocrat, didn't you? They all have crumbling old castles hidden away on their estates. If you let him know where you are, then you could just be trading your uncle's imprisonment for his. At least here you're free.'

'I know, but I think it's a risk I have to take. I can't spend the rest of my life looking over my shoulder. Besides, he'll want an heir and he won't want one with a woman who's behaved the way I have. And he *seemed* reasonable.'

'Mmm.' Nancy still sounded uncertain. 'Well, I suppose I'll just have to rescue you if he *does* lock you up. Anna and Henrietta can probably persuade Samuel and Sebastian to help, too.'

'Thank you. It's reassuring to know I have friends.'

'What will you say in your letter?'

'That I accept all the blame and that I don't expect any money.'

'That's not fair!' Nancy smacked her hand on the table. 'First you spend years being bullied by your uncle and aunt and now you have to just *give away* your parents' fortune to some husband you don't even know!'

'But at least I'll still have you.'

Nancy snorted. 'I may be a good friend, but even *I'm* not worth sixty thousand pounds.'

'I disagree. A true friend is worth several fortunes. I've had a lot of time to think since I came here and I've made up my mind. This is just the price I have to pay to be free.' She nodded her head emphatically. 'I'll write to him tomorrow.'

'Fine.' Nancy let out a heavy sigh. 'Who is *he*, by the way? You haven't told me his name.'

'Oh…no, I didn't.' Beatrix paused. 'This is the part you might need to sit down for.'

'I'm already sitting.'

'Yes…' She gave a tight smile. 'Well… You see, the thing is his name is Roxbury. Quinton Roxbury.'

'Just Quinton Roxbury? No sir or my lord?'

'Your Grace, actually.' She took a deep breath, admitting the truth in a rush. 'Quinton Roxbury, Twelfth Duke of Howden.'

It was funny, Beatrix thought, rummaging in a drawer for some smelling salts a few minutes later, but Nancy was the last person she would ever have expected to faint…

* * * * *

If you enjoyed this story, be sure to read the first book in Jenni Fletcher's Regency Belles of Bath miniseries

An Unconventional Countess

And whilst you're waiting for the next book, why not check out her other great reads

The Warrior's Bride Prize
The Viscount's Veiled Lady
Reclaimed by Her Rebel Knight
Miss Amelia's Mistletoe Marquess
Redeeming Her Viking Warrior